JUN -- 2017

At Fairfield Orchard

Center Point
Large Print

**This Large Print Book carries the
Seal of Approval of N.A.V.H.**

At
Fairfield Orchard

Emma Cane

CENTER POINT LARGE PRINT
THORNDIKE, MAINE

This Center Point Large Print edition is published
in the year 2017 by arrangement with Avon Books,
an imprint of HarperCollins Publishers.

The text of this Large Print edition is unabridged.
In other aspects, this book may vary
from the original edition.
Printed in the United States of America
on permanent paper.
Set in 16-point Times New Roman type.

ISBN: 978-1-68324-346-5

Library of Congress Cataloging-in-Publication Data

Names: Cane, Emma, author.
Title: At Fairfield Orchard / Emma Cane.
Description: Center Point Large Print edition. | Thorndike, Maine :
Center Point Large Print, 2017.
Identifiers: LCCN 2016059625 | ISBN 9781683243465
  (hardcover : alk. paper)
Subjects: LCSH: Large type books. | GSAFD: Love stories.
Classification: LCC PS3603.A5375 A95 2017 | DDC 813/.6—dc23
LC record available at https://lccn.loc.gov/2016059625

Brainstorming the plot of a book is always a delicate dance greatly aided by my critique buddies, but helping to create the entire world of a series? I don't know how many writers are up to the challenge, but these ladies are! This book (and series) wouldn't exist without my wonderful writing friends—the Packeteers (Ginny Aubertine, Laurie Bishop, Theresa Kovian, Michele Masarech, Maggie Shayne, and Christine Wenger) and the Purples (MJ Compton, Kris Fletcher, Carol Lombardo, and Christine Wenger). They are all writers extraordinaire. I've been blessed to have them in my life.

— *Acknowledgments* —

My thanks to all the people who helped me research this book: Jim and Angie Callen, Michelle Callen, Mark Kloecker, and Elisa Konieczko. A special debt of gratitude goes to Kris Fletcher, who thought an orchard would be the perfect setting for a new series; Danielle Fleckenstein of Beak and Skiff Apple Orchards, for giving me details of the inner workings of an orchard; and David Konieczko, for helping me to understand an archaeologist's world. Any mistakes are certainly mine.

— Chapter 1 —

Jonathan Gebhart got out of his car and breathed in the crisp air of Fairfield Orchard, ripe with the sweet scent of apple blossoms. In the distance, the Blue Ridge Mountains undulated into the disappearing mists of midmorning, their haze the mysterious blue they were named for. But everywhere else he looked, surrounding this oasis of buildings and a barn, the foothills were covered in the pink and white of blossoming trees, following long lines like the teeth on a comb. Had Thomas Jefferson known what would become of the land when he'd sold it almost two hundred years ago? Jonathan intended to prove it wasn't what other historians said it was.

He'd driven the half hour west from Charlottesville, Virginia, to Fairfield Orchard, rehearsing his most persuasive speech over and over. He wasn't known as the most outgoing of guys, but he was passionate about history and hoped that would be enough. But strangely, he didn't see a soul. A huge old barn that looked well over a hundred years old stood open and deserted. It had a lower level made of stone with its own entrance in the back, and the soaring upper level framed in weathered gray boards was stacked with crates and bins for the autumn harvest. A food shack and small store were obviously closed. There were picnic tables and benches, all positioned to take in the beautiful view of central Virginia during the harvest season. But in the spring, the public grounds were deserted.

Past a copse of towering oak and hickory trees was a dirt lane, which he followed around a curve until he saw a big house with white siding, blue shutters, and a wraparound porch around the original building. A two-story addition had been added to the right side. A battered blue pickup truck was parked nearby. He climbed the front steps, but no one answered the door. Jonathan hadn't called in advance, assuming that a request like his was better handled in person, but that had obviously been a mistake. There must be a business office or warehouse somewhere else on the grounds.

And then in the first row of apple trees next to the house, he saw a ladder disappearing up inside, and a pair of work boots perched on a rung, their owner partially hidden by branches and blossoms and bright green leaves. He'd done his research, knew that the owner was Bruce Fairfield, a Vietnam vet in his sixties.

"Mr. Fairfield?" Jonathan called as he approached the tree. "Bruce Fairfield?"

Sudden barking startled him, and a dog came up out of the straggly grass growing through a dark loam of what looked like fertilizer around the base of the tree. The medium-sized dog resembled a cross between a German shepherd and a coyote, its pointy ears alert.

"What's up, Uma?"

The voice from within the tree was far more feminine than "Bruce" should have. The dog sat down and regarded Jonathan, her spotted tongue visible as she panted, her head cocked to the side.

A woman pushed aside a branch and peered down, wreathed in pink and white blossoms, her sandy brown hair pulled into a ponytail beneath a ragged ball cap with the Virginia Cavaliers logo. She had a delicate face with a pointed chin, and a nose splattered with freckles. She was already tan from working outdoors, with eyes clear and deep blue and narrowed with curiosity. She wore a battered winter vest over a plaid shirt with a T-shirt beneath, and a faded pair of jeans with a tear at the knee. She held clippers in one hand.

"What can I do for you?" she asked, then added apologetically, "We're still closed for the off-season."

"I know. I've come from Charlottesville to speak with the owner."

Brightly, she said, "I'm one of them."

That rearranged his conclusion that she was just an employee.

"Hope you don't mind if I keep working while we talk," she added.

He blinked as her face disappeared behind

the branch she released. Soon, he could hear occasional snipping, and saw a branch drop to the ground. She seemed like she was examining, more than pruning. He was used to talking to students who tried to hide their texting during a lecture, but he couldn't force this woman to pay attention to him. At least the dog watched him with expectation.

"My name is Dr. Jonathan Gebhart, and I'm an associate professor of history at the University of Virginia, with a specialty in colonial history, particularly Thomas Jefferson."

She gave a snort of laughter. "Of course."

He stiffened. "Of course?"

"Thomas Jefferson founded the university, right?"

Did anyone from the area *not* know that?

"I hear he might as well still be alive," she continued, "the way some people refer to him. I guess you're one of the worshippers."

"If you consider historians worshippers," he said dryly.

She peeked out from behind a branch and gave him an amused smile. "I didn't mean to offend, but you caught me on a bad day. I'm trying to remember my pruning skills. It's been a while, and it's not exactly the season for it."

"May I ask to whom I'm speaking?"

Her smile widened. "My, don't you have a pretty way of talking. I'm Amy Fairfield."

"Daughter of the owner?"

"Technically one of the new owners, remember?"

She disappeared behind a branch again and continued pruning. Bees buzzed about her, alighting delicately on blossoms, but she ignored them.

"It's all a mess right now, of course," she continued. "My parents have just retired and left to have the time of their lives in the RV they always dreamed of." She peeked at him again. "Don't get me wrong, I'm happy for them, but they caught the whole family off guard, and now everyone has to decide who's coming back when, taking leaves of absence or quitting their jobs altogether, so we can keep the orchard going. And though I always worked weekends in the fall, it's been a long time since I was involved in the spring." She wrinkled her nose. "Way more than you wanted to hear, sorry."

And then she became silent as she examined her work critically. Her family problems were none of his business, though his curiosity began to formulate questions that he tamped back down.

"I'm here to ask a favor of you." He paused, but she didn't reappear. Taking a deep breath, he said, "I'm writing a book on the land Thomas Jefferson owned, and how selling it changed the course of Albemarle County and Virginia itself. As you know, your ancestors purchased this land from him."

"I know."

"You have an incredible inheritance here. One of our founding fathers walked this very land."

"I know that, too. But he walked a lot of land around here. I spent the last thirteen years in Charlottesville, sometimes running campus trails. I'm sure I walked lots of places TJ walked."

TJ? Though he corrected his students when they were so disrespectful, he found himself amused by Amy's irreverence. He well knew that Jefferson wasn't a saint, simply a flawed, though brilliant man.

But there were more important things on the line, like the book he needed to finish for his tenure portfolio. Without tenure, he could lose the career he'd worked so hard for, be let go from UVA. But even more important was his big hypothesis, the one that could turn his book into a bestseller and give him the prestigious career he'd always dreamed of.

"So what do I have to do with TJ?" Amy asked.

"I'd like your family's permission to interview them and look through the historical records you've kept through the years."

"Historical records?" she echoed. "Don't you find that stuff at courthouses or online?"

"You cannot find family Bibles or original land deeds so easily, not to mention family stories passed down through generations." He glanced at the house again, knowing it was far too recently built, and hoping Google hadn't misled him. "I believe there's an older house than this?"

"Yep, but we've closed it up to keep people from getting hurt."

A headache started to form. "Is it in disrepair?" He hoped Amy Fairfield and her family appreciated their own history.

"Not really, but no one is living there now, and we don't want vandals disturbing it."

The pressure between his eyes eased. "You get many vandals out here?"

"I didn't think so, but I'm not the one who made the decision. My father was. And then he left, leaving it to my siblings and me to continue family tradition—whether some of us wanted to or not," she added dryly.

He wasn't sure where she fit in on that spectrum, but it wasn't his concern. "Can I reach your father by phone or email?"

"Sure, but maybe you'd rather talk to my grandfather."

He smiled with relief. The elderly had a better grasp of the importance of the past. "Do you think he'd speak with me?"

Amy spread the branches and gave him a long look from head to toe. He felt an odd connection, her gaze almost a physical touch. He was baffled to experience an awareness of her as a woman, when he could barely tell she *was* one beneath her farmer's garb. Those vivid blue eyes studied him as if judging him. He'd been judged and found wanting before, and he wouldn't go through that again.

"I can't speak for Grandpa, Jon, but—"

"Jonathan." He withheld a grimace, knowing that he shouldn't be correcting her when he needed her help.

"Sorry. I don't know if now's the best time to be stirring things up. The orchard . . . well, we have a lot of work to do this summer, and it'll be time for the harvest before you know it. I just started working here again a couple days ago. How about next winter?"

"I can't wait until next winter," he said patiently. "This is the last section of the book, and I have to submit it by this fall to even have it ready in time for my tenure review next year. You do know what tenure is."

Those dark blue eyes narrowed, and she cocked her head. "Gee, maybe you better spell the word for me."

He briefly closed his eyes, knowing he was making things worse. "Forgive me."

He took a step toward her, trying to find the right words. He startled the dog, who jumped up and hit the ladder, which began to fall sideways. Amy let out a yelp and grabbed a branch even as the ladder crashed through several branches and hit the ground. Her feet struggled to find a thick enough branch to support her, and Jonathan reached for her. She was still too high to grab around the waist, but when he ducked under a thin branch and stepped beneath her, her toes brushed his shoulders.

"Step right on me," he urged.

For a moment, he thought she would refuse, but at last she let herself drop a bit, and her big muddy work boots settled on his shoulders. She wasn't even that heavy, and he realized she was probably smaller than he'd imagined, being half-hidden by the tree and wearing layers of warm clothing.

"If I was still a cheerleader," she said, "I'd have a spotter to help me jump."

At least she didn't sound upset with him. He needed her goodwill. "I'll squat, and you should be able to jump easily."

"You forget, I'm still in between all these branches."

"I'll go straight down, and you be careful." He sank slowly onto his haunches.

Using the tree for balance, she swung away from him and landed lightly on the ground. Still bent over, he came out from beneath the tree and practically ran right into her. Straightening, he stared down at her and she stared up, not six inches away from each other.

"You're taller than I thought," she said.

"And you're shorter."

"I am," she said ruefully.

Though smiling, she backed away as if he

was contagious. To his surprise, he regretted that.

"I made a mess of your jacket," she pointed out.

He looked down at his shoulders. "It's just dirt. It'll come clean."

She flashed that teasing smile again, and he realized she might be flirting with him. The thought was surprising, a little disorienting.

"You'd say anything to get my cooperation," she said.

He looked into those intelligent blue eyes, and imagined many a man would. He would, too— for his research. Right now, it had to come before anything else. "Your cooperation is crucial. I have a theory that Jefferson might have escaped to here during the American Revolution, instead of to his land to the south."

She tilted her head. "But he didn't have a house here."

He widened his eyes in surprise. "No, he didn't. You know more about *TJ* than you let on."

He'd thought to put her at ease with a light-hearted tone, but those intriguing eyes suddenly seemed to shutter. He decided right then that going into detail about his research might put her off.

"No, I don't know all that much," she said, looking away.

"I'll be conducting research at the library at Monticello, and also here, if you'll permit it. I need to find proof that I'm right. Can I count on your cooperation?"

"I'll think about it."

She was already retrieving the clippers and righting the ladder. He tried to help, but she gave him a distracted smile.

"I can do it. This is my job now, you know."

"What did you do before?"

"Real estate."

He could see her as a friendly, outgoing saleswoman. "Did you always mean to come back to the orchard?" he asked, curious.

"Interesting question. I don't really know. As for your request, why don't you come back tomorrow, and I'll give you my answer."

And she maneuvered the ladder back into the tree and climbed up, disappearing within the spring blossoms until he could only see those muddy boots. He turned and strode back to his car.

Amy heard the crunch of gravel beneath Jonathan Gebhart's feet, and she ducked her head until she could watch him walk away. He'd been an interesting man, all sober and serious, and seemed a little taken aback when she'd teased him. She could still see his short, wavy black hair that looked difficult to tame. It was hard to forget his eyes, green as spring in the orchard—and that moment when he'd really looked at her as a woman. That had been surprising and unsettling. He didn't have laughing eyes—she imagined he didn't laugh much at all, which was a shame, when he looked so gorgeous.

Would he be one of those boring professors who droned on and on about something that no longer mattered to anyone? No, he'd sounded too passionate about his request. Maybe he brought that focus to kids who only needed his course as an elective, who stared out the window on a gorgeous day and wished to be anywhere else. That had been her, once upon a time . . .

But not where history was concerned. That was an interest she had once had in common with the professor. But she'd let it all go, pushed it from her mind just as she'd pushed her family and friends away. She was surprised how much the amateur genealogist inside her had tried to come creaking back to life when he'd told her his hypothesis about Jefferson and her family land. But she wouldn't let it.

When the professor reached his car, Amy saw that his broad shoulders were squared, and he moved like a man who always knew exactly what he was doing, had everything planned out. She always found confidence sexy. He'd been professionally attired in a button-down shirt and chinos beneath the jacket she'd ruined, while she was grubby, with torn jeans and old shirts. He'd been dignified and educated, and she'd dropped out of college to spend her time with a man who hadn't proven worthy of the sacrifice. It hadn't been a sacrifice at the time, of course; she'd been giddy with what she thought was love. Amy knocked her forehead into the nearest branch, as if that could knock some sense into her. It had taken far too long for that sense to take hold, and it had proven costly.

She heard his car start, and then he was gone, dirt rising up behind as he traveled at a respectful speed down toward Spencer Hollow, the little village between the orchard and Crozet, the nearest small town. She used to take the quiet dirt road as an invitation to speed, roaring down the hill, the rolling countryside stretched out below her, rows of apple trees rising and falling as far as the eye could see. Life had been full of excitement and possibilities then—full of the promise of foolish mistakes, too, but she hadn't known that. Otherwise, she would have stayed holed up in her childhood bedroom forever.

She was back there now, in that same bedroom, her cheerleading trophies and school certificates still on the wall. She'd chosen this path, of course. When she'd gotten the call that her parents had wanted to retire, she'd been only too glad to run home for a fresh start. She'd been so excited to help her family, to spend more time with her siblings, to prove that they were all so important to her. But underneath all those good reasons she had to admit that coming home also meant pretending she hadn't let her life get so horribly, humiliatingly out of control as she'd spent years with a man who'd developed the same issues with alcohol that her dad had once had.

No one knew, of course, not even her twin brother—which Amy worried was causing a certain distance between them these last few years. But no one was ever going to know how foolish she had been. Her ex-boyfriend, Rob, certainly wouldn't tell; he'd moved on to the next woman, one even more malleable than she'd been. Amy had quit college for that idiot, she thought, groaning aloud. But at the time, it had seemed like a great move. Her grades had suffered because all she'd wanted was to begin a life with Rob, to live with him and make a home.

It was Rob who'd introduced her to real estate, his family business. She'd started learning the ropes while still in college, helping out agents part-time. She discovered she loved working with people, and had a knack for knowing how to find the most important reason why someone looked for a home, and then delivering on it. She didn't need college for that, so she'd dropped out. Gradually, as things with Rob got worse, it was harder and harder to be a part of his family business. Breaking up with him had meant eventually quitting her job, and it was almost a relief to be done with anything to do with him.

Now she was facing a new future, and she didn't want to look back, to see again the mistakes she'd made.

But the professor wanted to talk about the past—her family's past, and the memories weren't always pleasant. Did she really want such a reminder? And, of course, there was the fact that she was always so quick to help a guy out, she thought with dismay. But she wouldn't let her own hang-ups interfere with her promise to give his request some thought. He was right about her family's link to Thomas Jefferson. If he had discovered new information, how could she deprive him of finding out the truth?

To clear her head, Amy took a deep breath of the apple blossoms all around her. *This* was the scent of springtime, fragrant and lush, of her childhood, of her family obsession for generations. She'd been molded by the rhythm of the seasons, of planting baby trees with her father in the spring, of morning walks through the orchard in the fall, examining apples to predict when each variety would be at peak ripeness. There definitely was a history here, the good kind—and the bad. She just didn't know if she wanted to talk about it with a stranger, for there were dark episodes, like her father's drinking, that warped some of her memories.

Yet being back at home with her twin brother, Tyler, made her feel all about family right now.

Late last year, her mom, Patty, had had a breast cancer scare, and though it had turned out to be a benign lump, everything had changed for her father. Though sober for the last ten years, he'd never forgotten how his wife had taken up the slack when he'd been hungover, when he'd forgotten family events, when he had to be guided home after parties. Now Patty deserved the retirement she'd always dreamed of, and Bruce had intended to give it to her—even though the orchard's finances were shaky. He couldn't just give the orchard to his children and leave; there was no money for that. He would have had to sell it, and the thought had horrified the whole family. As the professor had pointed out, there'd been a Fairfield on this land for one hundred and ninety-nine years—Amy did know a lot more of her family history than she'd let on. It was their heritage, their history, their children's future. Their sister Rachel, who'd been Dad's right hand for years, couldn't resurrect it all on her own.

So Amy's oldest brother Logan, who'd made a fortune as a hedge fund manager in New York City and was now a venture capitalist, had offered a financial gift to their parents so they could buy their RV and begin their adventures. He'd insisted it was his right to share what he'd earned, and they'd reluctantly, graciously accepted. But Amy and the rest of her siblings had balked when he'd tried to bail out the orchard, too. After all, he was in business with several partners—it should be an official investment, a loan. The siblings even insisted on offering a business plan for what they intended to do to make Fairfield Orchard a success again.

And Amy, who'd been away from the business for a good ten years—except for working weekends at the height of autumn harvest—was beginning to feel a bit overwhelmed. Coming up with a new idea to change things up at the orchard was now going to fall on her, Tyler, and Rachel. Thank God for Rachel, who knew everything there was to know about the family business. With her help, they'd come up with a great way to position Fairfield Orchard for the twenty-first century.

Amy took a step higher in the ladder so she could look across the tops of the other pink-draped apple trees and see the Blue Ridge Mountains, the backdrop of her youth. She took a deep breath of the sweet fragrance and momentarily closed her eyes with happiness. It was so good to be home.

"Hey, are you still up the same tree?"

And then there was Tyler. Amy looked down to find her twin leaning against the tree, arms folded across his chest. He was giving her that killer smile that had won over legions of soap opera fans before the show had been canceled.

He'd played Dr. Lake, dreamboat hunk and dedicated neuro-surgeon—who always seemed to be in the ER to treat every other kind of trauma, too. Both twins had the same light brown hair and blue eyes, but his short hair seemed tousled naturally, rakishly—although she knew he spent a half hour in front of the bathroom mirror every morning, complaining the whole time about the necessity. His agent had several screen tests lined up over the next few months and was confident they would lead to work. Most of the time, Amy couldn't even be bothered to blow-dry her hair, just tossed it up in a ponytail. Tyler took good care of his body, and had already been after Amy to start running with him. As if she could keep up.

They talked or texted several times a week where once it had been several times a day. When Tyler said he'd come home to help her run the orchard, she'd been so happy knowing they'd spend time together again. College and life had separated them, and it had been jarring at first. He was a part of her.

In many ways, he was the same old Tyler, charming and happy, but in other ways, she sensed . . . something else. Was he hiding part of himself? But of course, she hadn't told him what had happened with Rob either.

"Have you been watching me?" she called.

"You can see a lot from the house."

"But not enough to come join me."

"I'm here, aren't I?"

"After sleeping in," she teased.

He shrugged. "We famous actors have busy evening schedules. Have to see and be seen, you know—however annoying it is."

"No one to see you here at the orchard." She climbed down the ladder. "Or did you go out last night after I'd gone to bed? Oh, wait—didn't I see a Tweet about watching a TV show? Me and your thousands of followers?"

He rolled his eyes, then nudged her elbow with his. "It's part of the job, and my agent keeps hounding me about it. Keeping track of me?"

"Always," she said fondly, smiling. "It's *my* job as your big sister."

He snorted. "By five minutes."

"It's still five minutes," she said sweetly. "Think we'll have any groupie interruptions today?"

He grimaced. "I hope not. Sorry."

Yesterday, a group of forty-something women had supposedly been on a wine tour of the region, and "accidentally" gone out of their way to see Tyler. He'd signed autographs, chatted personally, and Amy had gotten to watch her brother in action. He'd always been good with fans, just as she'd always been good with clients. Just another thing the twins had in common.

"I don't want them to interfere with the orchard," he said. "Come fall, when we're officially open, I can't guarantee what will happen. The public is welcome, after all."

Her smile fading, she touched his arm. "This is a temporary job for both of us. Six months. No one's asking you to leave Manhattan permanently."

He gave her a crooked smile. "I know. But I'm as glad to be here as you are. We're both running away from something, aren't we?"

Her eyes widened in surprise. "Tyler—"

But he already had the ladder in both hands and was walking to the next tree. "It's been a while since I checked for disease. Let's remember together."

She followed him, and soon they were trying to remember spraying schedules, how to keep ahead of apple scab, and when the beekeeper was supposed to arrive. Those were some of the topics of her childhood, and they should have felt safe as they prepared questions for their sister Rachel. But the topics were also part of the past, and it was difficult to feel safe there, when their father had so often let them down.

A couple hours later they went back to the house for lunch. Afterward, Tyler retreated to his room to return phone calls and messages, and so did she. It wasn't easy to abruptly walk away from a real estate career. She'd been a little concerned that it would be difficult not to be out in the community every day, dealing with buyers and sellers, being in a crowded office on occasion. So far, so good. It was peaceful to be with only a handful of longtime employees. And when the fall season began, she'd have more people around her every day than she knew what to do with.

For a moment, she stood still in her old bedroom. The sun shone through the windows, glinting off her MVP trophy from her senior year of competitive cheerleading. There was a good-citizen certificate from the Rotary Club, a cross she'd been given for her First Communion. There was even a stuffed animal some boyfriend had won her at the county fair. The blue-and-white checked comforter matched Rachel's old one, from when they used to share bunk beds in the same room. It felt familiar and comfortable. She was home, ready to begin her new—perhaps temporary—future.

She looked through the photos pinned to her corkboard: prom group shots, lots of photos with her siblings, especially Tyler, and then the family shot they'd taken at the fair, where they'd all dressed up in nineteenth-century clothes and posed with serious expressions.

She'd once had another photo just like that. Only it had been real and rare and a hundred years old. The professor would have liked that, she thought hollowly. Once, genealogy had been a passion of hers, and she had spent hours talking to her grandfather, going through old letters and photos with him. The discovery of *this* photo had been the culmination of her private research, a way to surprise her grandpa with a picture of his own grandfather and his family.

She reached behind the desk for the manila envelope where she kept the small pieces that were all that was left of the photo, of her attempt to do something to honor her family history for the two-hundredth anniversary next year. Her stupidity had ruined it all. She couldn't keep the evidence here where Tyler could find it; she couldn't throw it away, because it was proof of a life she never wanted to return to, of what her mistake had cost her. She'd find a hiding place, perhaps her old one in the barn. Now, the future had to be all that mattered.

But not to Professor Gebhart. He was all about the past—he wanted her family's past, and it only felt like another reminder of her mistake in trusting a man who didn't think he had a drinking problem.

— *Chapter 2* —

Jonathan got back to his Belmont neighborhood from his run to the university and around Grounds, since he'd needed to put aside the tension of his visit to Fairfield Orchard. Running was something he'd started just for his health. He'd taken it up in college when it was obvious he was sitting around more and more, his face buried in books or at the computer. But running had become a passion for him. He enjoyed the precise movement of his body, and it cleared his mind for thinking in a way nothing else did. Passing the flowers he'd recently hung on his porch, he entered the house, a nineteenth-century two-story with white clapboard siding, a big front porch, and lots of character. It had been perfect for him to slowly renovate and improve.

He took a quick shower and came down to the kitchen for a glass of water, but he still couldn't get Amy Fairfield out of his mind. He told himself it was because she held the future of his book, of his major discovery, in her hands. But there were other, more subtle things going on inside him, and he didn't like admitting that he found himself attracted to her. She was nothing like the women he normally dated, who were always professional and polished and expensively dressed—although he imagined she cleaned up well. But there was something about the way she'd come home for her parents, a loyalty he found rare and admirable. Those blue eyes had sparkled as she'd tried to tease him out of his serious nature. Not to mention the way the jeans had clung to her like those yoga pants women liked to wear. He didn't want such unwelcome feelings intruding on his work. His research had to come first.

He could always distract himself by attending the get-together tonight between the archaeology program and the anthropology and history departments—but that wasn't happening. He'd have to see his ex-best friend and his ex-fiancée, and awkwardness would ensue. Sometimes he thought he preferred historical people to real ones, who disappointed and betrayed. It had almost split the departments when their relationship had blown apart, since some professors had felt the need to choose sides.

He wasn't a monk; he dated occasionally, but he wasn't the kind of guy who could easily open up about something as ephemeral as "feelings." He thought he'd found the perfect relationship with his ex-fiancée, a partnership of intellects, of shared interests. But apparently that hadn't mattered as much to her.

He went to his office on the first floor and shook the mouse to awaken his computer. He had a desk that ran along two walls, and a rolling chair to move between it all. Books and papers covered one part of the desk, while his laptop was on the other. On the screen appeared the manuscript of his book, and he saw the chapter about the Blue Ridge Mountain property that eventually became Fairfield Orchard. It was while researching the Fairfields' history in the public domain—those land deeds Amy had mentioned, birth and death records, and information in Jefferson's own papers—that he'd begun to wonder if there was a discrepancy about Jefferson's flight from certain abduction by the British. Jonathan wanted the stories about the Fairfields, of course, but those stories would also help him set the groundwork for future work on locating Jefferson's exact retreat.

Amy was his gateway to her family. She'd been spunky up in that tree, unfazed when she'd almost fallen. His own heart had picked up speed at the near miss, but not hers—or not that he'd been able to tell. She'd been calm and matter-of-fact, hadn't seemed at all as intrigued by him as he'd been by her.

That was enough of that, he told himself, clicking to another section of his manuscript. He had more important work to do. The semester was almost over, and he had an entire summer for research and writing. He couldn't wait.

Midmorning the next day, Amy and Tyler walked alongside their sister Rachel through row after row of heirloom apple varieties, Albemarle pippins, Grimes Golden, and Baldwin, as they discussed the apple varieties they already grew, and the new acres that the workers had just finished planting. Amy took notes on a clipboard and wondered why Rachel looked so tired. Uma raced ahead, looking for rabbits to chase. Luckily, she seldom caught any. The sky was overcast but there was no feel of frost, and Amy hoped their worries about the weather could subside. But did it ever? She remembered her father waking them all in the dead of night to set up wind machines to pull warm air back down and combat a disastrous frost. The orchard was like a living being, to be nourished and protected and cared for.

Rachel was older than the twins by two years, her sandy hair on the blond side, cut short in a wavy chin-length bob that never got in the way as she worked. She'd never left the orchard, the one sibling out of six who wanted to work at Dad's side, to make a career of being a farmer. You'd think she'd be happy that Amy and Tyler had come home to work with her, but she seemed almost somber, hands in the pockets of her jean jacket, answering questions but not with any sort of enthusiasm.

Amy felt more and more concerned as the morning wore on. "Okay, Rach, out with it," she finally said, stepping in front of her sister, hands on her hips.

Tyler's eyes widened, as if he'd been unaware of any tension. *Men.*

But Rachel didn't look at all surprised. She only heaved a sigh, even as she straightened her shoulders and met Amy's gaze without flinching. "Ever since Dad decided to leave, I've been . . . unsettled."

"Unsettled," Amy echoed with concern.

Rachel winced. "Really, it started a long time before that. I've been feeling . . . restless."

And Amy knew, without Rachel having to say another word. "You want to leave."

Tyler's gaze narrowed. "Amy, stop jumping to conclusions."

"I'm not jumping to any conclusions, am I, Rachel?"

Rachel met her eyes steadily. "You're not. I've decided that with the two of you here, I need some time away, time to do something just for me."

Though Amy was concerned about what had prompted her sister's life-altering decision, she couldn't help feeling a little panicky. "Rachel, this is the worst time for that. Tyler and I don't have a clue what to do year-round."

"Of course you do. You grew up here."

"We manned cash registers, we guided customers to the ripest apples to pick, we drove the tractor. I don't know anything about keeping the books or deciding what new trees to plant, or when the spraying should begin. And Tyler and I working

35

alone together? It's not like we had our own secret language, you know. The whole family is counting on us to improve the business and keep it going, but with you leaving us . . ."

Tyler gave Amy a warning frown and turned to Rachel. "She's just scared, Rach. We thought we'd have you with us."

"I *am* with you," Rachel insisted, "in spirit. You can always call me anytime. But you won't need to. You'll have Carlos and the rest of the crew. Carlos knows everything."

Carlos Rodriguez and her father had been the closest of friends ever since the two of them had returned from Vietnam together. Carlos had been drafted in the early seventies when he'd been a pot-smoking hippie. Though he'd won a Bronze Star, he'd come home from the war still a hippie, and it wasn't any of Amy's concern if the pot-smoking was still accurate. She might have been just as guilty a time or two in college.

But Rachel was right—Carlos knew every bit of the business. Yet . . . no Rachel? Amy associated the orchard as much with her sister these last fifteen years as she did their father. But she'd noticed the circles under Rachel's eyes from the moment she'd come home. Her sister must have been struggling with this.

"But why wouldn't you tell us you'd been feeling restless?" Amy asked quietly. "Didn't keeping silent make things worse?"

Rachel shrugged, hands in her pocket against the chill wind. "No . . . maybe . . . I don't know. I thought it was just me, and that it would go away. How could I tell you all that?"

Amy knew all too well how easy it was to keep secrets.

"When the others came home to give Mom and Dad the going-away party," Rachel continued, "I couldn't say anything then. I didn't know what I wanted. I'm just starting to feel like I don't know how to help the orchard recover from all the years Dad sort of ignored it," Rachel continued. "That's been weighing on me more and more. To distract myself, I found other stuff to occupy my evenings and weekends. I dated on and off, I skied, I swam. I even tried crocheting, for goodness' sake. I finally came to realize that the orchard needs fresh blood, new ideas, people excited to be here. You both seem so glad to come home."

"We *are* glad," Amy insisted. "I've forgotten how wonderful it is to be part of this land, our orchard. But . . . new ideas? We're supposed to turn the orchard around all by ourselves?"

Hastily, Rachel said, "The others are coming to help eventually. And I don't want to walk away permanently. I just need a break."

"Then you should have a break," Tyler said.

Amy opened her mouth, then closed it. Tyler was right. She felt a little dizzy, knowing that this made her and Tyler's responsibility for the orchard even more urgent.

"Where do you want to go?" Amy asked, focusing on happiness for her sister's sake. "What do you want to do?"

"You remember my friend Ella? She's a free-lance writer now. She recently discovered that she had breast cancer, and though she's under-gone treatment and is doing okay, I couldn't stop thinking about how it had almost happened to Mom. Illness made Ella realize she's never given herself permission to travel. So for a few months, she's going to be a travel writer, but she's still a little too weak to do it on her own. I'd like to go along and help her."

"That's really kind of you, Rach," Amy said, feeling her heart soften for her sister.

Rachel winced. "I'm getting more out of it than I'm giving, trust me. But suddenly, I'm so very excited about the future, about seeing places around the world I've never been before."

Tyler gave Rachel a hug. "That's just great."

"Thanks."

But Rachel was staring at her worriedly, as if Amy's reaction would make or break her decision. Amy's nervousness was her own problem. Rachel was right; Amy had Carlos and the phone numbers of Dad and Rachel when she had questions.

Amy smiled, the same smile she used when a nervous client needed to be reassured. "I think it's an awesome idea. I'm very jealous, and looking forward to all the photos."

Rachel let out a sigh and threw her arms around Amy. "I'm so glad you're okay about this," she whispered fiercely.

Amy hugged her back, meeting Tyler's gaze. He looked a bit too knowing, as if he understood everything in Amy's mind—he usually did.

They continued to walk farther into the orchard, Rachel's arms slung through both of theirs as she chattered away about the plans she and her friend had begun to make. Uma gave an occasional bark as if to tell them she was still around somewhere. Amy only half listened, for she could see the original homestead nestled so close to a curving row of apple trees. The three of them used to play haunted house inside, while Logan, the oldest, did his best to scare them, and they all tried to keep the littler ones, Noah and Michael, away from their game. It was kind of mean now that she thought of it, but back then it had been a silly challenge.

Life was simple then, a true cliché if she'd ever heard one.

They reached a rough patch of land that had been allowed to stay wild, a meadow surrounded by trees and an outcropping of rocks too big to easily remove. It had been a pretty place for a picnic, and their mother had brought them there often, calling it their picnic meadow.

But now, Amy saw that the wild grasses had been flattened, and someone had built a fire with rocks surrounding it, leaving charred sticks in the center.

Rachel came to a stop. "What the hell is this?"

"I was just going to ask you the same thing," Amy said. "Did someone ask permission for any of this?"

"No, not that I heard," she said, frowning.

"It's probably just teenagers," Tyler pointed out. "I might have partied with my friends in the woods a time or two."

"But this isn't the woods," Amy countered. "This is a working orchard. They could have damaged the trees."

But they didn't see any damage. The three of them walked around the meadow, but everything seemed pretty normal, except for the blackened ashes of the fire. Uma bounded in and started sniffing.

"We can ask Carlos," Rachel said. "He's back at the garage working on one of the tractors."

They found Carlos in the large garage behind their little store, looking into the open engine of a tractor. His dog, an old black-and-white border collie named Barney, lifted his head and thumped his tail until Amy stopped to pet him. Uma, as usual, ignored most other dogs, and went to sniff in the shadowy corners.

Carlos was a wiry man who was still pretty

strong for a guy in his sixties. Outdoor work at the orchard surely helped. He was only a few inches taller than Amy, with black hair threaded through with gray, which he usually wore in a ponytail at the back of his neck. He wore a flannel shirt over jeans that looked as if he'd gotten some grease on them. A tattoo was partially visible at the neckline of his shirt and he wore small studs in his ears. She and her siblings had always thought of him as the fun-loving uncle who understood them when their father hadn't.

Carlos glanced up when they walked in. "So, you told them," he said to Rachel.

"I did."

Amy realized Rachel had confided her travel plans to Carlos. She wasn't surprised—he managed the orchard and the warehouse, and would need to know about such a major change.

"And it didn't go as bad as you thought it might," Carlos added.

"No, it didn't," Rachel said with relief.

Amy took a deep breath and it wasn't too difficult to put on a cheerful expression. "So Carlos, *you're* not planning to leave us, are you?"

He smiled from within his day's growth of gray whiskers, his dark eyes gleaming. "You couldn't chase me away, especially not with the two of you here to cause trouble. How could I leave you on your own?"

"You could decide to retire," Tyler pointed out.

41

Amy could have elbowed her twin hard.

"Retire? No way. What would I do all day? No grandchildren yet. I don't think Carmen's ever going to find a dude to put up with her."

"How's Carmen doing?" Amy asked, feeling a twinge of guilt. She and Carmen had been the best of friends growing up, since the Rodriguez property adjoined the orchard. They'd run wild together, watching tadpoles grow, hiding out in the tree house and keeping out boys, eventually keeping watch for each other below that same tree house when a teenage boy had been admitted. Neither of them had been girly girls, both tomboys, with Amy at her orchard and Carmen with her goats and chickens.

After dropping out of college, Amy had moved to Charlottesville and focused on her future with Rob, slowly leaving her friends behind, though she hadn't planned it. Carmen had gotten a business degree, and that made Amy feel both a little envious and even more foolish. Soon their friendship had degenerated to the occasional texts. And since Carmen wasn't big on technology, she'd never joined Facebook, the best way to fool yourself that you were still friends with someone.

Amy could pinpoint the exact moment she'd stopped texting anything personal—when Rob had started drinking. She couldn't find a way to explain to her old friends how a dark pit of worry had formed inside her. At the time, she'd told herself it was just a few drinks, that Rob would never be like her father. But her worry had turned to an isolation that had not only separated her from her friends, but which had distanced her from her family. Oh, she'd been there for holidays and working weekends in the fall, but . . . it hadn't been the same. She was so relieved and glad to put that painful part of her past behind her, reconnecting with her family on a deeper level again. But how to do that with her friends, when their break had been much deeper and permanent?

Part of her expected Carlos to frown, to show his disappointment in her. Carmen's final texts had been full of hurt and accusation, and much as Amy had tried to smooth them over, to pretend there was nothing wrong, Carmen hadn't believed her, and had never gotten in touch again. Neither had Amy, and the gulf between them had seemed uncrossable.

"My Carmen is doing great!" Carlos said, pride in his twinkling eyes and booming voice.

Amy let out her breath with relief.

"You've seen her goat cheese in the store, right?"

Amy knew he meant the orchard store, because no other store could go so easily unnamed. "Of course! It's delicious."

"She's in the MacDougall General Store in Spencer Hollow, too, and she's negotiating a few stores in Crozet."

"Soon she'll be in Charlottesville, if she has her way," Rachel said, grinning.

"She's always been a businesswoman—even in her tie-dyed fashion," Amy said with amusement. "We had the most successful lemonade stand ever."

"Because you held it during harvest at an orchard," Rachel reminded her.

Amy rolled her eyes good-naturedly.

Carlos said, "And now she's just begun a line of homemade goat milk soaps. She's got me using it now, too."

"No wonder you smell pretty," Tyler teased.

Carlos laughed. "I do. I can't keep it a secret."

"And your son?" Amy continued. "Has he graduated high school yet?" Carlos and his wife had accidentally gotten pregnant in their late forties, and she'd died of complications after the birth. Some men might have had a hard time raising that child, but Carlos considered Mateo a gift from God, a wonderful reminder of his wife. But he'd never remarried, which Amy always thought was sad.

"Mateo is finishing up his junior year," Carlos said, then shook his head. "That boy . . . always in trouble at school. His pranks are harmless, but . . ."

"Is Miss Jablonski still the principal?" Tyler asked. "She was a hardnose who cracked down on us for no good reason."

"No good reason?" Amy said, elbowing him playfully.

"Denise Jablonski," Carlos said, rolling his eyes. "She's gotten old and brittle and understands nothing."

"Says the man whose son is often sitting outside the principal's door," Rachel reminded him.

"The Denise I once knew would never—oh, never mind," Carlos said, waving a hand.

"So you knew her as Denise, huh?" Tyler asked.

"Don't get him started," Rachel urged with a groan.

"I know everybody in Spencer Hollow," Carlos said firmly.

"But you don't have feuds with everybody in Spencer Hollow," Rachel said.

Carlos gave her a cocky smile. "I don't have feuds with old women. Mateo only has another year at the school, and then he's done."

Amy's own smile gradually faded. The discussion about teenagers had reminded her. "Carlos, what's going on with the old picnic meadow? Apparently we've had trespassers and someone's lit a fire there."

Carlos frowned, then bent back over the tractor. "I noticed. Don't worry about it. I'll take care of it."

"Teenagers?" Tyler asked.

Carlos glanced sideways at him. "If I remember correctly, boy, you weren't above getting yourself lost in the woods."

"Me?" Tyler responded with wide-eyed innocence.

Carlos snorted. "I could tell your sisters a thing or two."

"Please don't," Amy said. "He already tells me everything, and there's only so much a sister can take."

"You only *think* I tell you everything," Tyler said.

Suddenly, Uma started barking at the door of the garage, a high-pitched friendly bark, rather than one of warning. Carlos's dog, Barney, got up to follow her.

Uma trotted out into the overcast day. A man stepped into view, tall and broad-shouldered, and Amy felt a ripple of goose bumps. How weird! She told herself it was only Jonathan Gebhart, back for an answer to his request. But there was something about the way he walked, so confident and precise, a man at ease in his body.

Uma joyfully let him rub her ears. Barney leaned against the man's legs until he had his own turn. When Jonathan glanced up and met her gaze, her pulse gave a jump.

"Hello, Amy," Jonathan said.

She nodded and spoke casually. "Professor."

He looked a little less proper today, in his neat, well-fitting jeans, hiking boots, and a puffy vest over a long-sleeve shirt. The wind ruffled his dark hair, and his green eyes squinted as they studied her, little lines in the corners that marked him as a man who'd seen some of life. She wasn't sure he'd seen more than there was in books, but still. She felt a little tingle in parts of her that hadn't tingled in a while.

"You told me to come back today," he said. "I hope you've given my request some thought."

She'd given it some thought, all right, and was mildly disturbed by how much she'd given *him* some thought as well. It had only been a few months since she'd broken it off with Rob, after all, but apparently her traitorous body had decided that the drought had gone on long enough.

"Amy?"

Amy winced as she heard her brother's call, and could practically feel her family gathering behind her with all the pressure of a storm front, looking over the professor with acute interest. And Jonathan looked back at them, probably estimating with clocklike precision who would be most willing to spill the family's dark secrets.

Not that there were that many secrets that she knew about—unless they were still secrets.

Tyler stepped forward and reached out a hand. "Hi, I'm Tyler Fairfield, Amy's brother."

The professor shook his hand, wearing a polite smile. "Jonathan Gebhart."

Amy introduced Rachel and Carlos, and even Barney the dog, who'd now decided to sit down on the professor's boot. Jonathan eyed Barney ruefully.

"So are you here for Amy?" Tyler asked, looking from Jonathan to Amy with interest.

"Not in the way you think," Amy assured him. "Professor, let's talk in private."

"Professor?" Rachel said. "Where and what do you teach?"

"Colonial history at UVA."

"Such an educated man," Rachel teased, elbowing Amy.

"He can say more later." Amy took Jonathan's arm, momentarily distracted by the strength of muscle she felt there. She dragged him away, but didn't get much farther than the old barn.

"This is surely over a hundred years old," the professor said, awe creeping into his voice.

"Almost one hundred and fifty," she amended.

"Amazing."

He walked inside the open double doors and saw all the wooden apple bins, stacked to the ceiling, some newly repaired, as they awaited fall harvest.

And then she thought about the ruined antique photo, its pieces hidden in the old hayloft, and she felt as if the professor could see it, judge her, and find her lacking. It wouldn't be any worse than she already felt about herself.

He walked along the wall, touching the hand-carved beams and the pegs that supported the whole structure without nails, his fingers dipping into the strikes made by an ax so long ago—she could imagine him thinking exactly that.

There was history at the orchard, almost two hundred years of it, and she realized that she could capitalize on that. If they were to prove that they had a plan to turn things around, to show that the orchard was worth Logan's investment, they would have every chance to be successful. Even mention in a history book might generate customers, especially if there was proof that a new discovery about Thomas Jefferson was involved. Then she realized that the professor was watching her muse. The green of his eyes was like a quiet summer morning, promising heat.

Whoa, now she was a poet?

"Have you given my request some thought?" he asked.

She couldn't read him—that was the curious thing. As a real estate agent, she was good at reading people, but his expression didn't betray anxiety or worry or even a plea. He just waited for her answer. He probably had a bunch of rebuttals all ready in case she turned him down. She imagined he was a man who planned every step ahead. And she liked that. In her Realtor days, she'd been known for the extensive calendar she kept, and how she never forgot an appointment.

"I've decided to discuss your proposal with my family," she told him, expecting a big smile of gratitude.

He nodded, saying nothing.

Trying to get some kind of reaction out of him,

she added with reassurance, "I'm pretty sure they'll be fine with it."

He cocked his head. "So you won't be dissuading them?"

"Of course not."

"I thought you might tell me you were too busy."

She forced a resolute smile. "We'll be very busy, no doubt about that. I just found out that my sister is following my parents out the door, temporarily anyway. That leaves Tyler and me, who've been away for years and years. I'll be honest, Professor, the two of us won't have time to help you much, and I feel bad about that. I understand how important this is to you." She expected a smile at her words, but he was all business.

"You said your grandparents would be interested."

"You know how grandparents are. They love to talk about the family history."

"Actually, I don't know that."

"I'm sorry," she said contritely. "They're dead?"

"My mother's parents are, but my paternal grandparents don't live nearby, and we never spent much time with them. My parents aren't as . . . family-oriented as yours seem to be."

This was a recitation of facts he'd obviously dragged out of himself, as if he thought a personal touch was necessary for her cooperation.

"Oh. I'm sorry again." He didn't even look

upset about it, which was sad and strange. She couldn't imagine not seeing her grandparents on a regular basis. Even her mom's parents, who lived in West Virginia, had been regular visitors across the state border. Her grandpa had died a few years back, but Grandma wasn't slowing down at all, still on the road, judging figure skating.

"I'm assuming the grandfather I would be speaking to owned the orchard before your dad?" he asked.

"He did. So he was here all the time when I was growing up. If I wasn't with my parents, I was with the grands."

He arched a brow. "The grands?"

"My grandparents have always seemed like such a solid unit, the ideal couple, that we gave them their own word."

"Interesting. Then it sounds like they'll be the people to talk to."

"Good." She caught herself glancing from his wide shoulders and down his body. There was a silence that lengthened as they watched each other. He was almost stern, and she wondered if part of that was a reaction to the effect of his handsomeness on women. She imagined he wasn't a man who flirted.

Uma gave a soft doggy whine of uneasiness, then took off after something within the bins. Was that a hint of relief in the professor's eyes as his gaze followed the dog?

Hesitantly, awkwardly, he said, "I'm sorry Rachel's departure is making it more difficult for you. You said you were in real estate. Was it around here?"

"Close enough, Charlottesville."

"Which neighborhood? I'm in Belmont."

Her eyes widened. "I'd rented a house in Belmont, but I let my lease run out last month and put my stuff in storage. What a coincidence."

He nodded. "I'm surprised you gave up your career to come back to the orchard."

She spread her hands wide. "It can seem crazy, I know. I felt like I really helped people. I liked evaluating the houses, too. Sometimes the inspectors said I could do their job for them!" She laughed self-consciously. "Sorry, I didn't mean that as a brag. I just love historic houses. I was considering specializing in them, when my parents sent out the call."

"The orchard must really have a hold on you."

"It's a tradition, our history, my family business. You should understand that."

To her surprise, those green eyes seemed to cloud, and he looked away. "Family businesses can be difficult to escape. Did you *want* to be here?"

There was more behind his question, she knew, but she wasn't going to pry. She couldn't help smiling her enthusiasm. "I lived here my whole childhood. Then . . . adulthood got in my way.

Except for holidays and events, I didn't come back all that much. But these last few days . . . I had no idea how much I'd truly missed being a part of this land, a part of making it a success." She took a deep breath. "Can't you just *smell* how special it is? Apple blossoms and even the earth itself. Yeah, it's dirt, I know, but . . . it's ours. I was glad to return, even if only for the six months Tyler and I have promised the others. After that—who knows?" She cleared her throat, feeling a little foolish for going on and on to a man who obviously only cared about his research rather than human emotion. "Do you have a cell, Professor, so I can let you know the family's decision without you having to traipse all the way out here?"

"I don't mind. It's a beautiful drive, with the mountains looming larger with every mile. It felt good to escape the tension of impending finals on campus."

"So it's not just tense for the students." She should have shown him the door. Why was it so easy to keep talking to him? Maybe because she could sometimes hear real emotion in his voice, like when he described the beauty of the drive, and it intrigued her. "Your cell number?"

He recited the number as she entered it into her phone. He even spelled his entire name for her. She had to bite her lip to prevent a smile. He was so earnest.

"I'll await your call," he said.

She turned to walk out of the barn, saying over her shoulder, "My family are all very busy. I can't guarantee how quickly they'll get back to me."

"I can keep myself occupied. The book is coming along."

Questions occurred to her about his book, but she held them back. She was so busy reminding herself to play it cool that when he reached his car she literally ran into his solid body. He caught her by the shoulders to steady her, and for a long moment, they stared at each other. His hands didn't leave, and they were warm against her upper arms.

"Uh, sorry," she said, blinking up as she stared too dreamily into his green eyes.

Yet she didn't move, and he didn't either. When he looked at her mouth, a little subtle current of desire threaded through her. She took a deep breath and stepped away.

"See you later, Professor."

"You don't need to call me that," he said, his voice a little deeper, huskier than before.

She couldn't help teasing him. "Whatever you say—Dr. Gebhart."

Shaking his head, he got into his car, turned around slowly on the gravel lot, and drove away. She shivered, though it wasn't cold.

— *Chapter 3* —

After the professor was gone, Amy caught sight of her brother taking a selfie with the orchard in the background.

Rachel came to stand beside her. "Tyler's communing with his fans," she said nonchalantly, hands in her pockets. "Instagram, I think."

"Poor guy. Not his favorite thing to do, but he's getting pressure from his agent. I thought he'd be able to take a break from the promotion for a while, but he has some auditions lined up. He told me that how many fans and followers he has is now being taken into account by casting."

"Mmm." Then Rachel glanced past her to the dust rising from Jonathan's car. "So who was that?"

"I believe I introduced you."

"I mean who is he to you? You dating him?"

"No," Amy said too quickly. "Does he look anything like my type?"

"Do you have a type? You were with Rob a long time, but he was only one guy. And it's been a while, right. How long?"

"Six months," Amy said, struggling to sound unaffected.

"What really happened?"

Amy's stomach clenched, but she continued to

breathe normally. She was used to faking her way through such conversations. "We just didn't have anything in common anymore."

"Did you ever?"

"Well, that's a nice thing to say," Amy said with exasperation. "You didn't like him?"

"He was okay. He never made an attempt to get to know any of us."

And apparently I didn't know him either. "We were together a long time, but it just didn't work out. I did love him . . . once."

"Well, I'm glad he didn't break your heart."

Oh, he'd broken it, all right, Amy thought bleakly.

Tyler approached them, sliding his phone into his pocket. He reached down to pet Uma.

"Did you appease your adoring fans?" Amy asked dryly.

"Always. But let's talk about the teacher."

"Professor," Amy corrected. She explained Jonathan's research. "He needs our info for his book. He's pretty excited about proving his new discovery—not that I know how we can help with that. Grandpa probably will be able to help the most, with Dad gone. I know any kind of attention has to be good for the orchard, but I admit it's hard to imagine finding time for this, myself."

Tyler frowned at her.

Rachel nodded. "Anything would help. Apple-picking season doesn't seem to be the draw it once was. So many U-Picks and wineries that it's hard to stand out."

Amy and Tyler exchanged a sober look.

Rachel clapped them each on the back. "But the wholesale part of our business is as brisk as ever, so don't worry too much. And with Logan's investment, we should be set."

That was easy for *her* to say. Rachel didn't have to come up with new, exciting reasons for Logan's partners to understand his investment.

Amy put on a smile—she'd always been good at that. "Then I guess I'll text everyone and make sure they're all right with the professor's work."

"I don't know why they wouldn't be," Tyler said. "I'm surprised you're so reluctant, Amy. You used to love this kind of stuff."

She shrugged, wishing he'd be distracted by his phone again, but he was watching with a twinkle in his blue eyes. She would have punched him in the arm if they were still teenagers. Maybe she still would.

To her surprise, their brothers Logan, Noah, and Michael got back to her almost immediately with their approval, and then she texted the professor. He wanted to know when he could begin, and she told him she'd have to check with her grandparents first.

"Do you both mind if I go see the grands?" Amy asked.

"Go ahead," Rachel said. "I'm going to start saying my good-byes to the warehouse staff. And since Carlos is going to open the next CA storage room, Tyler, you can get a reminder about how it's done. We have apples to pack and ship."

"I know what a controlled atmosphere room is," Tyler said with exasperation, even as he followed her. "Our apples stop ripening in there. What else do you need to quiz me on?"

Rachel and Tyler continued to bicker as they headed for one of the dirty, rusty pickup trucks. Amy stood and watched them until they'd disappeared down the dirt road, farther into the orchard, where the warehouse and cider mill were. She couldn't stop thinking about her sister really leaving the orchard. And apparently soon. Now that Rachel had made up her mind to go, she wasn't going to linger.

Amy's little Prius looked cute when she drove around Charlottesville in her Realtor capacity, but wasn't much good on the uneven roads of the orchard, where it tended to bottom out if she wasn't careful. She drove the couple miles into the village of Spencer Hollow to visit her grandparents. Spencer Hollow had stop signs but no traffic lights. The main road, Jarmans Gap Road, went right from the mountains, past the orchard, and through Spencer Hollow before eventually arriving in Crozet. The Hollow, as the locals often called it, was a crossroads around which clustered a connected series of nineteenth-century brick storefronts: the MacDougall General Store, Forget Me Not Antiques, Jefferson's Retreat Tavern, and Books to Buy or Borrow, whose owner, Betty Clark, loved books so much she'd divided her two parlors into both a bookstore and a library. They even had a doctor, though he was an old guy who was semiretired after a career in Richmond.

The Hollow was a peaceful place, with lots of dirt roads, horse trails, and rural charm. Nineteenth-century homes, both brick and those sided in clapboard, spread out from the main intersection, and the grands lived in one by Bucks Elbow Creek, beyond the general store and across from the public park. As Amy pulled into the driveway, she saw Henry Fairfield, her white-haired grand-father, sitting in a rocking chair on the front porch. He was close to ninety, a veteran of Korea who'd had the sad misfortune of watching his son and then grandson, her brother Michael, go off to war as well. Grandpa had returned from Korea renewed in his belief that feeding people was the most basic, fulfilling thing one could do, and he'd proceeded to devote his life to the orchard.

He raised his arm in a wave, his expression beyond pleased behind his glasses, and she felt a twinge of guilt. She hadn't visited as much as she should have the last few years. She'd told herself that real estate was a seven-day-a-week job, but being self-employed meant she could make her own hours. She had no excuses except her narrow focus on propping up the life and relationship that ended up falling apart anyway.

"Amy, dear, how good to see you!" Grandpa Fairfield called as she got out of the car. "Do you have time for some lemonade?"

She felt even worse. He thought she was just dropping by briefly, because of course that's all she'd done. "I have plenty of time, Grandpa. Tyler and Rachel have everything handled at the orchard."

"I'm coming into work later this afternoon," he said, giving her a big hug after she came up the stairs.

"I'm not surprised." She kissed his cheek and only pulled away enough to look up into his face. Though there were lines about his eyes and mouth, his eyes still shone that blue that he'd bequeathed to his grandkids. "You work too hard, you know. If you want to kick back on the porch and"—she saw a book on his chair—"read, then promise me you'll do it. It is a beautiful spring day."

He waved a hand. "And I've been enjoying it. But I want to ride through the orchard, see how the trees are doing this spring. It makes me feel better. Now come sit down."

In the shade it was a little brisk, so she was glad she'd brought her jacket. Grandpa was wearing a sweater and faded, comfy-looking pants. He insisted on serving her, fetching another glass and pouring lemonade from the pitcher on the little wicker table. She sat back with a sigh, looking out on the quiet, sun-dappled street, which ended just a hundred yards or so west at the creek. The grands had already hung baskets of pink impatiens and yellow begonias between the columns of the porch.

"So what's it like being back full-time at the orchard?" he asked.

She smiled. "It feels good. I don't know if I ever thought I'd leave it permanently, but the years did seem to add up, didn't they?"

"They did. Your father missed you—he missed all of you. But he wanted you to find your own way in the world."

"You raised him right," Amy pointed out.

A shadow passed over his face.

"Don't go there, Grandpa. You didn't turn Dad into an alcoholic. The fallout from Vietnam did."

"I don't know about that. Did you know that he didn't want to return to the orchard after his discharge, but I talked him into it? U-Pick orchards were just catching on, and I lured him with the thought of trying something new."

Her father had never said a thing. Gently, she said, "Grandpa, he suffered from nightmares for a long time. That wasn't because he'd chosen farming for a living."

Grandpa let out a long sigh. "Logically, I know

you're right, but I still feel somehow to blame, like I coerced my own son into something he didn't want. And when the drinking got worse . . . I didn't know how to help him. I offered to listen, as a fellow veteran even more than just his dad, whenever he needed it, but . . ."

"But he tried to go it alone, always a mistake when you've got family to support you." She heard her own words and felt a chill. Did she take after her dad so very much? She'd tried to go it alone with her failing relationship for years. And it had almost cost her her self-respect. And before that she'd tried so hard to learn from her father's mistakes, had never touched a drop of alcohol out of fear she'd be just like him. And yet, apparently, there were other flaws she could inherit.

She hesitated a moment before saying, "Was it very difficult to watch Dad fall down on the job where the orchard was concerned?" She didn't want to be the next descendent Grandpa was disappointed in.

He took a deep sip of lemonade, his white eyebrows drawn together in a thoughtful frown. "Difficult, yes, but it wasn't the orchard I feared for, but his life and what he was doing to his family—especially you children. Many a time I offered to attend AA meetings with him. Sometimes he even went. He was never cruel to you children or to your mom, so sometimes I just had to satisfy myself with that. But he wasn't dependable as a father and husband. It was difficult to watch. But it wasn't until tragedy almost happened that he opened his eyes and saw what he'd become."

"I'm sorry, Grandpa," she said, leaning across the wicker armrest to take his hand.

He gave her a sad smile and squeezed her fingers warmly.

She was more and more like her father with every word her grandpa said, she thought bleakly. For her father, that near tragedy had been when he'd been driving a tractor with a wagon full of children and almost flipped it over out of the carelessness of suffering from a hangover. He got sober, and though it had been a struggle, that had been ten years ago. He'd tried to make up for his failings every day of his life.

Could she and Tyler do the same? Could they make Fairfield Orchard even more successful? It seemed like a daunting task, and she wasn't sure she had time for a learning curve. Which was why she'd agreed to give history a try.

In a lighter voice, she said, "It would seem your generation was more stoic and solitary than my dad's. Guess that's just a generalization, huh?"

"Sure. People are people. They have to find ways to be part of the community."

"Really? What do you suggest?"

To her surprise, his gaze darted away from her

evasively. "Well . . . I go to the VFW down in Charlottesville every once in a while."

That was strange. Had she imagined his unusual reaction to her question?

He continued, "And of course I'm at the orchard every day in the fall."

"Are you taking classes through the university like Grandma is? I know she's meeting lots of people that way."

He made a face. "Neither of us went to college, but Grandma is the one it still bothers. I learn plenty of things in books. I don't need a professor telling me how to learn."

Uh-oh. She'd known he wasn't happy with Grandma's choices to take such unusual classes as documentary filmmaking or Life Beyond Earth. She'd thought it was about him feeling lonely or left behind. But would he hold such a thing against Jonathan and the chance that the orchard might get some good publicity out of this?

"Oh. Well, then maybe you won't be quite so happy with what I wanted to tell you next." She took a long drink of her lemonade. "I've had an interesting request from a history professor at the university."

At least Grandpa didn't scowl; he just waited to hear what she'd say before he reacted.

"It seems our orchard might be a little famous. Professor Gebhart wants to write a book about our ancestors' association with Thomas Jefferson."

Grandpa leaned toward her, arms braced on his knees, listening intently. "Go on, sweet pea. You and I have had these discussions before."

She felt a burst of nostalgia and pain, but she cut them off expertly to present a pleasant front, even to her grandpa.

"Well, he wants to explore our history, not so much births and deaths and land deeds, as he put it, but any stories that might have been passed down, any historic artifacts we might have. He thinks he found a new discovery, that Jefferson might have come to his land here to hide from the British during the American Revolution. I thought it might be good publicity for the orchard."

"Of course, of course. This sounds intriguing." Grandpa rubbed his hands together. "So he doesn't have proof yet?"

"Not yet. That's what he's searching for now."

"And of course you're all set to help him. You've always loved this sort of thing."

"No, I just can't. I'm too busy learning about the orchard. But would you be willing to be involved? No one knows as much about our history as you do."

He grinned. "I'd be honored. I have the family Bible here—not that it goes all the way back to Jefferson's time. And I remember my own grandpa telling me about a lost diary. Maybe this professor can help me find it."

"Well, he's motivated, I'll say that. This book

has to be submitted for publication by the fall for it to be part of his tenure portfolio."

"Then he needs our help! Good thing I'm not going on any long vacations—or an RV trip across country."

They both shared a chuckle.

"Now, Grandpa, you're not making fun of my mom's love of travel, are you?"

"Not at all. It's a beautiful country and we all should see it. I just believe in hotels and airplanes."

"She doesn't have to pack and unpack, and they can come and go as they please on their own schedule—what's not to love?"

"Those are the pros, all right. We'll see what they say about the cons in a year or two."

"It's only been a week, but still, they're loving it so far. Sounds like Cocoa Beach is beautiful this time of year. Have you seen the photos they posted on Facebook?"

"Of course. Your grandma might not have time to keep up with family, but I do."

Another little dig at Grandma. Amy didn't like it.

Apparently she hadn't hidden her concern well.

"That sounded just awful, I know," Grandpa said. "Don't you worry. Your grandma and I love each other, and teasing's a part of marriage. I . . . mostly understand what she has to do and she . . . mostly understands me." And he grinned.

What did Grandma have to understand about him? Amy didn't think it wise to ask.

She drank the last of her lemonade. "I guess I better go back before Tyler misses me."

"He's got Rachel, hasn't he—oh, not for long, I forgot."

"So you knew, too?" Amy asked with only a little exasperation.

Grandpa smiled with sympathy. "People like to confide in me." He gave her a pointed look over the top of his glasses.

She laughed. "I've got nothing to confide, Grandpa. But I promise I will confide if I need help."

Amy rose to her feet and Grandpa followed a little more slowly.

"I'll be there every day, sweet pea," he said, putting an arm around her shoulders as they walked across the porch and down the stairs. "There's nothing I don't know about that orchard."

But she wanted him to enjoy his retirement, and not think she was incompetent. She wanted him to be proud of her. She hugged him hard. "Thank you, Grandpa. I appreciate it. I'll get in touch with you with some dates and times that the professor is free. He says time's a little limited as he approaches finals, but after that, he'll be wide open."

"That's fine."

After leaving the grands' house, she turned onto Jarmans Gap Road right next to MacDougall General Store, another place she'd once hung out, when she'd been friends with Brianna, the owner's daughter. Another friend she'd left behind. Amy wasn't too impressed with herself these days . . .

Jonathan was no longer so surprised at the eagerness with which he drove up the winding road to Fairfield Orchard. It was a sunny Saturday afternoon, a few days after Amy had given him the good news about her grandfather's excitement to work with him. Jonathan had finished the school week and the prep for finals in a state of anticipation that was rare for him. He told himself it was the thought of finishing his book, finally being able to submit it for publication. The completion of his tenure portfolio was closer than ever.

But he'd never been one to lie to himself. It was also the thought of seeing Amy Fairfield again.

He was being an idiot. He knew such an attraction was primal in nature, something to be avoided as he worked toward his book deadline.

But . . . it had been a year since his fiancée left him, a year where he'd questioned everything about himself. The fact that he was interested at all in Amy surprised him. His ex, Geneva, had proved to him that he wasn't capable of the intimate emotions a woman needed, not after everything his parents had put him through.

But apparently his sex drive was just fine. He would ignore it.

He parked near the main barn, and only Uma greeted him. She came racing out, barking excitedly, and tried to jump into the car when he opened the door.

As he held her back, he scratched both sides of her neck. "You trying to get away, girl? I thought it was nice here."

"She loves to go for a drive."

Jonathan looked up to see Amy standing near the car, smiling with good-natured exasperation at her dog. It was a warm spring day, and she was wearing another pair of faded jeans tucked into her work boots, and a long-sleeve T-shirt that hugged her and gave him the best view he'd had so far. She was short, but proportioned well. The brim of her Cavaliers ball cap shaded her eyes from him. He imagined the cap gone, her hair tumbling down around her shoulders . . .

That was enough of that. He wasn't used to vivid imaginings about a woman he'd just met. But he kept getting caught in her expressive eyes, and that made him want to understand everything about her. For work purposes, of course, he reminded himself.

"Good afternoon, Amy," he said, slamming the car door shut.

"Afternoon, Professor." She eyed the leather bag hung from his shoulder. "Is that your man purse?"

"It's a satchel. It holds my laptop and whatever else I bring back and forth to work." As her dog trotted away, he added, "I guess I bore Uma."

"It's not you," she said with warm reassurance. "She's not one for lots of petting. She's happy for a moment's attention, to smell any new smells, and then she's done."

"I don't have a dog, so I must be a disappointment."

She eyed him, then flashed a teasing smile. "We'll see." She turned and started walking, saying over her shoulder, "The grands are up at the house. It's down this lane, away from the public section of the orchard."

He was listening to her, but was finding himself distracted by watching her walk in her tight jeans. He had to get it together, behave like a professional instead of a high school boy. Although it wasn't as if the college boys were much different. Apparently neither was he.

"Amy!" called a woman's voice.

Jonathan saw an elderly couple, arm in arm, come around the bend past the oak trees, and the woman raised a hand in greeting. They were dressed casually, the man in jeans and sweater, the woman in slacks and a fleece. Though their wrinkled faces betrayed their ages, they weren't bent over, as many might be. He imagined that years of hard work at the orchard had kept them strong. Their eyes were bright and interested, and showed a love they couldn't deny when they looked at Amy. Jonathan felt a momentary disconnect, for he hadn't seen that look even in his parents' eyes since he'd decided on his career and destroyed their hopes. And even before that, it was more of a look of pride and arrogant satisfaction because of his intelligence, not love. It had taken him a long time to realize that.

"This is Dr. Jonathan Gebhart," Amy said, "the UVA professor I was telling you about."

Her grandparents glanced at each other with amusement over something inexplicable, then gave him gracious smiles.

"How nice to meet you, Doctor," Mrs. Fairfield said, stretching out a hand. "I'm Frances Fairfield and this is my husband, Henry."

He shook hers, and then her husband's. "I'm grateful to meet you both. And please, call me Jonathan."

"We're thrilled to talk about family history," Mr. Fairfield said. "I even brought the family Bible."

He held up the old leather-bound book as if in offering.

Mrs. Fairfield exchanged an amused glance with Amy.

"Let's be honest," the elderly woman said, "*Henry* is thrilled. I'm simply glad someone wants to listen to him, since I've had to be the one doing that for almost seventy years."

Mr. Fairfield shook his head, although his gaze was fond upon his wife.

"And it's not like I haven't made him listen to me prattle on," Mrs. Fairfield continued. "I'm taking classes through UVA, Doctor—Jonathan."

"I hear she even missed an outing to Charlottesville's best cemeteries to meet you," Amy said. "You should be impressed."

"I am," Jonathan replied. "What classes are you taking?"

"One of them is Drawing Concepts and Practice. Perhaps you could be one of the models." Her eyes shone as she eyed his chest.

"Grandma!" Amy said, aghast.

Jonathan could feel his face heat up. When was the last time he'd blushed?

Mr. Fairfield shot his wife a look, then held out the book. "I'm excited about your project, Jonathan. I don't know how much help I'll be, since the Bible isn't two hundred years old. But it's at least a hundred."

Jonathan accepted the book and felt a surge of awe at holding something historic. It always took him by surprise, yet it happened every time.

He loved history, and words emerged before he could censure them. "When I hold something like this, I find myself in the past. I like to imagine who first purchased it, who wrote the names of their children on its shiny new pages, who read to those children from it, how they took care of it to make sure it stayed safe for your whole family to enjoy."

Mr. Fairfield nodded with understanding, but Amy looked at him from beneath her ball cap with an amused expression. He'd always been different and known it, practically from the moment he learned to read his first words at two years old.

Amy said, "Okay, I can see why you were drawn to history."

He nodded, then glanced at her grandfather again. "Is there a place we can sit and talk?"

"It's too beautiful to be indoors," Mr. Fairfield said. "I like to smell my apple trees. There's a picnic table in the shade by the Snack Shack."

Jonathan followed the Fairfields—who moved at a pretty brisk pace for their ages—already opening his satchel. The Bible seemed hot in his hands, full of secrets. He set it gently on the table so that he could open his laptop, then looked at the two objects side by side: two different items that people wrote in, but a century apart. He remembered not to say that out loud. He was still a geek, but he was trying to be a little more subtle about it.

Out of the corner of his eye, he noticed Amy. She had followed them, but at a slower pace. Maybe she'd heard every one of her grandfather's stories before and just didn't want to hear them again. Or maybe she had orchard business to attend to. Or maybe it all bored her. She looked at her watch.

— *Chapter 4* —

Amy didn't know what to do with herself as she watched the professor and the grands sit together at the table. Jonathan brought out his laptop, as if he couldn't wait to record everything her grandpa said. She ached to sit down with them, be a part of the conversation, go back and forth with Grandpa to get all the details right. Could Jefferson really have come here during the actual American Revolution? The very thought made her awestruck, even as it caused so much pain. She'd spent a long time putting her love of her family history out of her mind. Every time she mentioned it to Rob the last few years, he'd thought she was rubbing his nose in her family success, rather than simply sharing something she was passionate about with the man she| loved. She learned not to talk about it. And after she'd let Rob ruin her antique photo so spitefully, she couldn't bear to permit herself enjoyment of her family history again. It was too painful.

But Jonathan's research was still a wonderful thing, she reminded herself, both for her grandpa and perhaps for the orchard, when the book someday hit the shelves and gave them some local publicity. Because it *would* get local publicity—everything about Thomas Jefferson did. He was the pride of Charlottesville, once president of the United States, the man who'd designed the university, who'd built Monticello.

But in that Bible were the names of the family who'd been captured in the antique photo she'd managed to find. And her carelessness had let it be destroyed, before she could scan it. What her grandfather would have given to see his own grandfather staring somberly at the camera, as old-timers used to do. And it was all her fault. It could have been the centerpiece of their two-hundredth anniversary, and instead it signified the depths she'd let herself sink to.

She didn't go to the picnic table, even though she knew she was being rude. She did have a lot of work to do, after all. A tractor trailer would be arriving soon to pick up the apples they'd packed the last few days. But as she stood to the side, pretending to look at her phone, she was reluctantly watching the professor. His fingers flew on the keyboard, and sometimes he didn't even watch himself type as he asked questions of Grandpa and absorbed the answers. He was in his element, focused, as if the past interested him much more than the present. Which was ridiculous. He was a young, good-looking man, after all. He was making parts of her tingle without even trying. Surely he had an active social life, women who appreciated the strong, silent type. But she found herself wondering about that. He made her wonder far too much.

"Amy, if you're so curious, why don't you join us?" Grandma teased. "Grandpa and I will fetch some cider and snacks and be right back."

"Let me do that for you," Amy insisted.

"We need to stretch our legs," Grandpa said. "You come sit down here and keep Jonathan amused."

After her grandparents had started their slow walk to the main house, Amy eyed Jonathan. He didn't seem to notice her, focused as he was on his laptop and whatever he was typing furiously. His dark hair fell over his forehead, those green eyes squinted with concentration, those cheekbones—damn, she had to stop staring at him. She felt like one of Indiana Jones's students, who could only stare at him dreamily while he taught. The professor must get a lot of that. She turned away, the pickup truck and escape calling her.

"I thought you were going to keep me amused."

Was he teasing her? She turned around and regarded him, falling back on a flirtatious tilt of her head to hide her uncertainty. "I thought you were a big boy who could amuse himself."

He gave a crooked smile that was far too endearing.

"Don't you want to tell me all your family secrets?" he asked.

She reminded herself that he only cared about

his research, then gave him her real estate smile, bright and polite and interested. "I don't know anything more than my grandparents do, that's for sure. You'd just be wasting your time with me."

"I don't know about that."

And then he glanced down her body, and she was very aware of her rough old jeans and faded shirt, and how farming wasn't the most glamorous life. She'd worn adorable business-casual clothes in her old real estate life, sunny dresses or cute blazers and cropped pants. She had to get away from these crazy thoughts. She put a foot on the bench of the table and leaned her forearm on her thigh.

"I've got to ask," she began, "how did you choose history? It's not a topic a normal college kid chooses, like business or education or nursing."

"Maybe I wasn't normal."

He crossed his arms over his broad chest, as if daring her to ask more.

And she wasn't backing down from a dare. "Now you've got to explain that."

Was it her imagination, or did his gaze briefly slide away, as if he was reluctant to talk about himself? Men always liked to talk about themselves—didn't women learn the fastest way to interact with a guy was to ask him about himself?

He shrugged. "I learned to be passionate about

history after visiting Civil War battlefields as a kid."

"I've visited a battlefield or two, but thought Kings Dominion was a lot more exciting. I like roller coasters."

"My parents preferred intellectual field trips rather than ones that were simply fun."

She winced. "Doesn't sound like a fun child-hood."

"It was. If I could make it sound intellectual, my parents were for it—hands-on science centers, museums, battlefields—every weekend. I persuaded them to take me to the glass museum in Corning, New York, once."

"You were a strange kid."

"I know. But the history fascination never left me. I liked seeing how people lived, that they were just like us, even as far as living through wars. Of course, the American Revolution and the Civil War were on our home soil. That made them different."

"And these trips decided your profession," she said dubiously.

"Yes, and some intriguing classes both in high school and college."

"Your parents must have been very proud that their intellectual trips affected you."

"You'd think so."

She cocked her head. Before she could ask further questions, he continued speaking.

"Another thing I like to do is write, which is an important part of my job. You can't teach at a major university without being able to write about your research."

"When do you possibly have time to write—oh, wait, in the summer, right?"

"I try to do it all year round, so I don't lose the sense of my work."

"You're ambitious, and writing helps you advance in your career."

He nodded. "True. But don't think this is hard for me. I'm not only good at writing, I like doing it." He frowned. "I'm not bragging, just stating a fact."

"I know." She wrinkled her nose. "Writing was never my favorite thing."

"Then what was your favorite thing? I'd like to know more about you."

"Are you flirting with me, Professor?" She kept her voice light, but she took her foot off the bench and straightened up.

"No. I'm curious about the members of a family I'll be spending a lot of time with."

"Should I bring Rachel and Tyler in on this, then, so they can answer your questions, too?"

"I'll get to them in time, but for now, I think you're avoiding my question."

"There's nothing to avoid," she insisted. "You're here about how my family history is connected to Thomas Jefferson."

"History is about people. We'll all be history someday. I guess I'm just fascinated about why people make the decisions they do. For instance, I know you became a Realtor, but did you go to college?"

"I did. Although I guess you didn't leave a family business behind, or you'd understand it's a complicated decision."

She thought he went a little still, as if she'd hit a target she didn't know she was aiming at.

But all he asked was, "What did you major in?"

"Business."

"To bring back knowledge to the orchard, I assume. Yet you didn't come back until this year."

"And I didn't get a degree either. Guess that makes me a failure to a professor." She chuckled.

His dark brows lowered in a concerned frown, and to her surprise, he reached and put his hand over hers.

"I don't think you're a failure."

His touch connected her to him in a way that seemed more intimate than it really was. She pulled away, but he went on as if he didn't notice.

"A lot of people wouldn't have given up a career they enjoyed to come home, even if their families needed them."

"Sure they would," she insisted.

"Really?" He shook his head. "I should stop questioning you. I'm being too intrusive. Next I'll be asking you if there was a man involved—and that's just ridiculous. You're beautiful—of course you've dated."

Her mouth sort of sagged open. Her jeans had a hole in the knee; she wore no makeup. Her best feature, her hair, was always out of her face because she couldn't be bothered. And he thought she was beautiful?

She looked into his deep, spring-green eyes as if she could see the truth there, and soon she realized the moment was stretching on too long. She should look away, should *walk* away, and instead she dropped her gaze to his mouth.

"Amy!"

The call from the direction of the house caused a rush of relief. The professor looked back toward his laptop, but all he did was stare at the keys, as if he'd forgotten how to use them.

Amy turned away. "Yeah, Rachel?"

"Supper! Bring Jonathan."

Great. Just when she felt the relief of impending escape.

"You heard my sister, Professor," Amy said. "Do you have supper plans?"

"No, but I don't wish to intrude."

"Of course you're not intruding. Come join us."

He hesitated before nodding, and she wondered if he was only being polite. But she hadn't imagined the warmth of his hand on hers, or the way they'd looked at each other. This probably wasn't such a good idea. If the professor knew what kind of fool she could really be . . .

And how could she trust her own intuition? It had backfired so spectacularly already, leaving her shaken and doubting herself more than she ever had in her life.

But he scooped up the laptop and put it back in his man purse. She turned and walked briskly down the lane, not looking back to see if he was following. Uma trotted at her side, full of expectation. Jonathan caught up with her easily, his long legs moving almost slowly next to her short ones. They took the curve around the trees, and the family home came into view, surrounded by oak and hickory trees. The house had a long front porch where her parents had often spent their evenings relaxing. But they'd never been far from their orchard, their business, twenty-four hours a day. Amy wondered if that might have contributed to their need to escape.

"Nice house," Jonathan said as they went up the stairs.

"Even if it isn't historic?" she asked. "You might as well have spoken that part aloud."

"Well, I must confess that I am looking forward to exploring the old family homestead."

"This one is much more comfortable."

Inside, they entered the "formal" living room, which her parents always insisted be reserved for guests. But their guests were usually orchard patrons, and they never came inside. So the room had ended up being used for sprawling Barbie homes or Thundercat forts made of sheets. It was really the family room in the back that was the heart of their home, and Uma led them both through the dining room where Tyler was setting dishes, and into the kitchen, where her grand-parents were removing items from a tray.

"We were all set to return with the cider," Grandma Fairfield said, "when Rachel announced dinner was ready. Jonathan, you can still have cider with your meal."

"Or he can have wine," Tyler called.

As they decided what to drink, Amy leaned over the Crock-Pot and sniffed appreciatively, bumping shoulders with her sister. "Pork roast and veggies," she murmured. "You make the best, Rachel. Who'll make it when you're gone?"

"You will. I'll give you the recipe."

They'd been taking turns cooking for each other, but soon it would be only her and Tyler. She could see them degenerating into salads or quick hamburgers, or some pasta sautéed with vege-tables. Or maybe Tyler would eat at Jefferson's Retreat more. It was Rachel who made supper a family event.

Right now was still a family event, and she realized that Rachel had outdone herself as a sort of good-bye. Amy put her arm around her sister in a quick hug, and Rachel patted her hand, blinking her eyes rapidly before looking away. Amy hoped Rachel found what she was looking for.

Soon they were all sitting around the dining room table, passing the platter of sliced pork, and the bowl of veggies and potatoes. Tyler traded barbs with Rachel, Grandma tried to talk about the drawing class she was taking, and Grandpa wanted to know if they'd found any fungus on the trees. Uma sat alert on her little rug and silently prayed someone would notice how starving she was—or at least that's what Amy always imagined.

Voices rose and fell, but Amy found herself watching the professor. He didn't say much, and he seemed more reserved than when they'd been together outside. Of course, they'd been alone then. Once or twice, he opened his mouth as if to speak, but the conversation continued to swirl around him, and he let it go. It made her think he must not come from a very big family. Or maybe his was polite and let everyone else talk, instead of speaking over each other, as the Fairfields good-naturedly did. The longer she was near him, the more she saw that he was serious yet quietly confident, at ease with the success he'd made of himself. He was far too appealing to her.

"Did our tour of the orchard give you guys any brilliant ideas?" Rachel teased.

Amy regretted that all their voices hushed, and Jonathan watched her with interest. She made them wait as she finished chewing a slice of pork. Tyler kept his eyes on his plate and ate with determination. He could have answered the question, too.

After Amy swallowed, she chuckled. "I don't know enough to know what I'm doing, let alone have ideas to improve the place that would make Logan and the others relax."

"Logan is our big brother," Tyler said to Jonathan. "He's the new money in this operation."

"He's a venture capitalist," Amy explained, then said deliberately to Tyler, "An *investor,* not just 'the money.' We want to prove to him that we have ideas, that we know what we're doing."

"We're even going to write a business plan," Tyler said. "Very official."

She glanced at the professor, who was studying her with interest. "And maybe our guest is bored by all of this."

"If you need a writer, I could help," Jonathan said.

"Oh, no, we'd never bother you like that," Amy said quickly.

They passed the bottle of wine around, but Amy stuck to sweet cider, as usual.

"Logan is using this investment as a way to stay in New York," Tyler said dismissively.

"No, he's going to take his turn here, too," Amy insisted.

"Now, children," Grandma began, "disagreeing in front of a guest is impolite. Perhaps he'd rather hear the memories of your childhood in the orchard."

"We're not historic enough for him," Amy said, eyeing the professor with amusement.

Jonathan cleared his throat. "But the things you did here on this historic land are important. They're your own family history."

"But you're not writing about our generation," she said.

"No, I'm not."

"You could." Tyler leaned back in his chair with an air of bad-boy laziness.

"No, he could not," Amy emphasized.

Grandpa looked eagerly at Jonathan. "These kids loved their tree house. That's my biggest memory of their childhood. When I'd be out on my tractor, and got anywhere near, I could see them acting like pirates, hanging from the ropes. My son built it for them when Logan was old enough to enjoy it. There's even another wing, higher than the main floor of the tree house."

" 'Another wing' might be stretching it," Amy said. "It was only a platform, with railings but not a roof. I could stick my head out between the branches and see the whole countryside, clear to Charlottesville."

Back when the world outside the orchard had seemed exciting and full of promise, instead of a place where she'd made mistakes.

When supper was over, Grandma and Grandpa headed back to Spencer Hollow, and Tyler started doing dishes. When even Rachel deserted her to go pack and Uma dozed happily before the fire, Amy was left to walk the professor back to his car. It was still light, but the sun had set behind the Blue Ridge Mountains, and the sky had pale streaks of orange and purple. She inhaled deeply the smells of damp earth and sweet apple blossoms, the scent of the childhood they'd just been discussing. She tried not to think about how the professor loomed above her, tall and substantial, and not easy to ignore.

"You were pretty quiet in there," she said. "If you thought this was overwhelming, you should see it when the rest of the family is home."

"I wasn't overwhelmed so much as enjoying all the interplay. I'm not used to so many boisterous people."

"Do you have brothers and sisters?"

"None."

"Oh, I'm sorry." And then she thought about how that sounded. "Sorry again. That sounded like my idea of a family is better than the one your parents formed."

"I think it is," he answered.

He walked with his hands behind his back,

emphasizing his shoulders. She kept noticing that—was she turning into a "shoulders" woman? She had to focus on the conversation.

"Surely there were lots of reasons they didn't have more kids, maybe personal ones."

"Only one, and you're looking at him."

They came to a stop beside his car and she eyed his shadowed face, teasing, "You were that bad as a toddler that they swore off any more kids?"

He shrugged. "I was that good."

"What, no one could ever live up to the example you set?"

"They didn't want another child to even try. They wanted to focus all their attention on me—their weekend attention, that is. They both worked long hours, so I had a succession of nannies and housekeepers as I grew up."

This was sounding weird—and sad. "Well . . . some people believe all they can handle is one child."

He shook his head. "Never mind. It's very dysfunctional, nothing like your family."

She snorted. "My family is plenty dysfunctional. You've only seen a few of us."

"I study people for a living. Historic, contemporary, it doesn't really matter. I can tell you're a close family, even if you feel it's dysfunctional."

She didn't feel close, not like a good daughter should. She'd let Rob separate her from her family, making her feel almost like a stranger in her childhood home. She would *never* let that happen again.

Her thoughts were so entwined with Rob and the regrets of her past that when the professor lightly touched her shoulder, she was startled.

"Good night, Amy," he said.

"Good night, Professor."

He gave her a crooked smile before getting into his car and driving away.

She watched him for far too long.

— *Chapter 5* —

Rachel and her friend Ella left the next morning, driving to Richmond to fly out to California. Rachel's eyes had gleamed with both excitement and some worry, as if she knew she was leaving a mess behind. Amy and Tyler showed her only camaraderie and humor, and she hoped Rachel was at ease.

Afterward, Tyler had gone to the gym to work out. Not that the gym was up to New York City standards. It was an old storefront that the volunteers at the fire department next door had fixed up with some free weights and cardio machines, and was now called Feel the Burn.

At dinner the previous night, everyone had had an opinion about the orchard, but nothing seemed new and fresh. She'd spent too many years in the business world not to realize they needed something big and bold and different. But what?

While she and Tyler tried to figure that out, she still felt responsible to do *something* productive, even if that was just to discover what was going on in the picnic meadow. She knew Carlos had volunteered to take care of it, but he hadn't told her anything new. He was probably too busy squaring off against Principal Jablonski at a high school meeting.

If there were kids hanging out at the meadow, they needed to understand this was a business, and that they might damage the crops. But no one had come last night, and she'd huddled out there for hours in the old tree house. It hadn't been a total waste of time. She'd been lulled into a peaceful trance by the song of crickets and the scent of apple blossoms on the breeze.

After taking a morning drive through the orchard with Carlos, Amy drove into Spencer Hollow. If she really wanted a full grocery store experience, she could head into Crozet, but the MacDougall General Store always had the basics. And besides, maybe Brianna would be there.

Sometimes it felt like everyone she knew worked for their parents. Except the professor.

She gripped the steering wheel tighter and wished she could bang her forehead against it. She had to stop thinking about him. He'd be around for a few weeks, and then would go back to his own life, taking his hunky shoulders with him.

Amy parked in the packed-earth parking lot next to the store and stared up at it. Had they added another wing? What had started out as a tiny country store over a hundred years ago now sprouted a second story, a side wing to the south with a couple gas pumps beyond, and another wing in the back. Beneath the large name of the store were two slogans: "Groceries, Gas, Gadgets,

Guitars" and "Everything for the Hunter." It would have been easier to simply write "Everything," because that's what the store sold, and it always amazed her when Mr. MacDougall could find absolutely anything Amy wanted, even in the tiniest box at the back of some random shelf. Brianna took after her dad.

Amy walked in the side entrance of the store, where double rows of guitars gleamed atop one another. She knew that musicians came from miles around to purchase from the extensive and even rare collection of guitars Mr. MacDougall's grandfather had begun. A young woman was standing near the display counter, strumming a guitar, and looked at Amy like she was out of place. Amy'd been gone a long time.

The main section of the store was a mini grocery store: health and beauty products, canned goods, fresh produce, and cleaning supplies. Kayaks and fishing equipment hung on the walls. Beyond, into the next wing, Amy knew there was a glass-fronted deli case, a counter with stools, a few café tables and chairs, and an ice cream machine. It looked the same, crowded, but clean. If you couldn't find it at MacDougall's, they'd order it for you.

Brianna MacDougall stood behind the main counter, ringing up the purchases of a customer. She didn't see Amy at first, and as Amy wandered the aisles putting what she needed in a tiny

93

grocery cart, she eyed her old friend. Brianna's bright red hair had mellowed to a beautiful auburn, and it hung in waves to her shoulders, parted in the center and tucked behind her ears. She still had freckles dotting her pale skin. She wore a spotless apron that said "MacDougall General Store" over slacks and a button-down shirt, with the sleeves rolled up to the elbows. She looked pleasant and confident and smart, a woman who'd taken her business degree and improved her family store.

Though Brianna and Carmen had been Amy's two closest friends, and they'd all gone for the same major in college, Brianna and Carmen had rubbed each other the wrong way. Brianna was too straitlaced and professional, whereas Carmen was a free spirit, willing to try unconventional ideas and always pushing the other two into adventures.

When the customer had gone, Amy stepped up to the counter and placed her basket upon it. "Hi, Brianna."

Brianna gave her the same polite smile she'd give any customer. Amy inwardly winced, knowing she probably deserved that.

"Hi, Amy. I hear you're home for a while." Brianna's voice was smooth and placid, without a hint of emotion, whether disappointment or pleasure.

"I bet you still hear all the gossip at the counter out back."

Brianna just nodded.

"I'm home, yes, for at least the next six months."

Brianna only arched an auburn brow. Amy felt like she needed to babble to fill the silence.

"My parents decided to retire, and the orchard needs me—us. All my brothers and sisters will eventually take their turn at home."

"I heard about the retirement. Your parents stopped here on their way out of town to see my dad."

"Is he thinking about retiring, too?"

"You must not remember my dad too well."

Amy inwardly winced. Brianna said it politely, but it stung.

"Sorry. I was just curious," Amy said. She looked around. "Things look great here, as always."

"Thank you."

There was a long awkward pause. But at least Brianna didn't just ring up her purchase and ignore her.

Then Brianna spoke again, perhaps not with the same cool confidence of a moment ago. "I get the impression that your mom didn't tell you about my dad's diagnosis."

Amy's eyes went wide, and the awkwardness was forgotten. "No! Oh, Bri, I'm so sorry. No one has said anything."

And then Brianna's eyes welled up with tears. "They're pretty sure it's Alzheimer's."

Amy gasped and, without giving it another thought, hurried around the counter and put her arms around her old friend. Brianna trembled, but Amy didn't hear her crying. "Oh, Bri," she whispered.

Brianna hugged her back, then straightened, and Amy let her go. She studied her friend's pale face and gleaming eyes, watching as Brianna glanced past Amy at an elderly black lady with a cane who limped through the door and began to browse.

"I'm okay," Brianna said quietly.

"I can't believe that," Amy said, just as quietly.

"Well, I have to be, don't I?" Brianna sounded so very tired, even though it wasn't noon yet. "Dad still comes to work, of course, and he's on medication, but he doesn't remember things like he used to, and he gets so upset with himself."

"Your poor dad."

Brianna nodded. "Mom spends more time with him, of course, so that leaves me here."

"What about your sister?"

Brianna shrugged. "Theresa comes home when she can, but—oh, did you know she has a baby now?" Her voice grew warmer.

"I saw on Facebook. She looks so happy in the pictures."

"She is. Mostly. But I feel bad for her, like she can't even enjoy little David, because she's worrying about Dad."

"She's probably happy you're here working with your parents and helping them, and partly jealous because you get to spend time with your dad."

Brianna blinked at her in surprise. "I . . . hadn't thought of it that way. I guess that direct way you have of seeing to the heart of things hasn't gone away."

Amy flinched, but tried to hide it. "Thanks." Oh, she'd inconveniently lost that talent where Rob was concerned.

As if reading her mind, Brianna said, "I saw you broke up with Rob."

Apparently Brianna hadn't lost the spooky talent of reading Amy's expressions.

"I can't say I'm unhappy about that," Brianna continued.

"You never thought he was right for me. Guess you're the one who can see through to the heart of things, not me."

"In this instance, I wish I'd been wrong."

Amy nodded. "Thanks."

The door opened and in walked Tyler. He glanced around, his expression impressed, then grinned at the two young women.

"Hey, girls," he called.

He walked toward them with that nonchalant, easy stride that said things were all right in his world.

He slung an arm around Amy's shoulders, but

his sparkling eyes focused on their friend. "Hey, Bri, good to see you again."

"You, too, Tyler."

The elderly lady peered around the end of an aisle and stared wide-eyed at Tyler, but didn't come closer. It was bothering Amy how she was blanking on the woman's name. Amy was good with names, which had always helped in real estate.

Tyler glanced at the groceries with interest. "Whatcha making for dinner, Amy?"

"You mean what am I making myself for dinner?" she asked sweetly.

"We're living at the house together. I just thought we'd take turns cooking. Since you're the one here shopping, I assumed you wanted to go next, now that Rachel's gone."

She elbowed him lightly. "Guess neither of us should assume. Okay, taking turns sounds good. I'll let you be surprised by everything I whip up with this."

He nodded, then looked at Brianna again. To Amy's surprise, she thought a faint blush touched Brianna's pale complexion. Amy wanted to roll her eyes. Did Tyler affect every woman, even Brianna, who'd known him since he was skinning his knees in kindergarten?

"I really like those protein shakes on the café menu, Bri," Tyler said. He glanced toward the back room, where the girl working the counter was staring at him with lovesick eyes. "And Megan is a big help."

"Then go distract her," Brianna said briskly. "But not too much."

"I won't."

After a last squeeze of Amy's shoulders, he sauntered toward the back room, where Megan gave a little chirp of excitement and ducked behind the counter.

Brianna shook her head, and Amy couldn't decide if Tyler's interruption had been good or bad.

The elderly woman lined up behind Amy, so Brianna started ringing up Amy's purchases.

Amy hesitated, then asked, "Do you have a lunch break soon? We could eat at the diner. I think they still have that Sunday brunch menu."

Brianna set the laden bags on top of the counter, and their eyes met. Amy realized how very important it was to her that Brianna said yes. She had so much to make up for, and her friend deserved that.

"Okay," Brianna said, giving a small smile.

Amy grinned, hefting all four bags at once. She stepped aside, watching as Brianna smiled at her next customer.

"What time?" Amy asked.

Brianna glanced at the wall clock. "An hour?"

"Perfect. I'll drop the groceries off and come back."

"You're going to leave Tyler behind?"

Amy settled for an innocent look. "Should I lead him around on a leash?"

Brianna smiled, then lowered her voice. "Not sure how you lured him home when he's famous in New York City—in the whole country."

The old woman who was paying for her groceries said, "He deserves to be famous. He was wonderful on *Doctors and Nurses*. I watched him every day, our local boy who became so successful."

Amy stared intently at the woman, trying to remember, then brightened, belatedly recognizing the stooped owner of Books to Buy or Borrow. "Mrs. Clark, it's so good to see you. I didn't know you were a soap opera fan."

"I most definitely am." Mrs. Clark's glasses reflected the light as she glanced into the back room, where Tyler perched on a stool while Megan waited on him. "And it's a travesty that *Doctors and Nurses* was canceled. I miss seeing your brother every day."

"Well, here he is," Amy said. "Come on up to the orchard this fall and you can see even more of him."

"I'll have to do that," Mrs. Clark said. "I do like the fudge. And I'll bring my friends—Tyler has a lot of fans."

It was still hard for Amy to imagine her brother the center of adoring fans. To her, he was still her goofy twin brother, who couldn't always be relied on to get up with his alarm clock or return a text. But the longer she was back, the more she saw villagers regard Tyler with speculation. His job situation was more difficult than hers. He'd left for fame and fortune, and now he was home. Soon, their customers would see him driving a tractor or placing ladders against apple trees—not the sexy, celebrity life they probably thought he should have. But he was a man who supported his family, more than anything else. That counted for so much more.

She glanced at Brianna. "See you soon. Bye, Mrs. Clark. See you at home, Tyler," she added in a louder voice.

He waved, but didn't look away from where he was cheerfully charming Brianna's employee.

Amy rushed home to unload the groceries and answered some work emails that had built up the last couple days. She texted Tyler that he should drop by the bookstore; it would make Mrs. Clark's day.

At the Spencer Hollow Diner, all the booths had been reupholstered a deep green since the last time she'd eaten there. A counter ran the length of the kitchen, its stools like green-topped mushrooms. Chrome gleamed, the tabletops sparkled, their little paper placemats full of advertisements for the area—Fairfield Orchard was there, but there were wineries, too, and she wondered if that had a lot to do with the good-size crowd that was there for brunch. Somehow she had to find a way to bring those same crowds to the orchard this fall.

Brianna slid into the bench opposite her, her expression a little more reserved again. Amy could imagine her thinking that just because they'd connected over the grief of Mr. MacDougall's illness didn't mean Amy deserved complete and easy forgiveness. And Amy could accept that. She was just happy to have the chance.

"My mom says hi," Brianna said, picking up and eyeing the single sheet that was the Sunday brunch menu.

"Please tell her the same from me."

They each studied the menu, while faint music played in the background, and a teenage boy brought them water.

"Thanks, Seth," Brianna said.

The acne on his cheeks practically disappeared within his blush.

When he'd gone, Amy said, "He looks like a Delahunt."

"Bingo. They all have that square, Captain America jaw."

"Even the girls," Amy added.

Brianna gave a small smile but didn't laugh.

Amy hid a sigh. When the silence lingered a bit, she was relieved when Brianna broke it this time.

"The Delahunts just put in a pool, and they're not the only ones. So we set up a shelf of pool supplies."

For a conversation starter, it had all the depth of a summer-shower puddle, but it was something.

"Where do you find the room?" Amy asked. "That place is packed to the rafters, and I don't think you could build another addition without sacrificing parking space."

"True. But we have our ways. Dad even set aside a corner of the guitar display room for drums. Drums! No idea why, but we've actually sold a few. Even the big bass drums used by marching bands. Strange."

Seth came back to take their order. Amy ordered a veggie omelet and Brianna a shrimp salad. They waited awkwardly, quietly, until their iced tea arrived. Amy was just about to ask, *So tell me about your nephew,* when Brianna spoke.

"I can't believe you persuaded Tyler to leave New York."

Amy relaxed. "I didn't have to persuade him. He volunteered. All the sibs are taking turns, and it was easiest for the two of us on short notice to make some time."

"But his career . . ."

"He keeps up the promotion part of it as much as he can, because he's been doing some commercial work since *Doctors and Nurses* was canceled last year. His agent has him lined up to audition for some other stuff."

"And he's okay with being here?"

Amy shrugged. "Sure. We've agreed to six months, and it's only been a couple weeks. Though we grew up at the orchard, there's so much more to learn about the business side of things. And with Rachel gone—"

Brianna gasped. "Rachel left?"

"You didn't know? I thought MacDougall's was the center of town."

Brianna stuck out her tongue and Amy laughed, relaxing even more, slouching back in the booth to cross her arms over her chest and raise an eyebrow at her friend.

"I didn't know we still did those things," Amy teased.

"Only when certain foolish people bring it out of us."

"True."

Brianna rested her forearms on the table, leaning forward. "Why did Rachel leave?"

Amy told her about Ella's wish to travel the world, leaving out her illness, in case she'd kept it private.

"Oh, the cancer," Brianna said solemnly.

Guess it wasn't too private.

"Ella's doing so much better but she's not up to full strength yet," Brianna continued. "How wonderful that Rachel could go with her. I've been thinking the last couple years that Rachel seemed a bit . . . restless."

"Really?" Amy demanded, flinging her arms wide and just missing her ice water. "*I* didn't see that! Am I blind?"

"No, certainly not. But it's occasionally easy for all of us to see what we want."

Amy winced.

"I'm not criticizing," Brianna hastily added. "Sometimes we can assume the people closest to us are always how they *have* been. And it's a shock when things turn out to be different." She hesitated. "I wrote off my dad's symptoms for a long time as just being overtired or distracted or any number of things. But then he went for his usual walk and didn't remember how to get home." Brianna's voice cracked at the end.

Biting her lip, Amy reached across the table and took her friend's hand.

"He forgot his cell phone, and we all forgot about him." Her voice trembled. "I just thought he'd gone to work at his home office. It was hours later that someone found him wandering down by the creek. He could have fallen in."

"Brianna, you couldn't have known," Amy said with urgent sympathy.

"No, I know that."

Their server brought both their plates, standing a few feet from the table as if he was hesitant to intrude.

Brianna gave him a forced smile. "Bring them here, Seth, I'm starving."

When he'd set down their meals and hastily retreated, Brianna met Amy's eyes and said, "Dad's better now. The medicine has helped, and it's still very early. He doesn't like that we keep track of him, though, and he's grumpy about it." She used her fork to stir her salad.

"Maybe Rachel's been grumpy for a while, too," Amy said, "and unlike you, maybe I *deliberately* didn't want to notice what was going on. I guess I didn't want to imagine what it would be like if Rachel left the orchard and it was just my parents. And now all three of them have left." She forced herself to take a bite of her omelet. It steamed in cheesy deliciousness in her mouth and it made her feel better. Food always did. She'd better start working out again, and soon.

"And your boyfriend has left," Brianna said, watching her.

The omelet hit Amy's stomach like a cheese ball. "Nice transition," she said dryly. "And for the record, he didn't leave on his own. I asked him to, something I should have done a long time ago. And no, I don't really want to discuss it."

"Okay, we won't. Let's talk about the orchard."

"I'm not sure how interesting a subject *that* is," Amy replied after chewing another bite of the omelet. "I'm just diving in and feeling overwhelmed." She held up a hand. "Whining, I know. Mom and Dad and Rachel had done enough, and I'm glad they're taking time for themselves."

"I don't think you're whining. I think you're genuinely concerned. But you don't need to be. You still have Carlos, right?"

"Can you imagine if he quit?" Amy gave an exaggerated shudder.

"Well, your parents wouldn't have left, then. I only brought up the orchard because I get the impression that with so many U-Pick orchards—"

"You even know the lingo!"

"I'm a quick study."

Amy grinned.

"Anyway, there are lots of orchards and wineries to choose from nowadays."

"I know," Amy said. "I've done the occasional afternoon at a winery. There are so many around here. How can apples compete?"

"I don't know, but I think you need to find a way. I get the impression that except for families with little kids, people are getting sort of . . . bored at regular orchards."

Amy sighed. "I know things need to change, and Tyler and I plan to do that. We just have to figure it all out."

"You will," Brianna said, sounding relieved. "I'm glad to hear you want to switch things up. That'll be important, and it will keep you interested in your job."

They ate for several minutes, and the quiet felt more peaceful this time. Amy hadn't realized how much better she'd feel, reaching out to Brianna to try to make up for the past.

"I really do want to apologize, Bri," she said quietly. "I've been a bad friend for too long."

"You weren't bad," Brianna said, wearing a crooked smile. "Did you see me driving the quick twenty-five minutes to Charlottesville to hang out?"

"But Spencer Hollow is my home. I should have come back more."

"I think we should agree that both of us could have tried harder. I let the business overwhelm me a little, maybe."

Amy's eyes widened. "Is everything okay?"

"Oh, yes, fine, we're busy—busier than we've ever been, and I probably have those wineries to thank. But I need to relax more, too, and I'd love to go to Charlottesville and maybe explore the Downtown Mall with someone who's lived around there. I love that historic Main Street feel, the boutiques and the open-air cafés and taverns. I never get there—I'm always too busy."

"Then it's a date!" Amy made a vow to herself that she wouldn't leave any more friends behind, including the ones she'd made in Charlottesville. "Do you mind if I contact a few C'ville friends to join us? They'd love to meet you."

"Sounds good."

Reconnecting with old friends was important, but she didn't want to abandon her newer ones either. She had to find a way not to be too busy with the orchard, and much as she was happy to be home, it sometimes felt strange and scary and lonely. Thank God for Tyler—even though he drove her crazy sometimes.

And as if she'd conjured him, her twin walked into the diner with Grandpa Fairfield—and Jonathan Gebhart.

Brianna frowned at whatever Amy's expression showed, looked over her shoulder, and saw the newcomers. Tyler waved, but the other two men were taking their seats in a booth and didn't notice the women.

"Who's that?" Brianna asked.

"Professor Gebhart from UVA. He's doing some research on Jefferson—of course—and since my ancestor bought our land from our illustrious president, he's picking my grandpa's brains for old family stories. He's writing a book."

"A smart man, too," Brianna said musingly, casting another glance at the far booth.

"You're going to get a strain in your neck from twisting it that way."

Tyler waved at Brianna, who returned it, then quickly turned back to Amy.

"I could introduce you to the professor," Amy said, feeling a strange uneasiness as she said it, and not sure why.

Brianna shook her head. "Not necessary. You can tell me all about him, and if it's fun having such a good-looking guy hanging around."

"Uh, it's only been a couple times, and . . . he's good-looking?"

Brianna rolled her eyes. "Wow, that was a deliberate attempt to avoid my meaning. Has he asked you out?"

"No."

"Do you *want* him to ask you out?"

Amy remembered the way Jonathan had glanced down her body, at her mouth, and the feelings that had begun to awaken inside her, both unnerving and very tempting. "Th—this isn't a good time."

Brianna giggled—an actual giggle, Amy thought.

"You stuttered," Brianna pointed out.

"I did not."

"You did, but I won't make a big deal of it."

"You already did," Amy said with an exaggerated sigh.

Brianna's gleeful smile faded a bit. "Is this because of Rob? How long has it been since the breakup?"

"Six months," Amy answered, taking another bite of her cooling omelet. After swallowing, she said, "It's more about the orchard, and how over my head I am, and how he'll be around a lot for the next few weeks, and that could make things awkward."

"You've given this a lot of thought—though he hasn't asked you out."

Amy glanced toward the other booth and realized that Jonathan had seen her, had perhaps even been watching her all the while she and Brianna had been talking about him. Did he read lips?

He nodded at her, and she smiled back before returning her attention to Brianna.

Brianna was watching her with satisfaction. "You'd go out with him if he asked. Look at you blush."

"Bri, let this go."

Brianna raised both hands. "Okay, okay, I will. Just remember that though you have returned to Spencer Hollow, and in some senses your old life, it doesn't mean you can't find room to meet new people and enjoy this life you're forging."

"I can barely keep up with the people I know," Amy reminded her, "as you can testify to."

"Okay, okay, I'll let it go. But he's gorgeous, and if he asks you out, you should say yes."

Knowing that Brianna's head blocked Jonathan's view of her, Amy made a face. "We have nothing in common."

"So you've talked to him."

"Sure. He had to persuade me to go along with his historical research."

"And you did."

"I wouldn't turn him down. He's up for tenure

and he's trying to prove some big discovery about Jefferson—I'm not unfeeling."

"Yet you already know you have nothing in common," Brianna said doubtfully.

"He's got all these degrees, Bri, and I'm a college dropout. I'm a part of a big, messy family, and his family is so small and polite he didn't seem to know what to do with mine. Can you imagine when the rest of my brothers are back in town?"

"What, do you think he'll disappear with shyness?"

"He's not shy, just . . . focused on his work."

"You don't think he can come out of his academic shell and learn to enjoy your family because they're part of you?"

Amy groaned. "Bri, we're not even—"

"Hello, Amy."

Jonathan's tall shadow suddenly fell on her table, and Amy looked up in surprise. Brianna's eyes danced when Amy helplessly gave him an appreciative once-over.

Amy cleared her throat. "Hey, Professor." Then she did the polite thing and introduced them both.

Jonathan shook Brianna's hand. "I think I've seen you at the general store. You're the owner?"

"Daughter of the owner," Brianna clarified.

"A fascinating place."

Brianna grinned. "Thanks."

She looked from Jonathan to Amy as if she was waiting for something exciting to happen.

Jonathan turned back to Amy. "I just wanted to let you know I'm interviewing your grandfather again today."

"You guys don't waste time," Amy said lightly.

He shrugged. "He had a free schedule and called me. Seems your grandmother has homework."

Brianna glanced at Amy with interest.

"She's taking courses at UVA," Amy explained. "Seniors can audit them for free."

"It's a great program," Jonathan said. "People should keep learning throughout their lives."

"Advertising the university?" Amy teased.

"It seems like it," he said dryly. "Regardless, your grandfather just wanted me to let you know what was going on."

"You don't have to do that," Amy said. "Whatever you two guys talk about, it's up to you both."

"Thanks. I think your grandfather just wanted you to feel included." He hesitated, frowning. "I think. I'm not sure. I can never read these things right."

Amy felt a quick glow of memory, of sitting on Grandpa's lap, listening to his stories about the old ways of the orchard and their family. For a moment, she yearned to be there with Grandpa and the professor, soaking up those stories again. Startled to feel such a longing, she reminded herself that she had too much work to do.

Jonathan gave a brisk smile. "It was nice meeting you, Brianna. Amy, I'll see you later."

And then he was gone. Brianna just arched an eyebrow. Amy raised her knife threateningly, then cut another piece of her omelet.

"He'll see you later," Brianna whispered.

"Shh! You sound like a teenager." Brianna's smile was a little sad, and Amy relented. "Sorry. I guess sometimes we need that."

"We do. Let me distract myself from my problems by imagining your love life."

"Don't you have your own distracting love life?"

"No, and I should follow the advice I'm giving you. Maybe you can introduce me to someone in Charlottesville next weekend."

"I'll do my best."

And then Amy's gaze darted back to Jonathan, and he was watching her again.

Stop that! she wanted to say to him. His interest was unnerving and far too flattering, and it was getting harder and harder to remind herself that she didn't need the complications of a new man in her life.

But he was already in her life, wasn't he.

— Chapter 6 —

Amy headed back to the orchard and spent some time riding a pickup with Carlos up and down the rows of dwarf McIntosh trees, listening to him lecture about the thermal belt of warm air that aided their orchard. Uma and Barney sat on the back bench of the pickup, heads lolling out their respective windows. She wondered how she could ever absorb Carlos's years of knowledge and be as good a steward to her family land.

When she got back to the orchard office, housed beside the garage behind their closed-for-the-season country store, she found Tyler hanging out on the computer, frowning over his Facebook page as she approached. Uma went to her padded bed and sank down on it, head on her paws, eyes alert.

Tyler groaned. "I never know what to say on Facebook."

"Your fans love anything you say," she reminded him, looking down in amazement at the number of people who'd "liked" his page. She hesitated, her smile fading with her concern. "Carlos and I waited as long as we could and had to go on the tour without you."

Tyler clapped a hand to his forehead. "I wish you'd have reminded me at the diner."

"I guess I should have," she said, then added with mock seriousness, "You missed a fascinating lecture on the thermal belt and how it helps apples grow."

"As long as one of us knows it," he said dejectedly.

It was her turn to frown. "Everything okay, Tyler?"

He nodded, but didn't meet her eyes.

Knowing it was time to change the subject, Amy said, "It's weird being out with Carlos. I feel like he must miss Dad, that having to explain everything to me—us—has to be annoying. But he says it's good to pass on his knowledge to the next generation. After all, Carmen's only interested in goats—her kids, he called them."

"He loves the jokes."

"And then we stopped on a ridge overlooking the whole orchard, and he started pointing out the farms and homes beyond us, like I didn't remember, and of course, some of them I didn't. But did you know that Miss Jablonski lives pretty close by?"

"I'd forgotten, but okay, what does it matter?"

"She's one of Carlos's favorite topics. I can't imagine what it must be like when they're in the same room. It must combust. Today, Carlos went on about her resistance to the young people learning about civil disobedience."

"She doesn't seem the type to do much protesting," Tyler said. "If I remember, she's a work-within-the-system kind of woman."

"I said something like that, and Carlos smirked. He actually smirked! Like he knew something we didn't. I'd love to know the history of those two," she mused. "But the main reason I brought it up is that Miss Jablonski's property isn't all that far from the picnic meadow where kids—or someone—have been hanging out. Maybe she's heard or seen something."

"I don't know why you're going on about this, Amy. What does it matter if some kids made a bonfire?"

"Near our trees," she reminded him. "The source of our livelihood."

Tyler raised both hands in submission. "Fine, I get it. So how's Brianna?"

She told him about Mr. MacDougall's health issues, and they both shared a solemn moment thinking how lucky they were that they still had three of their four grandparents and that, along with their parents, they were pretty healthy.

"So I distracted Brianna by planning an evening out in Charlottesville," Amy continued. "Did you want to come with us next week-end?"

"Sure. How about if we invite Jonathan?"

Startled, Amy regarded her brother suspiciously. "The professor? Why?"

"He seems like a good guy."

She realized Tyler was watching her with equal suspicion.

She smoothed hers away and tried to deflect. "I have to admit, I didn't see a friendship between you two. He's more of a geek than you usually hang out with."

"I hang out with all kinds of people. I've grown since high school, you know. Or maybe your resistance to him isn't about me?"

She gave him a confused look, but had a sinking feeling she knew where this was going.

"Maybe you don't want us to become friends," he continued.

Now she really was confused. "I would never think that. You make me out to be a witch."

"Not a witch, just gun-shy where dating is concerned."

"Dating? Who's talking about dating?" she asked with exasperation.

"I'm not pushing you toward anything. I'm just . . . concerned about you, and want you to be happy again. He looks at you, you look at him—I'm not blind."

She ignored the last sentence and said earnestly, "I don't need anything else right now. I'm really happy to be here at the orchard, Tyler."

"I do know that. I feel the same. But it doesn't

change the fact that I didn't even know about your breakup with Rob until after it happened. You didn't confide in me, Amy, and that's not normal for us."

She bit her lip, unable to meet his eyes. "I'm sorry."

"You don't have to be sorry—I know it was bad. It had to be, the way you pushed us all away. You can tell me anything, remember that. I want things between us to be the same as they were before."

She almost said, *That goes both ways,* then stopped herself.

"You seem to be running from what he's actually here to do, and if it's not about the man himself, then it's about his research. Amy, you *love* that sort of stuff. You used to go on and on for hours after you and Grandpa talked about people long dead. It drove me nuts. Now you don't care at all? It's just weird and wrong."

She sighed and couldn't think of a thing to say.

"I hope you'll tell me when you're ready," Tyler continued. "So I'm just going to invite Jonathan to attend this get-together you organized. Okay?"

"Okay."

"And you're not angry."

"No, I'm not angry at all," she insisted. And she wasn't. But there were way too many mixed-up emotions whirling around inside her.

• • •

As Jonathan approached Amy's open office door, he couldn't help overhearing the last part of the conversation. Tyler wanted to invite him to attend something and Amy sounded . . . reluctant. Jonathan should take a hint from that. Obviously he was making her uneasy somehow, and he didn't want to do that.

When he'd walked into the diner earlier, he'd seen the way her eyes were sparkling as she spoke to her friend. She seemed so . . . alive, for lack of a better word, and he felt ridiculous trying to find some kind of poetic word that did her justice. He wasn't a man who knew how to pretty things up. He dealt with facts, and the fact was, he was blown away by how much he was attracted to her.

But she didn't want that, regardless of what those blue eyes said when she looked at him.

He knocked on the open door and saw Amy jump, then redden. Tyler just grinned at him. Jonathan liked Tyler, even though the two men seemed to have little in common. Jonathan had been with him earlier when a girl on the street had rushed up for an autograph, and Tyler had treated her like a friend, with no arrogance or impatience. For a celebrity, he was a pretty normal guy.

"Hello," Jonathan said, trying to act casual, as if he hadn't overheard a private conversation.

"May I speak with you, Amy, or is this a bad time?"

"Not at all. Have a seat."

She sat down behind her desk, with a little distance between her and him. Jonathan saw Tyler eye her with amusement.

"I'll let you guys talk," Tyler said.

"This isn't something private," Jonathan insisted. "I could say it to you, too."

"That's okay, I have stuff to do." At the door, Tyler paused. "Hey, Jonathan, a group of us are hanging out at the Downtown Mall Friday night. You're welcome to join us."

"Thank you. I'll check my schedule." And he'd politely decline, for Amy's sake, but he didn't need to say that now.

"I'll send you a text with details," Tyler added, then left.

Jonathan looked back at Amy, who was staring into her computer screen with great concentration. He didn't interrupt her.

It was a full minute before she glanced at him. "I'm sorry. I'm just looking over last year's summer purchases, and trying to plan what we'll need for fall. And figure out what questions to ask my parents, of course."

"You've been thrown into the fire, so to speak," he said. "I'll be quick. I just wanted to keep you abreast of what I'm doing with your grandfather."

"That's not necessary."

"I think it is. This is your home, and I might turn up in strange places."

Her eyes widened and she choked on a laugh. "Pardon me?"

"Well, you might turn a corner in the barn, and there'll I'll be, looking at something carved in a wooden beam."

To his surprise, her smile faded. Curious.

And then he "listened" to his own thoughts and told himself to stop trying to dissect every little nuance of a person. But it was Amy, and it was difficult not to be far too curious about her.

"There's no carving," she began. "Oh, you're just giving an example, and I'm being literal."

He smiled. "You are." And it was refreshing, because people always thought he was way too literal. He stopped himself from pointing out that they had something in common. "Your grandfather and I are going to Crozet today to photograph the original house deed in his bank box. Gradually, we're going to go through the trunks in the old house, and scour the cemetery and church records."

"You're certainly making Grandpa happy," she said. "Since Grandma started taking classes, he's seemed at loose ends."

"He's definitely a big help, and I'm grateful."

She sat back in her office chair and eyed him.

122

She wasn't wearing her ball cap, but her hair was still caught back in a ponytail. A strand trailed down her cheek, and he was surprised how much he wanted to touch it.

"You're going to know a lot about us, by the time you're done," she said. "Do you know as much about your own family history?"

"No, but then we're newer to the country, and we had nothing to do with Thomas Jefferson."

"Your obsession."

He smiled. "You could call it that. Or you could call it my job."

She returned the smile. "Guess it can be good to be obsessed with your job."

"And plus, my family doesn't care for history at all." Why had he said that?

She tilted her head. "Then they're not accepting of your career?"

She'd seen more deeply than anyone else ever had, and she barely knew him. And then he said the truth, something he'd only ever told his fiancée. "No, they don't like my career at all."

She frowned, and those deep blue eyes seemed like they saw to all the hurts in his soul. This wasn't good.

"But you're obviously a smart man. If history makes you happy, wouldn't they support that?"

"My father owns a pharmaceutical company. The sciences are what my family cares about. They were grooming me for the family business—

which perhaps you can relate to," he said wryly.

To his surprise, she came around the desk and sat down in the chair beside him.

"You've hinted at this before," she said, "that your parents focused on you. How were they grooming you? Making you take lots of advanced placement classes?"

"They didn't have to *make* me do that. I loved school and challenging myself."

She smiled. "Of course you did. I'm not surprised a bit. Guess you'd have to love school to make teaching your career."

"I told you my parents focused on my education, the best tutors and science camps."

"Let me guess—you were a child prodigy."

"I simply learned quickly."

"I bet you were reading by three."

"Two," he admitted reluctantly.

She gaped. "Wow. Impressive. Did you graduate school early?"

"High school by sixteen. My parents thought I should have gone even earlier, but I wanted to be a regular teenager sometimes."

"Where did you go to college?"

"UVA."

"Of course."

"Of course."

They shared a grin.

"And after that?" she urged. "Come on, brag to me."

He rolled his eyes. "I earned my PhD at Harvard, I did post-doctorate work at Yale, and then UVA lured me back."

"Wow, you really are a genius. I am very impressed. You could have turned out pretty self-centered."

"And maybe I am."

"I don't think so."

"That's kind of you."

She waved a hand. "I'm not being kind, just honest. So go on with your story. You were destined to be the next lord and savior of your family."

Eyes wide, he laughed, but it came out as a snort.

"Don't laugh," she said nonchalantly. "It's obvious your parents expected you to fall right into line with their plans, as if you had no freedom of choice. I'm glad you did what you wanted to do."

All he could think to say was, "Thank you."

"And I bet they didn't take it well."

"They did not."

"I'm sorry," she said quietly.

The thread of sympathy in her voice struck a pang inside him. He ignored it. "Why should you be sorry?"

"Because even when our parents don't treat us well, we love them and don't want to disappoint them."

Her family seemed so ideal—could her parents have mistreated her somehow? "I did disappoint them, but I cannot be sorry. You certainly have not disappointed your parents."

"You think not?" she asked with faint sarcasm.

"You're here, aren't you? You were the first one to volunteer so they could leave."

"It could have been Tyler."

"It wasn't. He already told me."

"There are other ways to disappoint parents," she said, looking out the window.

He studied her profile, her gaze far off and sad, and there might even have been a tremble to her soft lips.

He leaned toward her. "What happened?"

She turned sharply, and their faces were only inches apart. For a long moment, neither of them moved. Jonathan wanted to touch her, to soothe her, to taste her, and make her forget the sorrow that lingered, even when she was smiling.

Then she backed up. In a shaky voice, she said, "Nothing much happened, just the usual teenage stuff."

That was an obvious lie, but it wasn't his place to call her on something so private.

"I hope your parents are over their disappointment," she said. "After all, it's your life."

He was tempted to answer as he always did, something shallow that deflected the question away. Instead, he found himself saying, "No, they're not over it. I doubt they ever will be. We don't see much of each other anymore."

Her jaw sagged, and her eyes went soft and sad. "Oh, Jonathan, how terrible. I can't imagine how you must feel."

He shrugged. "I'm used to it now. There's much less drama this way."

"But with no brothers and sisters, and your parents out of the picture, you must be so lonely."

"Only a person with a big family would think that," he assured her, giving a crooked smile. "I have friends, a career I love, and my evenings are filled with the places and the times I write about. The past and its people come alive to me. I'm not lonely."

But he was. If she could lie, so could he.

"You should definitely come out with us Friday," she suddenly insisted.

"I don't want to make you uncomfortable."

She groaned and briefly closed her eyes. "I knew you overheard that part." She raised a hand before he could speak. "And I know you didn't eavesdrop deliberately. I'm sorry, Jonathan. My reluctance to date isn't about you, but . . . my last boyfriend and—everything going on in my life right now."

He hadn't heard Amy and Tyler discuss dating. It was far more appealing than it probably should be with the busy summer he had planned. But she was obviously against it.

"The orchard has to be my life right now," she continued, "until we get it situated to face the twenty-first-century customer."

"You just came back. Aren't you being a little hard on yourself?"

"Tyler and I will make it work."

Butt out—she might as well have spoken the words. So Jonathan rose to his feet.

"I'll let you get back to your purchasing," he said, nodding at the computer.

"Thanks. And I meant it about Friday. You don't live far from the mall. When Tyler sends you details, you should come. And I promise we're not going to the Corner and hang out at the bars frequented by your students."

"I am vastly relieved. Have a good afternoon." He sounded so formal. Why couldn't he just be a normal guy? Who was he kidding—he'd never been normal.

But he knew how to be polite and unobtrusive. He wouldn't complicate Amy's life—however much he found he wanted to.

— *Chapter 7* —

Late Friday afternoon, Jonathan was alone in the attic of the old homestead at Fairfield Orchard. He'd sent Mr. Fairfield down to rest and get something cold to drink. Much as it was a moderate May day, it was still hot in the attic, and the single window was stuck shut. Perspiration dripped from Jonathan's hair and stung his eyes. He'd worn an old T-shirt, and it stuck to his back like a wet beach towel.

"Hey, Jonathan, you still up here?"

"I'm here!" he called.

Tyler came up the stairs, then grimaced as he looked around. "It's a sauna in here. Why didn't you take stuff downstairs to go through it?"

Jonathan shrugged. "The trunks are heavy. It was easier to dig through them up here. They're mostly clothes and books anyway."

"Anything exciting?"

"Not so far. Your grandfather swears his great-grandmother's diary is here someplace, but we'll see."

Tyler shook his head. "This is real dedication to the cause, I gotta say. But go ahead and get your geek off."

Jonathan stiffened. Though he understood Tyler's words for the harmless teasing they were, he still felt that old sense of betrayal that he'd always experienced whenever his family dismissed his work. That wasn't what was going on with Tyler, and Jonathan was being far too sensitive about it. Just when he thought he was beyond such feelings, too. Perhaps immersing himself in the Fairfield family had disturbed him more than he thought, brought up memories of his family.

He regretted telling Amy about the estrangement. He'd thought he was used to the disapproval and the tension every time he made an overture to his family, but perhaps watching the Fairfields was reminding him too much of what he'd never had.

Tyler glanced at his watch. "You're still coming into Charlottesville with us, right?"

"I don't think so," Jonathan said. "And it's not because of your sister." Though it was.

Tyler grinned. "I thought you might have overheard the last part of our conversation the other day. Ignore her. I put her back up by telling her I see how the two of you look at each other."

Jonathan straightened so fast his head hit a sloped beam. Both he and Tyler winced.

"I didn't overhear that part," Jonathan said.

"Well, it's true. Although a word of warning: she had a bad breakup, and it wasn't that long ago. She's not even talking about it to me—and we used to tell each other everything."

"I understand." But regardless of her skittishness about dating, Amy was *looking* at him. He spoke without thinking. "Then I guess I'll go." So much for giving her some space.

"Good." Tyler frowned at him. "But you're a mess. You're not going to drive home like that, are you? Do you want"—he gestured at Jonathan's clothes—"*that* messing up your car? Did you at least bring a sweatshirt or something?"

"A jacket."

"Go take a shower and borrow one of m shirts. Not sure what else will fit you, but you're welcome to try. My room is the first one on the right at the top of the stairs. Amy is working in the office, and she said she was eating dinner at her desk. Workaholic," he added, his voice both amused and exasperated. "She needs tonight as much as you obviously do."

"All right, thanks."

Jonathan waited for Tyler to go first, then turned off the lights and went down through the old house's narrow staircases. The few remaining pieces of furniture were covered in sheets, looking like ghosts of themselves, rising up out of the past with stories they'd never be able to tell. He was in danger of being as old and unused as a piece of furniture in the corner, if he didn't do something about it. He didn't remember the last time he'd had a date.

Not that this was a date, he reminded himself. Just a group of friends having fun.

And Amy. He imagined seeing her away from the orchard, her long hair down around her shoulders instead of tucked away under a Cavaliers cap.

In the main house, Tyler headed for the kitchen, and Jonathan went up the staircase. Tyler's room was an interesting mix of childhood trophies and posters of the Washington Redskins and Nationals. Jonathan found it surprising that Tyler's parents hadn't remodeled, since he'd lived away for many years. During Jonathan's freshman year of college, his room had been converted into a fitness room, and when he'd come home he'd had a daybed to sleep on.

Next, Jonathan found the bathroom down the hall, and it wasn't until he was drying off that he realized he'd forgotten to grab the offered clean shirt. He pulled on his jeans and walked barefoot toward Tyler's room.

Just as Amy came up the stairs.

Amy came to a stop and gaped, all rational thought leaving her brain. Jonathan stood in her hallway, wearing nothing but a pair of jeans. Above the open snap—she swallowed heavily— his abs were a line of ridges sweeping up toward those broad shoulders she'd already drooled over, and impressive pecs scattered with hair. The muscles of his arms were lean but defined. Everything glistened with moisture, and his wet hair was slicked back from his face. For a man who spent hours with his face buried in books or computers, damn, he looked good.

"I'm sorry," they both said at once.

Amy covered her mouth and the laugh that almost escaped. Jonathan reddened, but his lips turned up on one side.

"This is awkward," she said.

"I've been in the attic in the old house for hours getting all sweaty, and Tyler told me to use the shower."

"I'm not complaining."

Their startled, shocked reaction was now changing, and Amy couldn't stop herself from letting her gaze meander back down his chest. The air was suddenly vibrating with the tension of two people who were thinking about sex. Amy didn't know about Jonathan, but on her part, she hadn't indulged in many months, and her body was coming awake, her breasts way too alert, her inner thighs suddenly hot.

She should duck into her room and slam the door, but she couldn't move.

Why didn't *he* move?

"Tyler said I should borrow a shirt." Jonathan's voice was low and husky.

Amy shivered. He sounded incredible and sexy and—was she thinking these things about the professor? Then she realized she was standing right in front of her brother's door.

"Oh, sorry." She reached for the doorknob and pushed it open, then stepped back. "Are you meeting us downtown?" Amy asked as Jonathan moved past her.

The width of his back compared to his hips made her breath catch. She wanted to touch him, perhaps even lick that line of moisture right up his spine. She jumped when he stopped in the doorway to glance at her over his shoulder.

"Yes. If you're sure you don't mind."

She wet her lips, feeling suddenly very dry. Or as if her moisture had all gone south. And that erotic thought made her blush. She'd even forgotten what she'd asked him. "If I don't mind what?"

His smile widened, his eyelids lowered in an actual smolder—the professor smoldered!

"That I meet you downtown," he said.

"Oh, right, yes, of course." And her face got even hotter. "I'll see you there." She escaped into her bedroom and closed the door. Leaning against it, she covered her face with both hands and gave a quiet groan. He was going to think— he was going to know—damn.

Snap out of it, she told herself. This attraction wasn't news to him. But this charged meeting was certainly going to make it harder to ignore. And it didn't help when a half hour later she was in the same shower he'd used, imagining his naked body up against hers . . .

When Amy was done showering, she forced herself to think more about what Jonathan had said in the office than about what he looked like naked.

He was alone. His family had abandoned him because he hadn't gone into the family business. She couldn't even imagine her parents ever treating any of them like that. She'd always known that although they would like some of their children to work at the orchard, it had never been a requirement. They wouldn't blackmail a child by withholding their love.

But that's what had happened to Jonathan. He'd played it down, like he was fine, but how could you be fine after that?

She continued to think about him, even as she discarded dress after dress, skirt after skirt, trying to decide what to wear. She settled on a skirt and wedges, with a little v-necked shirt that wasn't too plungy. Okay, maybe it was a little clingy . . .

This was ridiculous. She wasn't dressing to please Jonathan; she was dressing for herself.

If she'd gone overboard, her brother would have pointed it out, but he barely looked at her as he got into her car. It was a given that she'd drive, of course, since the strongest drink she'd have that night would be a Coke.

They picked up Brianna in Spencer Hollow. On the half hour drive into Charlottesville, they listened to music and talked about nothing in particular until Amy had a thought.

"Is this your first night out since you've been back?" she asked Tyler.

Tyler nodded as the approaching lights of a car briefly flickered across his face. Amy glanced over her shoulder to see Brianna listening with interest.

"Do you think your fans will bother you?" Amy continued.

He put on a pair of sunglasses and grinned at her.

"You don't think sunglasses at night make people look you over even more?"

"If he puts on a hat," Brianna said from the backseat, "he'll wreck his perfectly styled hair."

They all laughed, even as Tyler gave an exaggerated wince.

They ended up parking a couple blocks away from the Downtown Mall, which was really West Main Street that had been closed off to cars for seven blocks. There were lights hung in the trees outside restaurants and bars, scattered groups of wrought-iron tables and chairs down the cobblestone. Nineteenth-century buildings had been renovated into trendy boutiques and restaurants, the brick and stone picturesque. The college kids tended to stay closer to campus, to the bars on the Corner, so the mall was the perfect place for adults to socialize.

Amy was the first one to see the professor, of course, waiting beneath a lamppost. He wore chinos and a button-down shirt. But she was still remembering him with his jeans unbuttoned and a bare glistening chest. Oh, how was she going to get through the evening?

Tyler lifted a hand and waved. Jonathan returned the wave and came toward them.

"Good to see you again, Brianna," Jonathan said.

He nodded to Tyler, then glanced at Amy. She was so glad that the low lights of evening hid the blush she knew she was sporting. What was her problem? It wasn't like she'd seen him totally naked.

"Hello, Amy."

Did his voice sound deeper? Would everyone notice?

"Hey, Professor." At least she sounded normal, casual, and for the first time, it struck her how easily she could don a cheerful mask and hide behind it.

But Brianna was looking at her with a barely concealed smirk.

They ended up at a narrow bar with a little dance floor in the back. Soon they had a table in a corner, where Tyler and Jonathan ordered a couple flights of beer to taste. Tyler had to abandon his sunglasses once they were seated, and almost immediately a couple young women came over

for autographs. It happened occasionally throughout the evening, and Tyler handled it with his
usual casual good cheer.

"Would you ladies like to try one of these?"
Jonathan asked, holding up a small glass.

"Amy doesn't drink," Tyler said absently,
studying the next beer he was about to try.

"I could order you a glass of wine," Jonathan
offered.

She smiled at him. "That's nice of you, but I
don't drink alcohol. I just never acquired the
taste."

"Dad's an alcoholic," Tyler said, as if that
explained everything.

Were they going to discuss *every* old family
secret with Jonathan?

"Our drinks are coming," Brianna said, and the
server arrived not long afterward with her white
wine and Amy's Coke.

Amy tapped her foot to the beat of the music
and watched Jonathan and Tyler out of the corner
of her eye while she sipped her Coke. She was
relieved when some of her Charlottesville friends
arrived, and she could introduce them to the
group before heading out to the dance floor. It
felt good to use some restless energy that she
could privately admit was partly sexual in nature.
This lust for the professor wasn't her smartest
idea, but she couldn't seem to help herself.

It was a good half hour before Amy left the

dance floor. She still kept an eye on Jonathan and Tyler, who seemed to be having an in-depth discussion about beer every time she looked at them. Was Jonathan a drinker? She admitted to being overly sensitive after Rob, and her constant belief during their relationship that he could change because her father had.

There were times when Amy swore Jonathan was looking at her. She worried that every movement of her hips, every sway of her arms overhead, was like a come-hither call to him. She didn't want it to be. She was just happy to have a night off and reconnect with friends.

And then she saw that Tyler got up to dance with a woman, and Jonathan was left examining his flight of beer as if it contained all the secrets of the world. He was alone, and she thought that he must spend too much time that way—if you didn't count his students, and how could you? He took a long sip of beer.

Without thinking too much, she went back to the table, braced her arms on it, and leaned over him.

"Come on and dance," she said.

Jonathan gave her a little frown, even as his gaze dipped briefly to her cleavage and back to her face. Well, she *was* leaning over him.

"I don't dance," he said. "Go ahead and enjoy yourself."

"I'm not enjoying myself, watching you over

here alone. Everybody dances, even if you just sway while I do my excellent dance moves all around you."

He gave her that endearing crooked grin, the one that made something flutter inside her chest. Oh, this wasn't good. But she wasn't backing down now.

"I *am* enjoying watching you dance," Jonathan admitted.

She knew she was blushing again—how long had it been since she'd blushed this much? "Then watch me up close." She took his hand. "Let's go."

She thought for a moment he would refuse again, but with a sigh, he stood. She didn't release his hand, just led him behind her, moving between gyrating couples until they were closer to her friends.

And suddenly the music turned slow, Tyler took his partner into his embrace, Amy's friends left the dance floor, chatting as they looked for their drinks, and Amy and Jonathan faced each other.

He leaned down to speak near her ear. "It's okay. We can go back to our seats."

"Are you backing down from a challenge?"

They looked at each other for a long moment, and it was as if she was back in the hallway, staring at the water highlighting the contours of his chest.

And then Jonathan drew her into his arms, against the body that seemed burned into her

140

memory. He stared down into her eyes, his green ones half-closed. Their hips touched, their thighs brushed, and she could feel the heat of his palm against the small of her back. He took her right hand in his left, and it took everything in Amy not to tuck her head beneath his chin and snuggle her cheek against his chest. As it was, they were so close that her breasts brushed against him, and the friction began a slow burn that worked its way through her body, centering deep between her thighs.

Looking out at the bar, at the tables, anywhere but up into his eyes, she forced herself to speak loud enough to carry over the music. "For someone who claims not to dance, you're pretty good at this."

"This doesn't require too much coordination."

His voice rumbled out of his chest.

They stepped side to side, and every touch of his thighs against her made her want to tremble. This was surely the longest dance of her life— but she wasn't hating it. Oh, no, she wasn't hating it at all. This was the closest she'd gotten to sex in months, and even with all her clothes on, it felt way too good.

And this was the professor, a man she'd initially thought of as a stick-in-the-mud.

"I can hear you laughing," he said.

She could feel the movement of his jaw against her hair.

141

She looked up at him and raised her voice. "I can't believe you can hear anything in here."

" 'Hear' was probably the wrong word. I can feel it."

And she saw his gaze on her breasts, which were pressed to his chest. She should move away, but she didn't. It felt too good. "I wasn't laughing at you, but at our situation."

"And . . . ?"

"I don't know. I guess you're proving different than I imagined, and I'm laughing at my earlier assumptions."

"You're probably not wrong. I'm far too much of a nerd to dance well if the beat picks up."

"All I had to do was get a look at you today to know that if you're a nerd, you don't sit around most of the day."

"Amy Fairfield, are you complimenting my fitness regimen?"

"I think I'm complimenting something."

She smiled up at him. His own smile was fading, and he was watching her mouth with an intensity that gave her a little shiver.

He dropped his voice to a husky baritone. "If your brother weren't here, I think I'd kiss you right now."

Her mouth was dry, but she managed a response. "You kiss women in public bars, where any of your students might see you?"

"I've never actually kissed a woman in a public

142

bar, but I'm feeling buzzed, and I'm remembering standing there in your hallway, looking at you."

She looked down to the top button of his shirt, knowing what it hid. She wanted to unbutton it. "I can't forget it either, though I should." And she didn't like thinking that only alcohol might make him want her. That was ridiculous, she knew, but she was far too sensitive on the subject.

His hands dropped to her hips and he pulled her tighter against him. "Why should you forget it?"

The music was loud, there were people all around them, but his bent head felt like a tent that surrounded her, kept their words and their deeds private. She felt his erection against her stomach, and he made no move to hide it from her. His bold, arousing behavior was changing everything she'd thought she knew about him. Apparently the strong, silent type of guy had hidden depths.

"Hey, Dr. G.!"

Jonathan stiffened and stepped back, letting go of Amy. She almost staggered, deprived of his support and his warmth. But he was looking off the dance floor, his momentary frown smoothing out into a smile that almost looked friendly. Almost. Or maybe only Amy noticed the difference.

"Dr. G., I've never seen you here before!"

The speaker was a young man in a T-shirt and

jeans, holding a bottle of beer. He was standing with several similar young men, and all were looking at Amy with interest. Friendly interest, but interest nonetheless.

"Hello, Carter," Jonathan said. "Guess there's a first time for everything."

"You relaxing like everyone else after finals?"

"Of course. But just remember, I still have to grade them."

"Give me the benefit of the doubt, okay?" Carter shared a laugh with his friends, then turned his smile on Amy. "Shouldn't have interrupted your dance. Sorry."

"That's okay," Amy said.

"It's just that some of us were wondering what Dr. G. does with himself when he's outside of school. We pretty much thought it was study even more."

A returning frown disturbed Jonathan's forehead.

Amy took his hand. "Now you know different." She gave the young men her flirtiest smile, slid an arm around Jonathan's waist, and added, "Good night," before steering him toward their table.

Tyler, who'd obviously been sharing his flight of beer with Brianna and was now looking over Jonathan's, eyed the two of them beneath a raised brow. "A dance sure did wonders for both of your moods." Then he studied Jonathan more closely. "On second thought—"

"No mood problems here," Amy said brightly, releasing Jonathan and taking a deep sip of her Coke.

Tyler looked at Brianna. "Want to dance? Seems like the mood-killing slow number is over."

Amy could have sworn Brianna blushed. She hoped Brianna didn't have her eye on Tyler. Amy knew he wasn't planning on sticking around the orchard any longer than he had to. He had a career to return to.

Amy sank down in a chair and glanced back out at the dance floor. "I'm not sure I properly introduced you to my friends. I wonder where they—"

"Why did you act like that in front of my students?" Jonathan asked.

She raised an eyebrow at his cool tone. "Act how? I didn't think I was supposed to disappear into the background as if you didn't have a social life. I thought I was helping you out."

He suddenly pointed a finger at her. "There, did you hear yourself? Of course I didn't want you to disappear into the background, whatever that means. But why did you act like we had some-thing going on?"

"Well, that dance was pretty hot, although perhaps you didn't notice." She tilted her chin up.

"You know what I mean. You turned it on for those boys like you had to help me prove some-thing to them. That wasn't necessary. My students can believe whatever they'd like about my private life. It's none of their business."

She felt her defensiveness drain right out of her. "I didn't mean it to be like that."

"But that's how it was, wasn't it."

She swallowed and, to her surprise, felt a slight sting of tears. She wasn't upset about his anger; she was upset she'd hurt him. Had she flirted with his students as if she was taking pity on him? That's what he was implying. They weren't dating—and he certainly wasn't a man who needed pity.

"I'm sorry," she said quietly. "I didn't think it through, and I never meant to . . . to make it seem like you needed me. I thought we were just having fun."

He grimaced, then ran a hand down his face. For a long moment they said nothing, while the music kept up a beat that reverberated in her tight chest.

And then Jonathan covered her hand with his. "I'm sorry, too. I overreacted."

"No, you didn't. I screwed up. It won't happen again." She tried to pull her hand away, but he didn't allow it.

"Amy." He whispered her name. "That was the best dance I've ever had."

She gave him a tight smile and tried to relax, but she felt so mixed up inside. Why was she feeling protective of him? Why was she so affected by him?

"Of course it was your best dance," she said at last. "You said you never dance."

He gave her that crooked grin that made her heart beat way too fast. She should be mad at him. Look how easily they misconstrued each other. How could she trust herself to read any man's emotions, after what Rob had put her through? Half the time she kept expecting Jonathan to act like Rob, like downing the entire flight of beer in record time. That would have been Rob's style.

Jonathan was just a friend, she had to keep reminding herself. What could they talk about that wasn't so fraught with tension?

Jonathan spoke first. "I hope this misunderstanding doesn't make you think you should reject my offer of help with the business plan. You're giving me access to Fairfield Orchard and its past. I'll gladly do anything I can to help. I've been doing a little research about it and . . ."

He went on for a minute as she tried to control the rising heat in her face. He was making her feel like he thought she couldn't handle it herself. He was micromanaging her, just when she'd been taking control of her own future and trying to leave the past behind.

"That's okay, Jonathan," she interrupted. "My brother and I have got this."

She must have spoken a little too forcefully, because Jonathan straightened up in his chair.

"Of course you do. I was trying to find a way to

express my gratitude, but this isn't the right way. I understand."

Suddenly they were joined by a half dozen people all crowding around—Tyler and some woman who was clinging to his arm, Brianna, and Amy's Realtor friends, who seemed to be hitting it off. Everybody was having fun except killjoy Amy, and she felt like a fool.

Jonathan and Tyler ordered more beer for the table, and the laughter and good-natured conversation only increased. Amy kept trying to read what Jonathan was thinking, but she couldn't. She wanted to relax and just be a part of a fun evening, but she'd denied herself that, too.

Brianna, who'd been watching her too closely, said, "Let's find the ladies' room."

Amy didn't bother protesting. When they were in a narrow hall that led to both restrooms and the kitchen, and the music was muffled, Brianna stopped her with a hand on her arm.

"Everything okay? I thought you had a nice dance with Jonathan, but you've both been different since you got back to the table."

Amy put her back against the wall and sagged. "I am an idiot. Remind me that I shouldn't be allowed in public."

Brianna patted her shoulder, smiling. "I think you're being awfully hard on yourself. Getting back into the swing of things after a long break isn't always easy. Everything feels all surfacy with the new person, as if you couldn't ever understand what makes them tick."

"That's not far off the mark," Amy admitted.

"Then relax. He's feeling the same way, I bet."

"Bri, it's obvious I'm not ready to date again. Why am I doing all this"—she gestured back toward their table—"flirting and dancing and—"

"For the same reasons we all do. We don't want to be alone. We want to find someone who's like us, yet different enough to be interesting."

"We've got nothing in common," Amy said tiredly.

"Really? I see two people with a big-time physical connection. Isn't that a start?"

Amy tried not to smile but one appeared anyway. "Is it that obvious?"

"I couldn't see light between you two when you were dancing. I was waiting for hand-on-butt action, and I was about to take bets on how you'd react."

Amy snorted a giggle. "Or maybe how he'd react when I grabbed *him*."

"That's the spirit."

"Tyler told him to take a shower at our house, and I saw him without a shirt today. Let's just say I may have been underestimating the brainy guys of this world."

Brianna fanned herself.

Amy returned from the restroom in a better mood. She ended up in a discussion with Jonathan and Brianna about her flattened picnic meadow, and how she'd talked about it with Miss Jablonski, the high school principal who lived nearby.

"You can't find anyone better to sic on teen-agers," Brianna said. "She even scares me when she comes into the store, although she's nice and polite, of course."

"She's going to keep a lookout for me. It's a silly thing, but it's driving me nuts."

In another hour, things had mellowed, and though Amy hadn't asked Jonathan to dance again, she was back to lusting after him. She liked seeing him in the midst of a crowd, and although he wasn't the most vocal or expressive, he seemed to be enjoying himself. Though he was tasting different beers and discussing, he wasn't letting the alcohol get to him.

Occasionally he would glance at her, and she actually felt shy after their dance and their disagreement, but his gaze was full of appre-ciation. She was just starting to think about asking him to dance again when she saw him shaking hands with Tyler. He made his way up the table, saying good-bye to her friends, and then at last he got to her.

He leaned down to say something to her, but the song playing seemed twice the volume level.

"I'll walk you outside," she said, standing on tiptoes to reach his ear.

He went first, threading his way through a

crowd on the dance floor, and she didn't protest when he took her hand to guide her. He didn't let her go when they left the building, and the cool early-summer air made her shiver after all the heat built up from dancing.

To her surprise, he put her back up against the building in a shadowy corner and leaned into her.

"I've wanted to do this all night," he said in a hoarse voice.

And then he was kissing her, and it was no gentle kiss of tentative exploration. He slanted his mouth over hers with the force of a man who knew what he wanted. She met him eagerly, opening to him, tasting him, clutching the open collar of his shirt as if she didn't want him to get away. The taste of beer was a heady symbol of the evening; it reminded her of watching him, talking to him, rubbing against him on the dance floor. She rubbed against him now, and he put his thigh between her legs and pressed.

She moaned into his mouth, then gasped, head arching back. Then he was nibbling behind her ear, pressing openmouthed kisses down her neck, then licking his way back up.

"God, you taste good," he whispered.

"I'm all hot from dancing."

"I like it. Salty."

She held his face to hers and kissed him again, and for a long moment they just enjoyed each other. From somewhere in the distance, they heard voices, and a door slamming.

Jonathan straightened, his palms still cupping her face, his thumbs tracing her cheeks. "I should go. Your brother will be missing you."

"We've lived apart for over ten years. I don't think he'll even remember I'm gone." She hesitated. "And I don't think you should drive home."

Arching a brow, Jonathan released her.

"No, really. You don't live far away, right? Let's walk."

"You're walking me home?"

"I can protect you—I used to be able to beat up Tyler when I wanted to. Of course, he wasn't taller than me until he was thirteen."

"I don't think I can resist such an offer. Will I see you in action?"

"Only if someone dares to stop us."

He took her hand again, and side by side, they left the Downtown Mall and headed south, where the streets gradually grew more and more quiet. Just as Amy was remembering she'd left her sweater in the bar, Jonathan put his arm around her shoulders. After a brief hesitation, she slid her arm around his waist. They walked silently for several blocks into the Belmont neighborhood.

Amy wasn't sure where her impulses were leading her, and she didn't think about it too closely. She was having a fun night, except for a little hiccup of a disagreement in the middle. And she didn't like to think of Jonathan tipsy and walking home alone, even though it was a pretty safe section of the city.

He turned up the walkway in front of a two-story house with a flower-decorated porch. It had historic character, with lovely arches between the front porch columns, and a stained-glass window over the front door.

"This is it," he said.

"Nice. It has a turn-of-the-century feel. Perfect for a history professor." Now she was babbling. She accompanied him onto the porch, then shone her cell phone on his keys as he tried to find the right one. When he slid it in and opened the door, she backed up a step. "Have a good night."

"Wait a minute—you're not going to kiss me good-night?"

She felt a shock of eager excitement, but teased, "I thought we already—"

He drew her into his arms on the dark porch, and she wrapped herself around him. She slid her hands up the contours of his back and groaned her appreciation. His lips were warm and demanding, and she couldn't deny herself even though some distant part of her knew this might be a mistake. It was a kiss, a really good, throbbing kiss, and it had been too long. When he

153

cupped her butt and held her hard against him, she felt light-headed with pleasure.

"You're not going back alone," he said against her mouth.

She kissed him again, then gasped, "That was the deal."

Cradling her face with his big hands, he found her eyes and chin and cheeks with his kisses, whispering in between, "I thought your offer . . . to walk me home . . . was cute, but it wasn't the deal . . . Come on in and we'll . . . tell your brother where to pick you up."

She got her own nip on his neck. "I'm the designated driver."

"Then we'll call Uber to get you back there."

He explored her lower lip with his tongue, then sucked it gently into his mouth. Her thighs clenched. She couldn't even remember what he was saying.

"But the car can wait," he murmured. "Come inside."

This was a bad idea.

"Yes," she gasped.

— *Chapter 8* —

Amy didn't walk into Jonathan's home, she floated. She felt as light as snow in his arms, desired, needed. He kissed her with desperation, and she did the same with him.

It was a heady feeling, this low pull of desire, this awareness of being close to him.

The living room only had a single light on near the door, so the furniture were dim shapes in the darkness. Nothing mattered but Jonathan's touch inducing shivers, his lips making her moan. He was moving her across the room but she was barely aware of it, until he lowered her to the couch and sat beside her. It was like a high school make-out session, only far better when two people knew what they were doing.

When his hand moved from her hip and up her torso, just skimming the edge of her breast, she pressed herself into him, encouraging, begging, and if he didn't touch her soon—

She didn't have to wait. His big hand cupped her breast and she groaned. Her breath came in pants that matched his, and as he explored her, she gave little gasps and cries of pleasure.

"You're wearing too many clothes," he rasped.

"Then take them off."

He stilled. She hadn't planned those words, but

she didn't regret them. It had been too long, and they were both adults, and they wanted each other. She'd never felt so desperate and needy and desired.

"Are you sure?" Jonathan whispered. "Amy, you can change your mind—"

"I'm not going to change my mind." She pulled her shirt off. In the low light, the satin of her cream and pink bra glistened, and she could see Jonathan staring.

And then he rose above her and she sank back on the couch. She wanted him on top of her, pressing into her, but he slid his hips beside hers, finding just enough room so that she didn't fall off the couch. And then he was kissing her again, and his hand was roaming, and everywhere he touched he left what felt like a trail of fire and yearning. His fingers traced paths between her breasts, and up and over the covered peaks. She arched up and reached behind her, and then her bra sailed over her head. She wanted his mouth on her, but though he did a quick intake of breath, he didn't comply, just continued to tease her with his fingers. The first caress that brushed near her nipple and then slid away made her cry out her frustration.

"Please," she whispered urgently.

He bent and took her nipple deep into his mouth. With a cry, she held his head to her, felt the soft waves of his dark hair. While he pleasured her she fumbled to reach the buttons of his shirt, needing to feel more of him. She was pulling it up his back before he finally noticed and pulled it right over his head. And then all that delicious male flesh was against hers. Their mouths met over and over as his hand slid from her knee and up beneath her skirt. She wiggled, wanting his touch and feeling constrained by the couch and her tight skirt.

And then he leaned across her, pushed at the coffee table, and it fell over with a crash. He turned and took her with him to the floor. He came down on top of her, and though he obviously meant to move to the side, she held him against her for a long kiss, his chest flattening her breasts, their mouths slanting and devouring. He dropped down beside her, and she rolled him onto his back, greedy to explore the broad expanse of his chest. She licked and gently bit, then whirled her tongue over his nipples, all while unbuckling his belt and sliding down his zipper. She reached inside and ran her hand along the hard length of him beneath his boxer briefs.

He groaned. "Amy, my God, what you do to me. I can't wait much longer."

He rolled and came up on his knees, straddling one of her legs as he pushed her skirt up to her waist. In the low light, his eyes were intent as he watched his fingers trace the edges of her thong, then slide beneath to tease before slowly, far too slowly, sliding the thong down her legs and off. His hand cupped and spread her, he kissed her breasts again, and she knew she was going to come far too quickly.

"Now, please, now, inside me," she urged, and reached to pull down his pants.

When she touched his bare penis, he groaned and held still, trembling as she stroked him. He moved between her legs and stroked himself down the wetness of her body once, twice.

"Jonathan!"

He slid deep inside.

He gasped against her mouth and his voice was a low rumble as he said her name.

Oh, God, he felt so good, so right. She moved against him, urging him onward. Their mouths joined in a kiss as their bodies moved below. She surged up to meet him, every pressure spreading the pleasure higher. Hugging his hips with her thighs, she clutched his back and his butt in turn. She felt like begging him for the release that had her teetering on the brink of fulfillment.

And when it came, it was as thrilling and exhilarating as the plummet down the highest hill of a roller coaster. She couldn't hold back a scream, shuddering.

Somewhere in the depths of Jonathan's mind, he felt the satisfaction of knowing he'd given Amy so much pleasure, but then his instincts kicked in, and it was all about him and what he needed with a desperation that had gone beyond rational thought. His pace quickened, his breathing was a gasp. She felt so hot and tight around him—the sudden climax swept over him, through him, and into her.

At last he lifted himself up on his hands and looked down at her. Her light brown hair was wild about her head, but she was wearing a big grin, her teeth practically shining in the low light. She reached up and caressed his chest. Arching back his head, he moved inside her again.

And then he realized he was pinning her to the floor.

Rational thought returned in a flood. "Jesus, Amy, are you okay?"

He pulled out of her and sank back on his heels. It was far too easy to get distracted again at the sight of her open to him.

And then he shook those impulses away. "I took you on the floor!"

The coffee table legs were straight up in the air, his books and magazines scattered all over. Her skirt was wrapped around her waist; his pants were down around his ankles.

"I didn't even take off . . ." He gestured to his pants, stunned.

Amy's smile only widened into a lazy grin. "I know. It was pretty great."

But the worst part of it all just occurred to him. "I didn't wear a condom."

She sat up and took his hands in hers. "Don't worry, it's okay, I'm on the pill. I'm medically healthy. Can I assume you are, too?"

He nodded, but that only eased one part of his brain. "Amy, that's not the point—I mean, yes, obviously that's a relief, but . . . I've *always* worn a condom, and protection always came first. I let you down."

"We were both pretty thoughtless tonight."

They were silent for a moment, and he had to force his gaze to her face. He was upset by what he'd done, but he couldn't stop imagining taking her again.

"That was really your first time having sex without a condom?" she asked.

He nodded. "My ex-fiancée was always afraid one method of birth control wasn't enough. She didn't want a child until the right time in her career."

"So . . . did it feel different?"

"Incredible," he said solemnly.

She chuckled, and he stared at her in amazement. How could she not be upset by all of this?

"Relax," she said, coming up onto her knees. "It's too late, so stop thinking."

He fell back on his elbows as she leaned over and kissed him. She explored his mouth, her tongue stroking his, and his thoughts began to float away again. He dropped onto his back, and pulled her toward him by the shoulders. She looked beautiful, her hair falling all around her, her breasts right in front of him dangling like fruit—the worst, most overused metaphor, but he didn't care. He slid farther beneath her until they were right above his face. He felt her breathing pick up, heard her shaky sigh, and then he gently licked first one nipple and then the other.

"Oh, Jonathan," she breathed. "Yes."

For long minutes he focused on her breasts, until she was trembling above him. And then she lifted away.

"We have to stop," she said, regret in her blue, blue eyes. "They're probably wondering where I am. I'm supposed to drive everyone home."

Even all of their friends, her brother, had totally slipped his mind. "I can't think when I'm with you."

She looked away, and she might have been blushing, but it was hard to tell in this light.

"That's a pretty strong compliment coming from you," she said lightly. She looked around. "I think I threw my bra somewhere."

Jonathan rose and pulled his pants back up, still feeling uncomfortable that he'd never taken them off, not even his shoes. He flicked on another light near the couch, then turned around to find Amy bending to reach something behind a chair. She'd pulled her skirt down, but without underwear . . .

She came up with her bra in her hand and found

him frozen, just staring at her. She had a small frame, but her breasts were full and round and pink-tipped, then they hardened to points under his hot gaze.

Smiling, she put her bra on and continued to look for clothing. Jonathan found and held up the little scrap of lace that was hardly big enough to be called underwear. She took them and stepped in, then slid her top back on. Jonathan didn't do anything but stand still and watch her, as if this might be his last chance.

"So, you don't have any photos on display?" Amy asked, looking around. "No knickknacks? I see a lot of books."

Two walls had floor-to-ceiling shelves of them.

"You can tell what's most important to me, I guess," he said. "This isn't even my main collection."

She looked at the one painting of a plantation that hung over his couch, then shot an amused look at him. "Monticello."

"No laughing," Jonathan said.

"Hey, I get it. Thomas Jefferson is your obsession."

"He's not my obsession, I keep telling you. He's my job."

"You're cute," she said, shaking her head.

She walked to the door, and Jonathan realized what was going on.

"Wait, you can't leave."

She pulled her phone out of her purse and frowned at it. "I have to go. Tyler texted me a while ago. Damn, what am I going to say?"

"The truth."

She arched a brow. "He may be my twin, but we don't share every intimate detail of our lives."

"I meant tell him we went for a walk, that I had to clear my head."

"Oh, right." Her thumbs flew over the phone. "There, that's done. No time for Uber. I'll just walk back."

"My head's cleared. I'm coming with you."

She didn't protest, but she watched him put on his shirt with a gratifying focus. They stepped outside into the cool night and he saw her shiver.

"I left my sweater at the bar."

"Wait a second." He grabbed his coat from inside the hall closet and put it over her shoulders.

"Thanks."

They started walking, and this time the excited anticipation was gone. Jonathan found too many thoughts whirling around in his head as he grew more and more concerned about how much he'd lost control. He usually thought through everything well in advance, never took risks. Except for with Geneva, he'd always been careful not to get too involved with the women he'd dated. Otherwise, emotions got messy—an unplanned preg-nancy would be the height of complication.

Amy had wiped any of these considerations right out of his mind.

Amy slid her hand into his and leaned her head against his arm. "Hey, you seem far away."

"Sorry. I'm still—I really am sorry," he said suddenly.

He felt her stiffen.

"Sorry for what?" she asked coolly.

"Sorry that I was so caught up in wanting you that I didn't think about keeping you safe."

He felt the tension leave her, and though he didn't understand what was going on in her mind, he assumed her relaxation to be a good thing.

"We're both equally responsible, Jonathan," she said. "I didn't think about protecting you either."

"Sure you did—you're on the pill."

"Well, that's protecting me, after all, and protecting a child from being born into bad circumstances. I want kids, but I want to make that decision and be prepared for it." She paused. "Do you want kids?"

"Yes, I do. Someday."

She nodded and didn't say anything else. The lights of the mall gleamed ahead, and they could hear the buzz of music as they walked up a side street.

As they approached the bar, she suddenly stopped and put a hand on his chest. "Jonathan, you don't have to walk me back inside. I'm fine from here."

164

"I don't feel comfortable with that."

"You're a gentleman, I know, but I think the rest of them will take one look at the two of us together and know exactly what we've done."

He frowned.

"I'm not ashamed," she insisted. "Frankly, I had a great time. But this is my brother we're talking about."

"All right, if you think that's best."

He heard himself sounding stilted and didn't mean it to come out that way.

"Amy." He took her hand before she could leave, then leaned down and kissed her lightly.

She smiled. "You don't have to say you'll call me, you know."

She didn't want to see him again? He opened his mouth, but couldn't think of how to express his disappointment, his disagreement. But she wasn't finished.

"We can talk when you come to the orchard. We can . . . see where this is going."

He took a deep breath of relief. "All right, that sounds good. But I'll call you when I want to call you," he said, only half teasing.

Her smile broadened. "Fair enough."

He kissed her again, more deeply this time, tasting her as if he might forget. He murmured against her lips, "Good night."

He didn't want to stop touching her, but he did. She handed him his jacket, and he watched her walk into the bar, especially the sway of her hips, and the way her hair seemed to bounce around her shoulders. She smiled at him and then she was gone.

Jonathan put his hands in his pockets and, for a moment, wondered what it would be like to walk in there at Amy's side, and dare anyone to say anything about it.

But she didn't want that. Hell, maybe he didn't want that either. But they'd both wanted sex . . .

— *Chapter 9* —

Amy took some teasing when she returned to the table, but the place was loud and crowded and everyone was feeling their alcohol. No on looked at her too closely or asked pointed questions. She listened to the buzz of conversation and let her mind dwell on its own thoughts. She hadn't just relaxed and let things happen with a man since her breakup. She told herself she wasn't going to overthink this or analyze anything, like her brief panic when she'd thought Jonathan had meant alcohol was responsible for the sex, but that hadn't been true.

She could have sex with a man and not read too much into it. Other women did it all the time—or so she'd heard. She'd never been one of them. She'd dated a couple guys in high school and lost her virginity, but then she'd met Rob and they'd been all over each other. Focused, maybe even a little obsessed.

Sort of how she'd felt with Jonathan, how she couldn't get enough of him. Should this be a warning sign?

But he was nothing like Rob, she reminded herself. Every moment with him made that more and more clear. He was calm and rational and nice. And if she'd thought him a little too subdued before, she certainly knew now that he had a hidden fire of which she'd been the very welcome recipient.

Jonathan made her realize how much she missed the closeness of being with a man with whom she shared such a deep attraction. Frankly, she hadn't felt that for a long time even during her last relationship.

But this was all happening too fast, and it was a little scary. She didn't know Jonathan well— what had it been, a week? Ten days? She'd just told herself not to overanalyze, and here she was, doing that very thing, second-guessing everything, trying to plan out what her every action and reaction should be from now on. Had the sex been his attempt to prove something to her, after how she'd annoyed him when talking to his students?

She didn't have time to get involved with a man. She certainly had intended to know one very well before she permitted this kind of intimacy again. And she'd broken all of her rules.

She didn't blame Jonathan. He was a guy, after all, and sex was as important as breathing to them.

Sex was important to her, too, but she'd had no idea just *how* important. So important she hadn't thought of a condom, or the fact that she wasn't even dating the man. Or was it all about the man himself—and that was even scarier.

And then she had to let it go, or risk everyone figuring out what she was hiding. Within the hour, her real estate friends called it a night, and she and Tyler dropped Brianna off at her little house in Spencer Hollow.

Tyler was quiet as they took the gradual climb toward the orchard, the darkness complete but for a rare lamppost near an intersection. She was used to driving this road, and though she kept a watch out for deer, she was comfortable.

"So," Tyler began, "was the professor good in bed—or maybe you didn't even make it there."

Amy's mouth dropped open and the car veered a little.

"Careful there," he warned.

"Then don't say such crazy things while I'm driving."

"Crazy?"

She kept her gaze focused on the road.

"So crazy that you can't even look at me."

"I'm driving!"

A minute later she did glance at him, and he was waiting, giving her that smirk he'd been using since the day he was born. Of course he knew the truth—he could read everything in her face, just as she could read his. Maybe it came from sharing the womb, because it wasn't as if they had identical DNA.

"So a quickie with the professor," Tyler said slowly.

Amy winced. "Could you not refer to it that way?"

"I guess I'm not surprised. I told him I saw the way you two looked at each other."

"You told *him!* Tyler!"

"What? Hey, he's a good guy, and he deserved to know what I could see. And remember, he'd overheard part of our discussion, and I didn't want him confused."

She rolled her eyes.

"So where'd you go?" he asked. "Tell me you didn't find the nearest alley . . ."

She swatted at his arm. "Gross! He lives nearby," she admitted. "I was walking him home—"

"Walking him home? That's a pretty good pickup line."

"It's not a line," she insisted. "He'd been drinking and I didn't want him driving, and we sort of . . . walked."

"So he didn't force his drunken self on you. I don't have to beat him up or anything."

"Of course not. And don't discuss it with him! I'm not kidding here, Tyler. We aren't even dating, and I've never done anything like that before and . . ." Her voice trailed off. God, they weren't even dating.

"You've never had sex?" He chuckled.

She swatted him again.

"Hey, now don't be hard on yourself," he said

genially. "We've all been overcome by lust before. And it's not like he's a stranger."

"I've known him a week!"

"Ten days."

"Close enough."

"And you've had some good conversations, and I thought you'd eventually date him, if you could let yourself relax a little."

She'd been telling herself the same thing, hadn't she? She sighed. "I still don't feel right about it."

"Well, don't let him know that. He probably feels great and you'll hurt his feelings."

"So when have you been so concerned with another guy's feelings?"

"Hey, we men can be touchy about sex and our performance of it, all right?"

"Have *you* ever slept with someone when you didn't intend to do it?"

He didn't answer at first, and she glanced at him again as the car moved beneath a streetlamp. For once, he looked solemn.

"Sure, I'm a guy, after all."

But his cheerfulness sounded forced.

"So tell me details."

"Gross—to use your word."

"Not *those* kinds of details. You've always had a girl to date whenever you wanted. Why did you have sex unintentionally?"

He looked out the window and spoke quietly.

"Because she was a fan, and I don't normally sleep with fans. It feels like I've got all the power, you know?"

"Oh, yeah, I could see that."

"But one thing led to another—you understand that."

"Yeah, I understand too well." She pulled into the broad parking lot of the orchard and past the barn and the other buildings. She slid into one of the parking places beside the house and, after cutting the engine, looked at Tyler by the big light over the garage. "Did everything end up okay?"

"Turns out she was married."

She grimaced in sympathy.

"So no, it didn't turn out great, but it could have been worse. I got out of it without too much damage, and I don't think her husband ever found out my name. Or at least he didn't come after me."

"I'm sorry."

"Eh, taught myself a good lesson. Did you teach yourself a lesson tonight?"

"I don't know. I don't know what I'm supposed to be thinking—or doing. We weren't even dating. But now . . . are we? Is it automatic?"

"Do you want it to be?"

She let out a long breath. "I don't know. As you keep pointing out, he and I have been looking at each other. But that's just physical, and grown-ups should be able to ignore it. It's such a bad time for a relationship, Tyler. We're so busy with the orchard—" And then there was her horrible misjudgment about Rob.

"The orchard has gotten along just fine all these years."

"But I've been studying the last five years of business records, and our profits have slowly been going down. Why do you think there was no money for Mom and Dad to retire without help?"

"Well, I know that," he said with exasperation. "But things'll work out."

"Really? How? If we don't do anything differently, then this year'll be a little less than last year. Why would Logan want to keep throwing away money on a losing effort?"

"Because we're family and he's loaded."

"We told him that we don't need a handout, but a business investment. We have to work harder."

She saw his shoulders stiffen.

"Do you think I'm not?" he demanded.

"I didn't say that!" she insisted, surprised by how defensive he suddenly sounded.

He opened the car door and slammed it behind him.

She jumped out, bewildered. "Tyler, don't be angry, please."

He didn't answer. Amy stumbled to a halt and just stared as her brother went inside. Uma came

173

bounding out the door, and Amy patted her absently as she watched Tyler's progression through the house by where the lights went on, and knew he'd gone right to his room.

They didn't argue—they never argued. And if they had a few words, they always apologized immediately and good-naturedly.

But *should* she apologize? He was the one who'd gotten touchy when she suggested they needed to work hard. She hadn't meant to accuse him at all. But now she could privately admit to herself that she'd noticed that he was often late, and sometimes missed a meeting with Carlos. She knew the orchard was important to him. She needed an equal partner, someone to rely on. This wasn't high school, where the result of being late was detention. This was real life with real life consequences, like failure, and the ending of a two-hundred-year-old farm. She wasn't going to let that happen on her watch.

But what was going on with Tyler? He had her really worried.

And then she heard something and froze. Uma's ears pricked up. It sounded like the distant echo of voices. What voices? Only she and Tyler lived here now. And had that been the sound of some kind of instrument—a drum?

The picnic meadow.

She was about to jump into the nearest pickup to go investigate, but remembered how bad the muffler was. But what choice did she have? Her little Prius would bottom out on some of the ruts between the apple rows.

She grabbed the keys from the rack inside the back door of the house, let Uma jump into the truck, then set off into the darkness of the orchard, trying not to rev the engine as she shifted gears. High above, the black sky showed pinpricks of stars, and ahead, the Blue Ridge Mountains were a black uneven line blocking out the horizon.

But she was too late. By the time she arrived at the picnic meadow, just the wet remnants of a dead fire greeted her. There was no damage, besides flattened grass, not even a piece of litter. Uma circled around the meadow, sniffing, but grew disinterested fast. So someone was meeting for some fun under the stars. Why the orchard?

Amy drove back home slowly, feeling frustrated for so many reasons. And of course that brought her back to sex with Jonathan, and then her argument with Tyler—which had started because of the sex. She didn't want to go back into the house. Tyler's light was off now, and she couldn't even make things right with him tonight. She found herself walking beneath the parking lot lamppost, and heading for the barn. She slid open one big door, which creaked as it moved. Inside, she switched on the light, then walked past all the stacked apple bins to the hayloft ladder. Once she'd climbed up, she found the manila envelope with the torn family photo. She held the pieces in her hand, staring at the remains of old-fashioned serious faces, and the one face of a little boy, smirking. It was her great-great-grandpa, it had to be, but she hadn't gotten the chance to ask her own grandpa before Rob had ruined the photo.

She'd only seen what she wanted to see in Rob, and had proceeded to let her life get away from her. Jonathan was different in so many ways, but he was also intense and focused and managing, which made her feel skittish.

Those things shouldn't have to matter to her. Why couldn't she just be like other women and date without any kind of commitment? Or at least find an uncomplicated man?

Amy woke up in her bedroom, her Backstreet Boys poster making her feel like the boundaries of her childhood were closing back around her. As a kid she remembered feeling helpless and worried about her dad's drinking, but now it was about making a success of the orchard. She certainly wasn't helpless, not anymore.

And then Uma popped up from the floor and set her head on the bed, looking at Amy expectantly. Amy chuckled and ruffled her fur.

Well, if she was going to get on top of things, it was time for a meeting of all the employees to see what they thought of the business and what could be improved.

176

After feeding Uma, she showered, then called Carlos and asked him to keep everyone at the warehouse before dispersing for the day. She texted the plan to Tyler, but didn't hear back.

Her phone rang while still in her hands, and for some reason she expected Tyler (although why would he call her when he could just walk across the hall). But it wasn't her brother; it was Jonathan. She hesitated. Hadn't she told him they'd talk at the orchard?

Wimp, she told herself, and answered. "Morning, Jonathan."

"Good morning, Amy."

His deep voice was only friendly, but she shivered nonetheless. Just the sound reminded her of the way he'd said her name while he was inside her.

"I know you said we'd talk when I saw you next," he continued. "But . . . that didn't seem right to me after everything that happened last night."

"Always the gentleman," she said lightly. She could have kicked herself for the strain she could hear in her own voice. She was really a woman of the world, wasn't she, she thought with sarcasm.

"Well, no, if I was a gentleman, I would have at least bought you dinner first."

She had to smile. "I could have bought *you* dinner."

177

He paused. "Then can we have dinner this week?"

She'd known this was coming, and had hoped to be more prepared for it. "I don't know, Jonathan. I have a lot of work right now. Can we revisit this in a couple weeks?"

"Sure. Whatever you think best."

Did he sound disappointed . . . or relieved? She didn't know him well enough to hazard a guess. And maybe that was a sign she was making the right decision.

"Are you coming out to the orchard today?" she asked.

"No, I have finals to grade this weekend."

"Oh, okay, then I'll see you next time."

"Amy, I'm sorry this is awkward, and I don't know if I'm making it worse, but . . . I had a really good time last night."

"Thanks." She didn't return the sentiment, and by the time she realized it during the long awkward pause, it wouldn't have sounded true. "See you later, Professor."

"Good-bye, Amy."

Grimacing, she tapped her phone on her forehead a few times as if she could knock some sense into herself. What a mess—and she'd probably made it worse, hurting his feelings. She had to let it go and focus on work.

After she put on a little mascara—to look a little more like the boss rather than the regular worker she'd always been before—she descended to the kitchen. She felt worried when Tyler wasn't there. They needed to talk, and she hated to wait until later in the day. Of course, with the way her conversations were going today, maybe it was a good thing.

But her day only went downhill from there. Tyler showed up barely on time to the meeting at the warehouse, and they didn't get a chance to talk first. His hair wasn't immaculately styled, so she guessed he'd overslept—again. Poor guy. She was starting to wonder if he was having more problems with this career hiatus than she'd thought. While they all waited for Carlos, who was checking the malfunctioning controls on a cold atmosphere room, Amy asked their six full-time employees if they'd seen anyone hanging out at the meadow, and none of them had. Of course, they usually went home every night.

Grandpa Fairfield walked into the conference room with Carlos, deep in a conversation about the coming harvest. They broke off when they saw her, as if she didn't need to know these things. She tamped down her frustration. All in good time. Carlos's dog, Barney, ambled toward Uma, who ignored him as if he didn't exist.

The meeting with the employees was good, but not extremely helpful. Their suggestions were about putting in a maze, or expanding the playground or trying a new kind of fudge. Amy knew they were trying to be helpful, but many of them had spent their whole lives working for her dad, and knew how things had always been done, and couldn't think of anything . . . different.

When they all left—including Tyler, and she didn't try to stop him—Amy had the frustrating feeling that there was something she should be seeing. She thought some nebulous idea had occurred to her at the bar, but sex with Jonathan had put everything else from her mind, and now she couldn't remember.

They had to find a way to get old customers to want to return this fall, and bring all their friends. But apple-picking was such a family thing. So what were other orchards doing that was so successful?

And that was it—she'd have to go find out, and that called for some undercover spying. Well, that was a little melodramatic. Research on her competitors was more accurate. She went to find Tyler.

He was watching Grandpa Fairfield and Carlos huddle together over the controls for the malfunctioning CA room. In the distance, she could hear the machinery for the packing line kick into gear. She tapped Tyler on the shoulder, and he gave her a distracted smile.

"Can we talk?" she asked.

"Sure."

He followed her back to the conference room and she closed the door.

He smiled at her. "Amy, everything's okay with us. I know you're just worried about the business."

Well, that was true, but for some reason his saying it that way irritated her. Couldn't she be worried about him? But she let it go.

She gave him a big hug. "I hated how we ended last night. I don't like us to be upset with each other."

"I know. It was stupid of me to go to bed like that without talking. But I'd had a little too much to drink, and that was probably why I over-reacted."

That made her feel better. "Hey, want to do some research with me?" Seeing his expression, she added, "Fun research, I swear."

"Okaaay . . ." He drew the word out.

"Let's go tour some of the local orchards and see what they're doing. We could make a day of it."

"You do realize that most of them won't be open to the public, unless their country stores are year-round."

"I know, but we can see the grounds, maybe reintroduce ourselves, ask how business has been. Everybody only knows Dad and Grandpa, not us. And we can use this as research for the business plan, too. We have to know how saturated our market is, and if that's a problem going forward."

"Sneaky. All right, I'm in."

But Tyler wasn't in. Come Monday morning, he got a call from his agent about a last-minute cancellation by an actor for a soap opera fan celebration in DC. She found him in the bathroom, quickly running product through his hair.

"I have to go, Amy. You understand, right?"

"Of course I understand, Dr. Lake. Your public awaits." But would Tyler one day get an offer for a part and leave her in a lurch? No, that was ridiculous. He'd promised her six months. "Damn, it's a beautiful day, too. We'll just have to go another time."

"That's not necessary. I know how you are when you get a plan cemented in your head. So I called Jonathan a little while ago, and he's happy to take my place."

Her mouth dropped open. "Tyler!"

He smiled at her in the mirror. "What? Come on, Amy, you two obviously hit it off."

"Did you ever think to discuss this with me, or find out how we left things?"

"You probably said you were too busy to date right now."

She frowned.

"I knew it. But that's ridiculous. It's not like you're getting married. Go have a good day orchard-snooping."

She opened her mouth to protest, then closed it. He was right. She was making too big a deal of sex with Jonathan. She'd only thought about it all weekend, of course, and had dreams about it, and remembered running her hands all over his body, and wishing she could do it again.

Tyler kissed her cheek. "Wish me luck with my fans."

"Like you need it."

She was the one who needed luck.

— Chapter 10 —

Jonathan didn't know what to expect when he drove up to Fairfield Orchard to pick up Amy, whether she'd be mad that he'd accepted her brother's last-minute request. She hadn't called to cancel, so he took that as a good sign.

As he pulled up, she came out of the office, wearing skinny jeans with knee-high boots and a pink-and-green top with a black sweater. Her light brown hair was loose and tucked behind her ears. He was suddenly overwhelmed by the rush of pleasure and desire, and surreptitiously adjusted himself before getting out of the car.

Sunglasses hid her eyes from him, but she swung her purse strap over her shoulder and gave him a wave. "Hey, Professor."

Her nickname for him was a red flag that she was trying to keep her distance. At least one of them had some common sense, and he was irritated that it wasn't him.

"Hello, Amy." His voice was a little too husky, and he cleared his throat, hoping that would disguise it. But it was difficult not to stare at her, to drink in her pretty face and the body he'd known so intimately just a few days before. "I didn't know if I should take Tyler up on his offer today."

"Didn't finish your grades on time?" she asked brightly.

"No, they were due today, so they're done."

"Of course."

"But to be honest, I didn't know if you wanted to spend the day with me after we'd agreed to hold off on dating for a while." He'd asked her out because it had been the proper thing to do, and had almost been relieved she'd turned him down. He was wary of the way being with her had so addled his thinking.

But he'd also been disappointed in her rejection. He still wanted her, far too much.

She put her sunglasses on top of her head and looked directly at him with those dark blue eyes. "I know, but Tyler sort of goofed things up."

"You could have turned me down and gone alone. It's not like you need me. Today. Need me today, I mean." Once again, he was behaving like an idiot. Where was his vaunted mental prowess?

She smiled. "I guess we have to find a way to relax around each other, since you'll be at the orchard for a while yet. This is as good a start as anything else. Sure, being together feels a little weird. We both admit we've never been as impulsive as we were Friday night."

And by her simply mentioning it, Jonathan felt a greater upsurge of the erotic tension that hummed between them. He barely mastered his need to glance down her body and remember.

185

Amy's smile faded, and she licked her lips. He thought about kissing her, holding her against him, feeling every curve of her body. All his good intentions got lost along with his rational thoughts.

She pulled a tube of lip gloss out of her purse and quickly applied it. "How about if I drive?" she asked in that same friendly, overly casual tone of voice. "I know where we're going."

He took a deep breath and stepped back from the imaginary cliff. "That's fine, thanks. I've been wanting to see how your little Prius rides anyway."

On the drive, they gradually relaxed. Jonathan got her to talk about her childhood in the orchard, the chores she'd had to do, the things her father had expounded on about their family business. They stopped at a couple orchards near Crozet, and she talked shop with the owners. It was obvious how good she was with people, and she must have done well as a Realtor.

They arrived at an orchard that perched atop a mountain. Their store and tasting room were open year-round, so Jonathan followed Amy as she took a little tour. As she meandered through the store, she gave Jonathan the occasional aside about how the store's products compared to theirs.

"Did your father ever consider keeping your store open all year?" Jonathan asked.

She wrinkled her nose. "We aren't situated well for that. The orchard is partway up Calf

Mountain, and most of the traffic we get is people coming specifically to the orchard. He didn't think a store by itself would be enough of a draw if we aren't on a major road."

"Amy Fairfield, is that you?"

It was a man's voice—a young man's voice. Jonathan turned to see an Asian-American man about their age come striding down an aisle of pancake mixes and local jellies. He was shorter than Jonathan, but his polo shirt fit him well, and he certainly had a big smile for Amy.

"Alex?" Amy said, smiling back.

They shook hands.

"I don't think I've seen you since high school," Alex said, holding her hand a bit too long.

Amy glanced at Jonathan. "Alex Hwang, let me introduce Professor Jonathan Gebhart, who's doing some research out our way."

Which immediately made clear to the other man that Jonathan was an acquaintance to Amy and nothing more. Jonathan gritted his teeth. He damn well wasn't just an acquaintance, but what was he, after all? But he shook hands with a polite nod.

"Our dads are good friends," Alex confided to Jonathan. "Our families used to do things together, picnic, play ball. But what are you doing here, Amy? Checking out the competition?"

"Actually, yes, I am."

But her smile was lovely and self-deprecating,

187

and who could be upset with her? Jonathan watched Alex look her over with satisfaction.

Amy said, "My brothers and sister and I recently took over for my dad so he could retire."

"I heard something about that—but all of you came home?" he asked, eyebrows raised.

"No, we're taking turns. Tyler and I are here first. So I'm doing a little driving around today, just checking things out."

Alex glanced at his watch. "I'm sorry I don't have time to catch up. But I'll be out your way on Wednesday. We could meet at Jefferson's Retreat for a drink and you can pick my brain. Five o'clock okay?"

Amy pulled out her phone, scrolled through her schedule, and inputted the details. "Sounds good. I'll see you then."

Alex shook hands with Jonathan and left at a swift pace.

"Well, he's still a nice guy," Amy said, looking after him.

Jonathan had never felt more like being a jerk in his life. Amy did something to him, twisted him up inside, made his logical brain blow up in the face of the primitive, jealous, possessive man he felt like inside. After what had happened with Amy Friday night, and now these appalling feelings, it was a good thing Amy was keeping her distance. He should take a lesson from her. Let her have drinks with whoever she wanted.

"I bet you'll have lots in common," Jonathan said calmly.

Amy cast him a sharp look.

"Well, you want to pick his brain about the orchard, right?" He didn't want her thinking he was throwing her at another man.

He saw her gaze focus over his shoulder, and she walked past him. Jonathan turned to see her studying a collection of old family photos on the wall, showing the history of the Hwang family orchard. He stepped beside her to take a closer look, and saw that her lips were pursed in a tight line, before she saw him and let her expression relax. He didn't know what she was thinking, and much as he wanted to ask, he didn't.

"They don't even go back very far, now do they?" she said dryly.

"Well, it looks like they're here to stay," Jonathan said, trying to keep his confusion to himself. Why was she denigrating her friend's orchard history? Or was he reading too much into this? "Let's go see the tasting room."

She blinked as if coming out of a trance. "Tasting room?"

"They make vodka and gin out of their apples."

"Let's go take a look."

The tasting room was in a brand-new building, with an elegant patio outside, and a huge stone fireplace inside, situated between floor-to-ceiling windows. Jonathan followed Amy as she was

189

drawn to the French doors that opened onto a deck. Outside, she went to the railing, and he hung back, fascinated by this view of her framed against the countryside, which dropped away from the mountain below them. The rolling hills of Virginia had come to life with spring, and everything looked new and vibrant. Apple trees blossomed in endless rows right below them, their scent perfuming the air.

Jonathan felt his mouth go dry as he studied Amy, framed by the orchard so like the one that was part of her, the one that was in her blood. But she didn't care about its history. She only cared about what hadn't happened yet, and she focused all her considerable energy on that.

But . . . he'd never felt such a yearning as he did now, to hold her from behind and take in the view standing in solidarity with her, a couple.

And then she turned and stared at him, her eyes alight with a new excitement, her smile eager as she took his hand and pulled him to the railing to stand beside her.

"I just had an idea. We have this kind of view; we could create an incredible tasting room. We can't do spirits—that would take years of work. But, Jonathan, we already make the best cider in Virginia. What if we make *hard* cider?"

"Interesting thought."

He was having a hard time even coming up with the right response because of the way her deep blue eyes sparkled in the sun, framed in dark lashes. The pull of desire low in his gut made his brain go fuzzy. This was crazy. She was finally having an idea for her future that excited her, and all he could think about was finding a bed.

Her eyebrows lowered as she studied him. "Are you all right?"

"I am, definitely. I think that's a great idea, but . . . do you know anything about fermenting cider?"

"Not much, no, but I bet Carlos might."

"Why?"

"I remember he mentioned it to my dad years ago, but with my dad being in recovery, he never pursued it."

Tyler had mentioned their father was an alcoholic. Amy didn't drink, which was certainly a response to that. Had things gotten bad with her dad, before he'd sobered up? All this time, Jonathan had been thinking what a Norman Rockwell family she seemed to have, but perhaps it had taken a lot of work for their family to straighten out.

But Amy didn't seem to care about bad thoughts from the past. Her eyes were alight with excitement about hard cider—which she didn't drink.

Amy frowned with consideration. "Maybe Carlos did some research on cider so that he could discuss it with Dad."

"Good point. And if this works out, you'll

definitely have something to put in your business plan."

She rolled her eyes, but it was obvious nothing could kill her good mood. "You and that business plan. Come on, let's go do a tasting."

He arched an eyebrow.

"Okay, *you* do the tasting and tell me what you think. There aren't all that many cideries in the area, you know. And none of them can claim the fame of being made on the land once owned by Thomas Jefferson, who drank hard cider every day. We have several blocks of trees growing antique fruit varieties from that era. It's kind of a thing around here."

He put up both hands. "Wait—you're going to actually use your history to promote cider, if this all works out."

"Sure, why not?" She grinned. "I thought you might appreciate that. We can bring history into the present and you'll find there's a world of interesting, *live* people outside of your research." She took his hand. "Let's go taste. And then we'll head to an actual cidery. I want to see their tasting room."

He followed, unable to resist her warm hand and the brilliant smile she gave him over her shoulder. So she thought he was so focused on his research he didn't even meet people? Well . . . she might be right, to a degree. It was difficult for him to relax and enjoy the moment.

His mind was always going, always planning out the next logical steps, and often wrong when it was time to predict what other people were thinking—including her. He had no idea where he stood with her.

That wasn't quite true. She'd told him she didn't want to date right now. And she'd been far more intelligent about the whole affair than he had. It was his own feelings and needs he couldn't predict. But he was being drawn inexorably into her orbit, into caring about her family. He couldn't risk that; he damn well knew how it felt to be on the outside looking in, when he was no longer important to them. As she'd pointed out to Alex, he was just a professor doing some temporary research. In a few weeks it'd be over, and he'd go back to Charlottesville and his own life. And she'd probably be relieved.

Amy was almost giddy at finally—finally!—having an idea worthy of Logan's investment. Jonathan was being his usual calm self, and it was probably good that he was keeping her tethered to reality, when she really wanted to giggle and dance about. This felt so right. She wanted to stand at the railing and spread her arms wide and embrace all of Virginia.

Instead, she led him back into the tasting room, and while he ordered a selection of spirits, she studied the menu, the decor, the employees. She watched Jonathan sip from each small glass and discuss the properties with the knowledgeable woman behind the bar. What was her position called? Amy had so much to learn!

She tried to get a rein on her excitement, knowing she had to discuss it first with Tyler and Carlos, and then the rest of her family. Maybe her dad would even be against it, but he was off on his own adventure now. His most recent Facebook photos had been of the beaches on the gulf coast of Florida. Maybe he wouldn't even care what she did. The orchard needed to come into the twenty-first century, and tasting rooms were becoming the norm. Okay, usually they were for wineries, but she had an orchard and cider. Hard cider would bring in couples, not just people looking for family entertainment—another thing she could write in her business plan.

Jonathan had barely finished his flight of spirits when she led him quickly back to the car and headed for the closest cidery. This place was like Fairfield—it had started as an orchard, but only forty years ago. And look how much they'd expanded. She saw that their patio was new, and it was obvious they'd added onto the building recently.

Inside, they stood at the bar and Amy listened as the pourer discussed each cider, how some were a rounder mouthfeel, others had a fruity nose or a crisp finish. Amy studied Jonathan and the way he tasted cider as if he was part of her newest project, and it was kind of a relief to think of him as a guinea pig instead of seeing him in her mind, naked, as she'd been thinking of him all day. It was damned distracting. She still felt guilty for booking that meeting with Alex for Wednesday, right in front of Jonathan—and it really was a meeting to exchange business news. But . . . it hadn't felt that way, with Jonathan standing right there listening. He'd looked polite as always, but what had he been thinking?

She'd told him she didn't want to date for a while. Surely that had made their relationship clear.

Of course, could he have thought the meeting with Alex was a *date?* Jonathan had to know she'd never do that kind of thing right in front of him . . . didn't he?

She had to get her head back in the game and study the layout of the cidery and the menu. Jonathan offered her a sip of one of the ciders, and she'd actually found herself hesitating before turning it down. No, if this was going to be her business, she wasn't going to develop a taste for it. Not with all she knew about what alcohol had done to her dad.

She drove the rest of the way to Fairfield Orchard in an excited blur of chatter. Jonathan had good questions for her, and she made mental notes about things to research.

As they got out of the car, Jonathan said, "This was a pleasant afternoon, Amy. I'm glad you had such a great idea. You go ahead and tell Tyler."

"What? No, you're not driving anytime soon. You come talk to Tyler with me. You'll have observations I didn't have. You're the cool thinker, not me. I'm giddy."

And she did an actual twirl, right there in the gravel parking lot. Jonathan stared at her with a bemused look on his face, and when his gaze dipped down her body, she felt it like an impact in her gut, like a reminder that although they'd made a good team researching that day, she could never forget the attraction that always shimmered beneath the surface. It made him dangerous to her in ways that were forbidden and scary and far too alluring.

But she wanted his help telling Tyler, so she swallowed, put on her best fake smile, and said, "Let me text Tyler and find out where he is."

Tyler ended up being at the warehouse with Carlos, which was perfect. After fetching Uma, they drove the mile, and once inside, Barney the border collie rose sleepily from a corner and came over to sniff, and Amy petted him absently, while Uma ignored the other dog. She was able to drag Carlos and Tyler away from that temperamental CA room and into the office.

"Guess what," Amy said excitedly. "We came up with a brilliant idea on our fact-finding trip today."

Tyler and Carlos looked at her expectantly, and Jonathan wore a faint smile.

Amy took a deep breath. "We should turn our cider mill into a cidery and make the hard stuff. Do a tasting room, everything. What do you think?"

Tyler had studied her as she spoke, nodding more and more. "Great idea. You should taste Carlos's cider."

Carlos put a tattoo-covered arm on the back of the office chair next to his and looked cool and unperturbed.

"Carlos, you make your own cider?" Amy demanded in shock. "I know you mentioned making it once to Dad, but he turned you down."

"Sure, your dad knew all about my experiments." Carlos sobered. "But this big of a decision—it feels strange without Bruce."

"My dad retired," Tyler said. "He's left it up to us, and frankly, the place isn't in as good a shape as it could be. We need an infusion of excitement, a new idea we can advertise and bring in customers who want more for an afternoon than picking apples with their kids."

Amy stared at her brother, impressed.

"And besides," Tyler continued, "you've won awards at the state fair."

Amy gaped. "How did you know this and I didn't?"

"I drink cider—you don't."

She groaned and turned back to Carlos. "Would you be interested in helping us get started on an actual cidery? We'd discuss the financial details, of course, but if this works out . . ." She let her sentence trail off.

Carlos grinned, his earrings glinting in the sunlight coming through the window. "Sure. I've been experimenting for years now. Your dad let me take whatever cider I wanted for my fermenting."

"You should taste it," Tyler said. "It's incredible. And he has several varieties."

"Come home with me," Carlos said. "I'll let you see perfection."

Everyone seemed as excited about the cidery idea as Amy, and they all trooped out to their cars. She felt euphoric, like they were companions out to conquer the world.

"I better get back to the homestead attic," Jonathan said. "My research awaits."

"No way," Tyler told him. "We need a tasting buddy, and like you said, you've done some research on this topic. You're good at that."

Amy watched Jonathan grin, and felt that little tingle of awareness again that was never very far from her consciousness when she was with him. But her brother . . . was he deliberately keeping Jonathan with them because of her? Or was there really a friendship developing between the two very different men?

Carlos had a small farm outside Spencer Hollow. Amy drove both dogs and the three men, listening to them discuss Carlos's experiments. Her mind whirled at the variables: apple varieties, the differences in crops from year to year, yeast strains, spices, and juices. Amy was almost relieved when they arrived at the farm. There was an old farmhouse with several additions over the years, a big barn behind it, an old silo next to that—which hadn't been used in at least a couple generations—and lots of fenced-in pastures for goats and chickens. Those animals roamed and watched the new arrivals with interest, until Uma ran at the fence as if to chase them. If she'd wanted, Uma could have vaulted the fence easily, but she was a well-trained dog.

There were several newer buildings on the farm, large garages, and that's where Carlos led them. In the building with "Carlos's Cave" over the door, she saw several fermentation tanks and a table in the far corner with bottling equipment. Carlos talked about the hundreds of five- and fifteen-gallon test runs he'd made and how he monitored each like a science experiment. He had a laptop full of data, and both Jonathan and Tyler peered over his shoulder to look at the screen. Amy stood apart, bemused and a little bit overwhelmed now that she had a direction and a complicated future—if it all worked out. Did she know the first thing about beginning a new business that didn't involve real estate?

Then behind her, a woman's voice quietly said, "So, the Fairfields have come down from on high to take even more advantage of my father."

Amy stiffened in surprise, but she kept her irritation out of her voice as she turned around. "Hi, Carmen, it's good to see you, too. And no one's taking advantage of your father."

Carmen Rodriguez was a tall woman, curvy in all the right places, who had her own sense of Bohemian style. She wore a long patterned skirt over sandals, a short lace top with capped sleeves, and lots of bracelets on her wrists.

As she studied the woman, Amy saw into the past, when she'd line up her sleeping bag beside Carmen's so that they could stare together into a jar of lightning bugs. They'd shared all kinds of childhood adventures.

Yet now, Carmen looked at her like she was a stranger. Of course, it was hard for Carmen to remain cool when Barney bounded at her and flung himself against her thighs, the most excitement he'd shown for anyone. Carmen bent to rub his ears and kiss his snout. As she straightened and regarded Amy, her smile faded away.

"I'll make sure my father is treated well in this,"

Carmen said. "In fact, maybe I'll represent him."

"You do that," Amy responded just as coolly. "The fact that you think I'd cheat Carlos, who's been like an uncle to me—" She couldn't even go on.

"I didn't mean it like that," Carmen said stiffly.

They had the attention of Jonathan by this point, and he studied them with interest. Carlos and Tyler were still in a deep conversation about cider fermentation.

"Then how did you mean it?" Amy demanded, hands on her hips.

"I simply meant that my father is more about the resulting product, not the business behind it."

"And you with your business degree certainly know more about that than the rest of us."

Amy didn't mean to sound jealous of Carmen's degree, but then Carmen had persevered and graduated, unlike flighty Amy, who'd found her relationship with a guy more important.

Amy glanced at Jonathan, feeling again how much more educated he was than her. He still regarded the two of them with interest, arms crossed over his chest.

Carmen eyed him. "Who's that?" she asked Amy.

He approached and held out a hand. "Jonathan Gebhart. Unofficial cider taster."

Carmen bit her lip, a smile peeking out. She shook his hand. "Carmen Rodriguez. Goat milk entrepreneur."

Jonathan's smile grew broader, and Amy felt a sulk coming on. Good Lord, if this was anything like Jonathan felt when she chatted with Alex Hwang, then she and Jonathan had a relationship going, whether they wanted to or not.

Of course they had some kind of relationship going—she'd *slept* with the man, hadn't she? And she didn't think of herself as a one-night-stand kind of woman. She just wanted to . . . put off seeing what kind of relationship they had.

"Goat milk entrepreneur," Jonathan repeated. "What exactly does that mean?"

"It means she makes stuff with goat milk," Tyler said, "and they make great gifts." He came over and hugged Carmen. "Hey, babe, how are you?"

"Hugging a celebrity," she said, a little girlishly. She tossed her dark hair and batted her long lashes at him. "The day doesn't get much better than that."

"Be careful, Tyler," Amy said. "Carmen will think you're only hugging her to get on her good side before negotiations."

Tyler snorted. Amy felt churlish, but hadn't she just been insulted a few minutes ago?

"Thanks so much for your Christmas order last year," Carmen was saying to Tyler.

"Those soaps were awesome gifts for all the office staff I deal with in the business. You sure you don't want to go into mass production?"

"Not yet," Carmen said, "although Papa keeps urging me."

"I tell her how talented she is," Carlos said, "but she just wants to take her time."

"And now you're thinking of going into business, Papa," Carmen said, a little sternly.

"I already work for the Fairfields," Carlos said placidly. "Nothing new there." He glanced at Tyler. "Maybe I could take on another title?"

Tyler grinned. "Sounds like you could." He looked at Amy. "Are we going to go for this?"

And then everyone was looking at her, including Carmen, who frowned.

"I don't know," Amy said. "The idea just came up today. Don't you guys want to . . . taste or something, before we call the whole gang?"

"I thought you'd never give the word," Jonathan said.

And before she knew it, they were sitting on the Rodriguez's back porch overlooking the goat pasture, where the animals frolicked and grazed. Uma wandered the yard below them, and Barney watched her with panting interest, but made no attempt to exert himself to follow. They all discussed the cider, whether it was fruit forward enough or what food it might pair with. Amy didn't taste it, but she didn't feel out of place. She enjoyed listening to them talk, even as it gradually got a little sillier. Carmen didn't say much to her, and she didn't say much to

Carmen, so it was okay. Jonathan was talking about his Jefferson research and his big discovery, even as Carmen professed fascination with Jefferson, and had so many questions. Amy wanted to roll her eyes.

"Is the tree house still there?"

Amy suddenly realized Carmen was actually talking to her. "Sure. In fact, I was just up there the other day."

Carmen arched a dark brow. "Reliving your childhood?"

"No, trying to see who's been making bonfires in our old picnic orchard."

Carmen frowned and said, "Trespassers? Papa, did you hear?"

Carlos frowned, but before he could answer, Amy said, "Your father does enough. I'll get to the bottom of the problem."

"I've heard about this tree house from your grandfather," Jonathan said.

"It's not a historic sight," Amy said. "At least, not for another hundred years."

"It means something to your family, right?" Jonathan shrugged. "That's as important as something historical. My father wouldn't allow a tree house. He was worried I'd fall out and hurt my brain. I wasn't the most coordinated child."

Everyone chuckled.

"Wait a minute," Tyler said, "does that mean

I'm supposed to challenge you to a pickup basketball game with a guaranteed win?"

"You'd probably win that one," Jonathan admitted. "How about a game of pool? I'm pretty good at that so the odds are more even."

"Let me guess," Tyler said. "It's about math."

Jonathan grinned. "Exactly."

Jonathan was particularly relaxed and funny when drinking cider, and Amy found herself watching him with interest and even a little unease. She was being silly—adults could get tipsy every now and again—but when alcohol had been so detrimental in her early life, and then her only long-term relationship, it was hard to take it in stride. She could never stop wondering what a person could do under the influence. Was this even a good idea for Tyler, whose eyes were soon lowered in lazy amusement as he talked to Carlos?

Regardless, she had to do what was best for the growth of the orchard, and a cidery seemed different enough—yet close enough to what they already did—to be worth looking into it.

But was this the business direction she wanted to take Fairfield Orchard? What would her father say?

— *Chapter 11* —

Jonathan was feeling pretty laid-back and happy on the drive back to Fairfield Orchard, a far better frame of mind than he'd been in recently. Tyler was as excited about the cidery idea as Amy, and to see the two of them actually complete each other's sentences as they debated what had to be done next was actually like participating in twin research. When he said as much, he was told he'd had too much to drink. So he went back to quietly petting Uma and trying not to wear too broad of a smile.

When they arrived back at the orchard warehouse, Tyler headed to the office to do some research on the equipment Carlos told them they'd need to get started.

Jonathan opened the door for Uma, then got out of the backseat and stood beside Amy to watch Tyler hurry off. "You don't think he'll get on a tractor or something, do you? He's had a little too much to drink."

"I think he'll be fine," Amy said, but she gave him a dubious glance. "You, on the other hand, can't drive yourself either."

"Whatever will I do to pass the time?" he asked softly.

He felt all hot and aroused again, just taking in

her body in her tight jeans and those boots that molded to her calves. He'd been staring at her ass all day. His good intentions vanished and the primitive guy inside him took over.

She didn't move, and her expression got all soft and dreamy. He put his hand on her cheek, then slid his fingers back through her long, sandy hair.

"I like when you wear your hair down," he said in a husky voice.

She blinked as if trying to get herself under control. "We said this was a mistake."

"No, we just said we were going to start thinking about dating in a few weeks." He traced the outer curve of her ear. "On second thought, *you* said that."

"And you agreed," she insisted.

He had. But he could feel her trembling. "Right now, I can't seem to remember why it's a good idea."

"This is the cider talking." She stepped back. "Even the other night, you'd been drinking before we . . ."

He frowned. "Do you think I only want you when I've had something to drink?"

She didn't answer, and she didn't meet his eyes.

He cupped her head with both hands and gently tilted until she met his gaze. "I want you all the time, practically from the moment I saw you."

"Practically?" she echoed in a breathless voice.

"Very well, I noticed how incredibly gorgeous

you were, but I was concentrating on persuading you of the rightness of my cause."

"Your research cause."

He nodded.

"And what's your cause now?"

"I don't know. I just know that when I close my eyes at night, I still see you naked, and I can't sleep and I want . . ."

He trailed off and kissed her, slanting his mouth over hers, going in deep as if the taste of her was what he'd been missing all his life. It wasn't as if he didn't have questions about the two of them together, but being with her never felt wrong, even if he did things he never normally did, crazy things, like kiss her in broad daylight right in front of her family business.

She put her hands on his chest as if she needed his support. He understood how she felt, off balance, over his head, and every cliché in between.

A door slammed somewhere, and Amy pushed away from him. "That could be Tyler or someone else," she whispered.

Her lips were wet from their kiss, and Jonathan stared. "He's a man, he won't care."

"No, he won't, because he already figured out what we'd done."

That made Jonathan raise his gaze to hers. "Really?"

She nodded. "Sorry. It seems I'm an open book

to my twin brother. He wasn't fooled when I got back to the bar Friday night. Everyone else was," she hurried to add.

Jonathan smiled. "I don't mind. I like your brother. I really haven't had a friend like him since—" He broke off and frowned. The cider was not only making him act on his horniness, he was talking too much.

"Since when?" she asked.

She looked so concerned, so interested. He should stop talking—they weren't even dating. But suddenly he was speaking words he hadn't meant to say. "Since my best friend lured away my fiancée." Wow, that was a simplistic summary.

She drew in a breath. "I . . . that's terrible. I'm sorry."

He shrugged. "It's better in the long run, right?" Because he hadn't seemed capable of whatever Geneva needed. He should remember that, where Amy was concerned. Yet . . . they weren't even dating, and kissing her was incredible.

She was looking at him with sad, even glistening eyes, as if his pain hurt her, as if she felt sorry for him. He'd said the wrong thing. Damn cider.

He let out a breath, knowing he'd ruined any chance of another kiss. "So, I can't leave yet. I should look at something historical, right?"

She eyed him with concern. "I don't think you should be crawling around in a hot attic. And you probably won't come up with good questions for Grandpa Fairfield—not that you could even drive there right now."

"Then show me your historic tree house."

A smile tugged at one corner of her sweet mouth. "What?"

"I keep hearing about its place in the annals of your family. Show me. Unless you want to go listen to Tyler ramble on about how many fermentation tanks a cidery needs."

"I'm very interested in that."

"Of course you are. It's research. I appreciate research, too. But it seems that Tyler talks excitedly when he's drunk."

Her smile grew wider. "You know him well already."

"Then come show me the tree house."

"All right, if it helps you sober up. Let's go find a pickup."

"I think I need something to eat. You did say it was a picnic meadow."

"I have plenty of apples."

"Then go find me some. I'll just wait here with Uma." He was pleasantly tipsy, and the car held him up well.

She rolled her eyes with exaggeration, but came back a few minutes later with a bag. Once they were in the pickup truck, Uma hanging her head out the rear window, Jonathan rooted through it. A couple bottles of water, apples, and packages of cheese and crackers with the logo Rodriguez Goat Milk Company.

"Carmen's?" he asked.

She nodded. "She has a line of picnic-ready packaging. Pretty smart."

It was another beautiful day, and as they munched crisp apples, Jonathan remained silent and enjoyed the view. Endless rows of apple trees in even lines rose and fell with the landscape, looking like pink and white cotton balls on sticks, and with the car window down, the sweet, potent smell was incredible. And then Uma's damp nose touched the back of his neck and he jumped.

Amy cleared her throat. "So . . . I didn't know you'd been engaged."

He gave her a faint smile. "I imagine there's a lot we don't know about each other."

"When did you break up?"

"Last year."

"How long were you together?"

"Five years."

"Oh, I have you beat. I was with Rob for eleven years."

"So it's a competition?"

"Only a pathetic one," she admitted ruefully.

Their eyes met, and they smiled again.

"But we never got around to getting engaged," she added.

"Why not?"

"I think . . . though I loved him deeply those first few years, very gradually the bad times started outweighing the good. It happened so slowly that I didn't even know how much of my life was going by. I knew something was wrong, and I didn't want to just leave him. I was always trying to fix our relationship, to make it better— to help him."

He studied her profile as she frowned and continued to drive. "I'm sorry it was tough."

"Well, I finally saw the light. It's been better in the long run, just like you said."

He nodded. He opened the packages of cheese and crackers, made a little cheese sandwich, and handed it to Amy before eating some himself. He wanted to ask for details, because he was curious about everything to do with her, but he didn't ask; he didn't want to answer too many questions in return. Apparently Amy didn't see it that way.

"I was the one to break things off," she said.

"So did my fiancée. I guess you women figure things out quicker than we men."

She hesitated, then glanced at him. "Did you know something was wrong?"

"Not one bit."

"Oh," she said softly. "I'm sorry."

He shrugged. "No reason to be. Apparently I'm smart about some things, and not about others."

"So she was fooling around behind your back?"

He couldn't believe he was discussing this, but then, he'd never discussed it with anyone. He chewed a bite of cheese for a long moment before deciding that it seemed to ease something inside him to speak of it at last. "They said they weren't."

"You believe them?"

"He was my best friend since college. He seemed to feel pretty broken up about falling in love with her. He'd known her as long as I had, had been the guy we always hung out with. He said he had never imagined betraying a friend, but knew he'd done so with me."

"Oh, Jonathan, it sounds pretty rough all the way around—but roughest on you, of course," she added swiftly.

And now that he'd started talking about it, he couldn't seem to stop. "But my fiancée . . ." And then to his surprise, his throat closed up, and he couldn't get out the words. Geneva had cried when she said she hadn't known what true love was until her feelings for Mark became impossible to ignore. But Jonathan thought that was bullshit. He had known he wasn't an easy man to be with, that he'd been altered by his parents' withdrawal of love. He knew he'd pulled back from caring too much about people, had walled off a lot of his emotions. And he hadn't been able to bring down those walls with Geneva. He'd thought their relationship, built on similar careers and interests, had been ideal, not full of the ups and downs of crazy emotions like other people seemed to have. But in the end he just couldn't be what Geneva wanted. He couldn't be that for any woman, and Amy was right to push him away.

"You don't have to say any more about her," Amy said. "I can see that it's still painful."

Her compassion was even more painful. Maybe Geneva deserved compassion more than he did, by lasting as long as she had with him.

"I'm pretty much over it," he said, knowing that still wasn't quite true. He took a deep swig from the bottle of water. "How about you?"

He thought she gripped the steering wheel a little harder.

"I think I'm over it, too."

"Do you? So not wanting to date me has nothing to do with . . . what did you say his name was?"

"Rob."

"Rob."

"Sure, the breakup hurt. I didn't want to have to do it, but . . . he seemed to care more about drinking than he did about making our relationship work."

Jonathan grimaced. "Amy, that had to be tough, especially after what happened with your dad." With all the alcoholism issues disturbing her family, he realized she might be the one person who truly understood what he'd gone through with his parents.

Her lips twisted with bitterness. "Rob didn't have a problem when we first dated. It was gradual, and I thought he meant it when he said he would work on it, change things. But it's a hard addiction to kick."

"Your father did it. You had every reason to believe Rob could, too."

She glanced at him. "You make it sound like I wasn't too much of an idiot for holding on to hope."

"I hope you didn't think that about yourself." He reached across and briefly squeezed her hand. "If you loved him—"

"No, don't go there. We're always warned that we can never change a person with love. It took me a long time to realize the truth of that."

Maybe Geneva had even tried to change Jonathan with her love. It certainly hadn't worked. So who was he to give advice?

The dirt road they traveled opened onto a grassy meadow strewn with the occasional boulder. Amy pulled up next to a circle where the grass had been burned away, and the remains of charred wood lay like a clump of collapsed Jenga blocks.

Amy turned off the car, got out, and stared at the fire circle, frowning. Uma raced around the meadow, as if unable to decide what part smelled the best. Jonathan looked past Amy, and he could see the tree house, complete with half-wall sides and a roof.

"Wow, that's a good-size tree house," he said, walking toward it. He glanced over his shoulder at Amy. "We should date its history, of course. From the Federalist period? Or perhaps the Victorian?"

She glanced up from the fire pit, and her frown eased, as he'd hoped.

"I think it would be called the Eighties Punk architectural period," she said.

"All I remember about the eighties is balloon pants and spiky hair."

Amy caught up after a moment, and when they arrived at the trunk, he said, "It has a real wooden ladder. No slabs of wood nailed to the tree?"

"You haven't met my dad yet," she said. "He's a big believer in safety, especially when Logan was young and a little . . . exuberant. Which explains the half walls, rather than just railings."

"Let's go up," he said.

"Really?"

"Sure. You go first, so I can catch you if you fall."

"What a gentleman," she said with amusement.

Maybe she wouldn't think so if she knew a by-product of being a gentleman was watching her ass as she climbed. And he did that, with gusto. Maybe he should be concerned that the cider hadn't worn off yet, but he was still enjoying the pleasant buzz.

He followed her up, and was surprised when he only had to duck beneath the roof a little bit.

Amy noticed. "Well, Dad had to stand up here, too."

The little tree house was like a long semi-enclosed room bolted into the tree. There was a bench built along one wall, and a little cupboard on the floor, which when he opened it, revealed a collection of rocks.

"You know, it's strange," Amy mused. "Teenagers are probably the ones hanging out in the meadow, but you'd think they'd have climbed up here. It looks untouched."

There was an opening, like a doorway, in the back. He stuck his head out and saw a few steps in the tree, then another platform just behind, without a roof.

"Logan used to make Michael hang out there sometimes, because he was the baby," Amy called. "Yeah, we could be mean kids."

Jonathan turned around and saw her standing at the railing, looking out on the land that had been in her family for almost two hundred years. That kind of history called to him, spoke to him, and he couldn't imagine the pride and satisfaction of knowing it had been handed down from generation to generation.

And there had to be fear, as she struggled to make the orchard relevant in the twenty-first century. Yet she was handling it all, and he admired her for it. She'd come back to help her parents, even though it meant interrupting her career. That kind of family loyalty was foreign to him, but it was very appealing.

Seeing her framed by the blue sky and the Blue Ridge Mountains beyond made him remember watching her on another deck, where there had been too many people for him to even touch her.

Not now.

Coming up behind her, he put his hands on the railing on either side of hers and leaned against her. He heard her gasp, but she didn't stiffen or pull away. He dropped his face into her hair and inhaled. The floral scent of her wafted around his head and only increased his arousal. He rubbed his hips up against her and closed his eyes at how good it felt. He'd never been as distracted as Amy made him feel. He couldn't keep her at a safe distance no matter how hard he tried.

With a long sigh, Amy dropped her head back on his shoulder. He kissed the side of her face and behind her ear. He slid his hands up along her torso and cupped her breasts. When she gasped and arched into his hands, he took that as permission and began to play with her nipples through the fabric of her shirt and bra. She pushed back against his erection, then reached back to hold his hips against her.

But when he dropped one hand lower and tried to cup between her legs, she stopped their foreplay by stepping aside.

"I'm sorry, Jonathan, but the staff is mowing this week, and they could be right out there."

"You can't be seen, I understand. Of course, if we sink behind these handy walls . . ."

She grinned and shook her head. "They'll see my car and come investigate. I had no idea how persistent you could be."

He could see her nipples as hard points through her shirt, and he forced his gaze back to her face. "Do you wish I wasn't persistent?"

She glanced down, a sweep of her eyelashes as she blushed. "I—I don't know. I certainly don't seem to stop you enough. But . . ."

"I know. I overstepped my bounds." He glanced out of the tree house. "I think I'll head back to the homestead."

"I'll drive you."

"No, a good jog will clear my head. Do I head back the same way?"

"That will only take you to the warehouse. The homestead is actually closer. Head down that road." She pointed. "It's about a half mile."

"Perfect. I'll let you get back to your thoughts."

Jonathan climbed down the ladder, and Amy

couldn't stop watching until the top of his head disappeared through the floor. Then she turned to see him begin to run in the direction she'd guided him. He moved gracefully, powerfully, and she bit her lip as regret washed through her. She wanted what he offered, no doubt about that. It was too easy to picture him lying beneath her right here in the tree house as she rode him. She groaned and closed her eyes.

It took a lot of effort to remind herself that she had to stop rushing into this relationship, after all the mistakes she'd made in the past. Fairfield Orchard was spread out before her; the land—her family legacy—was what she should concentrate on. She and Tyler were shepherding in a new phase of the orchard—if she could make the case to her family. She didn't have time to sit around dwelling on her regrets or acting like a fool over a man. It was time to follow Tyler's lead and begin to map out what it would take to create a cidery.

The future was more important than the present, or even the man who could only be a distraction right now.

And here she was standing around being distracted. She stared down the road he'd taken. Oh, it was so easy to be distracted by him.

— *Chapter 12* —

After two days of intensive internet research about the equipment required for a cider house—and Amy knew that that was just scratching the surface—she and Tyler took a break and walked the public grounds of the orchard. It was a gorgeous day, not a cloud in the brilliant blue sky. It was easy to imagine new crowds swelling the walkways and buildings, instead of just Uma, who ran ahead of them as if trying to guess where they'd go next. She and Tyler debated building a tasting room from scratch, but in the end, the site of the beautiful old weathered gray barn with its stone foundation, which only stored apple bins during most of the year, seemed like the ideal home. She thought of the torn photo she'd hidden there and knew she'd have to remove it. But she didn't want it in the house with Tyler, who tended to roam when he couldn't sleep at night.

"The barn's fine *if* the renovations aren't more expensive than building from scratch," Tyler said.

"But just think what we can do. It's a bank barn, built into sloping ground, with each floor having its own road and entrance. We could eventually make the lower floor into a private banquet facility." Amy linked her arm to his as they stared at the barn. "I don't know about you, but I'm so excited I can barely contain myself."

He eyed her with amusement. "I can tell."

"If we can make this work . . . we've saved our family orchard. Two hundred years, Tyler. During next year's anniversary we'll have a lot to celebrate if we can pull this off." She hesitated. "Do you think it's possible to have it all done by September?"

He grimaced. "Three and a half months? I don't know. We'll have cider, but a renovated barn? We'd better start soon."

"How about a division of labor?"

"What are you proposing?"

"You handle the cider production, and I'll handle the tasting room."

"You want to run a tasting room when you don't drink?"

"I'm not saying that—I'm talking about the construction of it. We'll discuss who's running what when there's something to actually run."

His smile widened into a grin. "You've got a deal. You know buildings better than I do." He waved a hand at the barn. "This seems too much like decorating, and I don't decorate."

They both went back to staring at the barn, and she tried to imagine windows cut into the upper floor to let in the light. He was right—so many decorating details to be decided. It was pretty overwhelming. She hoped Alex Hwang wouldn't mind her questions later that day. But . . . she'd be his competition, wouldn't she?

She thought about Jonathan's offer to help with the business plan. She'd be wise to keep him separate from her business, but . . . wouldn't she rather work with him than a stranger, who wouldn't know her and her family, wouldn't understand how important this was to them?

And as if she'd conjured him, she saw Jonathan's car just cresting the hill and passing the grassy parking lots that she wanted to see overflow this fall. He pulled up beside the barn, and to her surprise, he jumped out of his car, not even bothering to shut the door behind him.

He wore a grin she'd only seen in more intimate moments, and she was surprised to feel her face heat. Even the memory of sex with Jonathan felt a little overwhelming sometimes.

"Hey, Professor," she said.

To her shock, he hugged her, lifting her clear off the ground. She didn't know what to do with her arms except pat him awkwardly on the shoulder until he set her down. Tyler was laughing, and she shot him a helpless look.

"So what gives?" she asked, a little breathlessly.

"Just actual proof about the most exciting research discovery of my career," Jonathan said.

When he turned to Tyler, her brother raised both hands. "I believe you, dude, no need to hug me."

Jonathan chuckled. "No hugging, I promise. Damn, but I knew every time I passed that tavern in Spencer Hollow, Jefferson's Retreat, that it was a good-luck charm." He turned back to Amy and put both hands on her shoulders. "I've just come from the Jefferson Library at Monticello."

"You mean you don't know everything by heart already?" Amy teased.

Grinning, he just kept going. "I've been focusing on Fairfield Orchard for my book, the property that was part of Jefferson's land holdings in the early nineteenth century. It's only an estimate of exactly how much land he owned or inherited during his lifetime, of course."

Knowing how important this was for him, she was excited on his behalf—and could admit how much it thrilled her, too. She made a hurry-it-along motion with her hand, and then regretted it.

"Sorry," Jonathan said.

She winced. "No, I'm not rushing you. I'm dying to know more."

"I see."

And there it was again, that connection, that feeling that they understood each other. He was so adorable in full professor mode.

Adorable. She couldn't have imagined thinking of him that way just a couple weeks ago, she realized uneasily. Tyler cleared his throat loudly.

"Anyway," Jonathan continued, "here's a

historical summary to set the stage for my news. Jefferson was elected governor of Virginia in 1779, during the American Revolution, then president in 1801. Needless to say, he was a little busy. But he always found time for hunting. He thought it was the best form of exercise, better for the mind than the violence of sports played with a ball—I'm paraphrasing him here."

"Only Amy would find this fascinating," Tyler said, "but keep going."

"I've been reading his letters—and believe me, there's only an estimate of how many there are, but it's over eighteen thousand—and for the first time I found an actual notation that he came to this property to hunt. It was just a hypothesis on my part, since I know it was your ancestors who broke ground and began to farm. But now my guess has been confirmed and actually enhanced. Amy, there's mention of a *hunting cabin!*"

He spoke those final words with reverence.

Amy felt an answering echo of his excitement and wonder. "Jefferson's hunting cabin," she breathed.

Tyler rolled his eyes. "You two."

Jonathan shook his head with good-natured impatience. "You don't understand what I'm saying. If there was a hunting cabin, then we can do an archaeological excavation. We might discover something about Jefferson, something scholars have never known."

Amy's smile died as reality intruded. "An excavation? What exactly are you saying?"

"I'd like to bring in an archaeologist here. It's almost summer, just when they'd have field schools to teach students how to dig. We don't know where to dig just yet, and I'll keep doing some research to see if the location of the cabin is mentioned. But archaeologists are trained to study the physical features of the land and can probably surmise the best area to begin digging our test pits."

"Test pits?" Amy said weakly.

Tyler spoke up. "The grounds right here have always housed the main buildings of the farm."

Didn't her brother realize that an archaeological dig could disrupt their plans for the tasting room? Just when her love of history was returning, it had to interfere with the most important thing in her life.

Jonathan looked around, rubbing his hands together. "I wonder if this barn was built on top of the original, or beside it."

"Or perhaps it *was* the original," Tyler suggested.

Amy couldn't bother with speculation; she needed details. "So, say we allow an archaeologist here. What would happen?"

Jonathan turned a frown upon her, and she realized how her words sounded. As if she might forbid it. She wasn't certain how the rules worked, but this was private property, and she and her family owned anything on it—or buried beneath it. If this excavation he was talking about was too extensive, she didn't know if she *could* permit it. Not, and be ready to open the tasting room on time for the fall season.

"Phase one of an excavation," Jonathan explained, "involves digging small test pits in a grid pattern, ten or twenty meters apart. The pits themselves would be less than a meter square. They wouldn't be in your way," he insisted.

She took a deep breath. "Okay, that seems easy enough. But what if the archaeologist finds something? What happens then?"

"Then it begins to look like what you see on TV. They lay out patterns with strings and stakes."

"Large chunks of land?"

"Maybe, but probably not. If there was a hunting cabin, it would have been very primitive. The structure itself obviously didn't survive, and any remains would be seriously deteriorated after over two hundred years in the ground. But if we could find proof that there actually was a structure here—remains of fire or wood pieces, musket flints, a garbage pit—and perhaps tie it in with Jefferson himself, that would be all the proof I need for my book."

"Why couldn't those remains be from our ancestors, not Jefferson?" Tyler asked.

"They might be. The trick would be to narrow

the time frame to before 1817, when the land was sold."

"You can be that precise?" Amy said. "And quickly?"

"Sometimes." Jonathan let out a deep breath. "You don't seem as excited as I am."

"That's not true. I'm thrilled you've discovered such a tantalizing clue to our connection to Jefferson." His shoulders relaxed until she said, "But. We've just been discussing where to put our tasting room, and depending on the cost, we might very well be renovating our barn. Heavy equipment would be all over the area, and soon."

"We could try to keep the test pits away from the main entrance to the barn," Jonathan said. "The archaeologists won't be in your way . . . too much."

He was so excited by the thought of cabin remains she could only imagine what he'd have done with the historic photo she'd allowed to be ruined through her carelessness and stupidity.

"What do you think, Amy?" Tyler asked. "It seems okay to me."

It seemed almost ironic that this had come up just when she was ready to move forward with the orchard's next stage.

"I think you should do it," Amy said.

Jonathan smiled with obvious relief.

"We'll let the rest of the family know," she continued, "but I'm sure they'll have no problems."

"And they're not here, are they?" Tyler said.

Jonathan regarded the barn now, crossing his arms over his chest. "So, this will be the tasting room."

Amy nodded. "If the finances work out. If it's financially impossible, then we build from scratch."

"I've seen other barns converted to tasting rooms," Jonathan said. "I'm sure you can make it work. And it's a beautiful building. The ax marks on all the interior beams will be a nice, rustic feature. You'll have to be very careful not to damage the historic elements. I'd be happy to consult with the architect."

"I might just go to a general contractor." He was already here researching her family history, she was seriously considering asking for his help with the business plan, and now the renovation itself? Pretty soon, she might consider him indispensable, and that was a bad idea.

But she noticed she was no longer thinking he was trying to manage or interfere with her life. She knew he was too good of a guy for that.

"Thanks," she said. "I'll keep that in mind."

He shot her a glance, and she wondered if she hadn't been so good at masking her uneasiness.

"I'll head to the homestead, then," Jonathan said. "Your grandfather is supposed to meet me there. Is he excited about the cidery?"

Tyler nodded. "It's given the old guy a boost.

He spent yesterday looking over my shoulder at the computer, discussing equipment. He's a master at making sweet cider, of course, and he already seems determined to learn the secrets of the hard stuff."

"So you've told the rest of your family?"

"Last night," Amy said. "We didn't have our figures together, of course, but we wanted to see if they're as excited as we are."

"Are they?" Jonathan asked.

"The kids, yeah." Tyler shrugged. "My dad seemed more . . . ambivalent."

"At least he didn't disagree outright," Amy countered. "Or perhaps he thought he couldn't, since he's pretty much sold the orchard to us kids."

"But he knows we need to do something bigger, something bolder," Tyler said. "He'll back us."

"I'm glad for you both. Will you be around tomorrow afternoon? I can bring Dr. Alberici over to meet you and see the lay of the land."

"Sure," Amy said. "Just text me when you arrive."

He nodded, and looked at her a little too closely. "I'll see you later."

Jonathan turned and walked toward the homestead, glad to have work to focus on this afternoon instead of thinking about Amy having drinks with Alex Hwang. It wasn't like she was his, he reminded himself. She'd made that perfectly clear. And she was right.

Time to focus on work, something that was usually easy to put first in his life. But being with Amy had altered his thoughts, his intentions. This new discovery should serve as a reminder of what had to be most important right now.

Later that evening, he'd have to call Mark Alberici, and he wasn't looking forward to it. They worked at the same university, but in different departments, and it had been pretty easy to avoid one another since Mark had married Jonathan's ex.

There were other archaeologists Jonathan could call, but the two of them had published several papers together. Jonathan had always been determined not to let his private life interfere with his career. He knew how Mark worked and, frankly, trusted him.

About work.

— Chapter 13 —

Jefferson's Retreat was an old-school tavern that had probably been built when it was the only building at the four corners of Spencer Hollow. It wasn't as if there weren't lots of buildings named after their famous local president, but never had it seemed so significant than after hearing Jonathan's news about the hunting cabin.

Amy sat at the bar, an iced tea in front of her. The interior was dark, the windows small, but the owner had given it a historic ambience with period pieces like lanterns and candles. There were even a few colonial-era items on the menu, like game pie and ale-potted beef. The tables and chairs were wooden, the bar paneled in weathered gray barn wood. A dozen people already sat at the tables or leaned elbows tiredly on the bar after a long day's work. Amy kept the stool open beside her, waiting for Alex.

"So that was your car in the parking lot."

Amy turned to find Brianna smiling at her, and at her side was Carmen, who was decidedly not smiling, but did give a polite nod. They were here together? Amy shouldn't be surprised that over the years they'd found common ground.

Amy smiled at both of them and answered

Brianna. "Yep, haven't been here in a few years. It hasn't changed."

"Are you alone? You could have dinner with us," Brianna offered.

When Carmen's face remained expressionless, Amy gave an inward sigh. Brianna had forgiven Amy for her silent absence these last few years, but Carmen wasn't going to be so easy. And Amy didn't blame her. Amy had let too much go in her pursuit to please and enable a man—she wasn't going to make that mistake again.

"I'm meeting someone on orchard business," Amy said.

Now why had she said it like that? As if she had to explain that it wasn't a date. Who cared—except perhaps Jonathan? Okay, and her. She apparently cared.

"Did you ever meet Alex Hwang?" Amy asked. "His family owns the Apple Valley Orchard near Charlottesville."

"They make great vodka," Carmen finally said.

Amy smiled. "So I hear. He's agreed to let me pick his brain as we try to bring our orchard into the twenty-first century."

"Good luck," Brianna said. "You know you're welcome to join us if your meeting ends quickly."

"Thanks!" Amy heard the brightness in her own voice and winced. Her professional ability to turn on the charm shouldn't have to be necessary with her friends. She couldn't look at Carmen, who'd always been too good at reading her.

By the time Brianna and Carmen had found a table near the stone fireplace, Alex was walking in. He was still wearing a polo shirt embroidered with the orchard name, and he shook hands with someone before his smile broadened when he spotted Amy. She stood up politely, and ended up being enveloped in a hug.

"I wanted to do that the other day, but thought the guy you were with wouldn't appreciate it," Alex said.

Surprised, she gave him a welcoming smile. "Don't worry about that. You and I . . . go way back." She'd been about to say "we're friends," but knew that had never been exactly true. Their fathers had been friends, and the kids were forced to hang together. Alex had always been with her brothers.

And she would have said Jonathan wasn't her boyfriend, but it would have sounded defensive. And maybe untrue. When you sleep with a guy, and aren't dating anyone else, does that automatically make him your boyfriend? She didn't think so, but it had been a long time since she'd been casually dating.

"Can I buy you a drink?" Amy asked as Alex sat down on the stool beside her. "After all, you traveled to my remote neck of the woods, so I owe you."

"Not that remote. I like it out here. And I'll take a Kilt Flasher," he told the approaching bartender.

Amy choked on her drink.

"What?" Alex asked. "It's a Scotch ale."

"Love the name."

He chuckled, then eyed Amy. "Does it seem strange to be back in the family business?"

Amy smiled. "Sometimes. Weird to be back in my old room full-time."

"But your parents aren't there."

"Nope, they headed south in a brand-new RV. They're soaking up the sun on a Florida beach."

"Good for them." Alex grimaced. "Sometimes I wish my dad would get that in his head, but he's still in charge. I'm just in training."

"Well, there has to be a lot to do at Apple Valley, considering that fantastic tasting room you have going."

"Thanks. The detour into distilling spirits from apples has really paid off. You can find us in all the Virginia liquor stores now, and eventually the whole seaboard. Although I'm getting ahead of myself," he added, winking at her. "It's just that that's my job, sales and marketing."

Just one of the many duties that would have to be expanded when the cider house was up and running, Amy realized. And that was right up her alley. She felt a little thrill of excitement.

"So what did you want to chat about?" Alex

asked. "I'd hang all evening with you, but I have dinner plans with some college buddies who are back for a visit to Charlottesville."

"Of course. Well, it's awkward to say, but we hope to begin to produce hard cider on a bigger scale by the fall. Not spirits!" she hastened to add. "We won't be competing with you there."

He laughed. "There are plenty of customers to go around, believe me. Our tasting room has been open year-round for a couple years now, and sure, it gets a little slow after Christmas, but I can't complain. So you're just brewing cider?"

She nodded. "We need to expand our customer base, and what better way than offering something for the grown-ups? You said I could pick your brain, and I do have lots of questions. Anything you wish you'd known before you started?"

And Alex launched into a half hour of tips and hard-won experience that had her glad she'd brought a notebook. By the time he kissed her on the cheek as he left, she was studying her notes and trying to clarify the ones she'd been too hasty to get down in full.

"Amy, come on over!" Brianna called.

Amy slid the notebook into her purse, then took the extra chair between the two women. The blonde server in her black button-down shirt and jeans approached and smiled.

"Hi, Amy."

Amy recognized her from high school, but her usual good memory deserted her. "I'm sorry, I'm blanking on your name."

"Valerie. We had some classes together."

Amy blushed. "I do remember that, sorry, Valerie."

The woman's smile was tired but polite. "It's okay."

"What have you been up to?" Amy asked.

"Just working here and raising my daughter."

"Oh, do you have a picture?"

By the time Amy had admired the picture of the adorable five-year-old on Valerie's phone, placed an order for a burger—though the other two women were just about ready for dessert—Carmen was at least looking a little less hostile. But still guarded, and it hurt Amy's heart—even as she knew she deserved it. Amy was the one who'd often let texts and voice messages go unanswered until it had seemed absolutely clear she was too busy. It hadn't been planned but . . . the result had been the same.

"I saw those recent pictures your sister put on Facebook," Brianna said.

"Me, too!" Amy cried, delighted. "Hawaii—Rachel's always wanted to go there. Did you see her climbing the volcano?"

Carmen nodded along with them, but didn't say much as they discussed Rachel's photos.

"So, Amy," Brianna finally said, "Carmen's been telling me about your idea to expand the orchard."

"I hope she told you how her father is helping make that possible. Tyler and Jonathan can't say enough about his cider."

"I've tried it," Brianna said. "It's delicious. You should give it a try—oh, wait, you don't drink."

Amy shrugged, then sat back as her small salad was placed before her. "Thanks, Valerie." She speared some lettuce and a tomato.

"Not being a drinker might make it hard to own a cidery," Carmen pointed out.

"That can't be true," Brianna said. "I sell cigarettes but I don't smoke."

"But people don't linger over cigarettes to compare them," Carmen said. "You don't need to discuss with authority whether there's acidity or sweetness, whether the finish is bold or lively."

Was Carmen trying to discourage her? Amy couldn't tell. "I'll be hiring a well-educated staff to man the tasting room. Tyler is in charge of the cider house at this point. And my other brothers will be taking a turn at the orchard, too. We'll make it work."

"And you're in charge of the tasting room construction?" Brianna asked. "I think that'll be the fun part."

"I hope so. I saw some beautiful ones last

week, but I still hope that the product is more important than the decor it's served in." She hesitated. "We're going to get some contractor quotes about having the old barn renovated."

Though Brianna gasped with excitement, it was Carmen who spoke first.

"And your dad is okay with that?"

"He doesn't know we've decided to try the barn yet. We're getting all our facts and figures together so we can present the family with a well-thought-out plan. I have a meeting with a contractor soon."

For the first time, Carmen's cool facade cracked and she looked a little uncomfortable. "Oh. My father's been feeling uneasy about the alcohol. I said if he felt bad, he should talk to Mr. Fairfield. They talk about everything, you know." The last was said a little defensively.

Brianna was frowning at Carmen, but remained silent.

Amy stirred some more dressing into her salad, not really seeing it. She couldn't blame Carmen for suggesting Carlos make a run around Amy's plans. "I guess I should have thought that he might want to talk to my dad. Well, it'll work out."

An awkward silence stretched out.

"So . . ." Brianna said brightly, "is Jonathan the first guy you've been interested in since your breakup with what's-his-name?"

A smile tugged one corner of Amy's mouth. "He's not Voldemort. We can say his name. It's Rob." It was important not to forget his name or what had happened.

Brianna chuckled. "When you and Jonathan danced together the other night, I thought your clothes were about to combust."

Brianna and Carmen shared a smirk before Carmen said, "Not that I noticed anything between them the other day during the cider testing."

Amy wasn't sure what Carmen was trying to say, but she let it slide.

"So have you started dating him?" Brianna asked.

"No. He's working with my grandpa on the family research. We're all busy."

"So he's asked you out," Brianna clarified.

"Well, okay, he's asked, but like I said, I'm busy and so is he."

After Valerie came back with the burger, Amy gestured to the onion rings. "Help yourselves."

"No, thanks," Carmen said. "So you're not going to date the professor."

"I didn't say that." Amy took a big bite of her burger and sighed. They were still as juicy as she remembered.

"He can't take his eyes off you," Brianna said. "There's only so much of that a girl can take before she succumbs."

Amy kept her gaze on her burger and didn't say anything. But her cheeks were heating, and she tried to think of chill winter winds.

"You slept with him already," Carmen said slowly.

Amy chewed forcefully. She couldn't look up.

"You did!" Brianna breathed.

Amy risked a glance. Brianna looked surprised, but not disdainful. Even Carmen was just proving curious. Amy let out a sigh. "I didn't mean to."

"Oh, I've heard that before," Brianna said. "So was he better than Rob?"

Amy blanched and wouldn't let herself go back there. "Hey, I don't compare."

"The professor looks buttoned-down," Carmen said. "I could think that makes for a bland roll in the sack."

Amy's face heated right back up. "It was . . . pretty great."

Brianna actually giggled, and Carmen fought a smile.

"But you're not dating him," Brianna said doubtfully.

"It's just such a bad time," Amy insisted.

"Why? Because of Rob?" Brianna's voice was kind rather than nosy.

And that was almost too much for Amy. She felt tears prick her eyes, but she refused to cry. She'd cried enough after the breakup, but she'd never shared the ugly secrets with anyone, and they were sticking in her chest like a lump that had gone down the wrong way. But she was at Jefferson's Retreat, where everybody could see her. And in this tiny town of just a few hundred, word of an emotional breakdown would spread fast. She cleared her throat and forced a tight smile. "It was a bad breakup. It's tough to want to risk myself again. I think I just need more time."

Brianna touched her arm in sympathy.

"But your body disagreed," Carmen said.

Leave it to Carmen to be the realist.

"Yes." Amy hesitated, then added wryly, "And I can't blame alcohol, can I?"

Brianna squeezed her arm gently. "Hope you're not being hard on yourself. We all have done stupid things we wish we wouldn't have."

"Oh, I know I have," Amy said with conviction, meeting Carmen's gaze deliberately.

Carmen's expression remained cool, but after a moment, she looked away.

"How does Jonathan feel about waiting?" Brianna asked.

"He's busy, too, trying to do the research that will help finish his book. But whenever I look at him, I feel . . . well, overheated doesn't quite sum it up. Yet I can't let myself hook up with him just for sex on a regular basis. And I don't want to hurt him," she ended on a whisper.

"Maybe you feel more than you want to feel," Carmen said.

"Maybe . . ." Amy's voice trailed off. With a sigh, she tossed a ketchup-coated onion ring in her mouth and tried to enjoy it, but it seemed her appetite was gone. She signaled to Valerie for the check.

"You can get dessert," Brianna said. "We'll wait."

"No, that's okay. I'm full."

"Wow," Brianna continued, "I never thought I'd hear that from you where dessert is concerned."

"Or maybe she's just changed," Carmen said.

Amy tried not to let her shoulders slump. "Yeah, I've changed. I guess everybody does over ten years. But I didn't let you guys see it. I didn't let my family see it much either, toward the end."

They were both watching her, Brianna with glistening eyes, Carmen with a frown. But it wasn't such a cold frown, more like perplexed.

"Amy, you know you can talk to us," Brianna said.

"Thanks, Bri. I appreciate that. But now I have to get back. My head is whirling with everything I have to do in only three and a half months. It's crazy but exciting, all at the same time."

"Can you make it work?" Brianna asked.

"I think so." Amy glanced at Carmen. "Your dad has seemed pretty excited about all the changes."

"He hasn't seen a contract yet."

"That's true. After we've talked to the family, I'll make sure that's done next. I haven't forgotten how special he is to us, you know."

Carmen only nodded and tossed her napkin on the table before rising. "I'll see you guys later.

After she walked away, Amy started to stand but Brianna took her arm again.

"Be patient with her," Brianna said. "She'll come around."

"She's hurt by my behavior and she has every right to be. You both do," Amy said soberly.

"Well, you're here, trying to make amends. I appreciate it and I know she will, too."

"I hope so."

But Amy wasn't feeling exactly confident in her relationships lately, not any of them.

— Chapter 14 —

The next day, after a productive meeting with the first contractor, Amy felt better about their prospects for renovating the barn, rather than building from scratch. She had another contractor coming in later that afternoon, and she would make sure both understood that she needed to see plans quickly.

And then Jonathan's car came up the hill, and she felt again that anticipation of being with him, being near him. It sometimes felt rather over-whelming, and far too much like the first time she'd fallen hard for a man. And look how that had worked out.

Jonathan's car was followed by an unfamiliar SUV. The archaeologist? She reminded herself to enjoy the land's history again, and not be so consumed about the orchard's future all the time. She would make all of it work out in the end.

Jonathan parked beside the barn, and his friend followed suit. To her surprise she recognized the man and went forward, holding out her hand.

"Mark Alberici," she said as they shook. "Jonathan called you Dr. Alberici, and I didn't connect the name. Good to see you!"

In contrast to Jonathan's slacks and button-down shirt, Mark was dressed in jeans and a long-sleeved UVA T-shirt over his sturdy frame. He wore his brown hair a little long, so it curled over his ears and at his neckline. His face and hands were ruddy from the sun.

Jonathan stared from her to Mark. "You two know each other?"

To Amy's surprise, Mark seemed to redden with discomfort, so she spoke up. "Sure, I helped Mark and his wife buy a house a couple of months ago."

Jonathan nodded, his expression impassive. "Got it."

This was really strange, Amy thought. Mark was the man Jonathan wanted for the job, but they didn't look all that comfortable together. Well, you didn't have to like everyone you worked with. There were certainly clients who made the house-hunting process miserable, but Mark and his wife had been genial and professional.

Mark rubbed his hands together and eyed her barn. "Beautiful old building."

She grinned. "And hopefully it'll be transformed into a beautiful tasting room. That was the contractor who drove past you as you arrived."

"How did it go?" Jonathan asked.

"Pretty good. I like his ideas. He's going to give me something official, and I'll compare it to another contractor I'm going to interview."

As she talked to Jonathan, she found it was

difficult to act like nothing had happened between them, to behave professionally in front of his colleague. She was still thinking about her promise to herself that she wouldn't randomly sleep with Jonathan, and wondering if she could keep that promise, because it was far too easy for her eyes to linger on his black hair, wavy as if it would only take the brush of her fingers to make it unruly. And those eyes, so green and mesmerizing when he looked at her. Of course there was her discovery that she was a "shoulders" girl, where he was concerned.

Mark cleared his throat, and she realized that she and Jonathan had been staring at each other. Mark looked both amused and relieved—a strange and curious combination.

"Sorry," Amy said briskly. "I have a lot on my mind. Jonathan told me you two have written papers together?"

Mark nodded. "I did some excavation near the Rotunda at UVA and Jonathan collaborated with me. We went to school there together. Took a lot of the same classes."

"Then you've known each other for a long time," Amy mused.

But Jonathan wasn't looking at Mark, although he did nod perfunctorily. She wondered if she and Jonathan both had the same problem with not giving enough time to maintain old friend-ships. But she guessed there might be a lot more to the problem between the two men than that.

"This is a fascinating revelation," Amy said. "I really hope it helps you make a big splash with your book."

He gave her that smile, the one that made her stomach churn and her palms sweat, and brought back incredible memories of their evening together.

"Thanks, Amy," he said quietly.

"Since Jonathan has explained the historical details to me," Mark said, "mind if I take a look around?"

"Go ahead," Amy said.

When they were alone, Jonathan said, "I appreciate what you just said."

"It's all true."

"You know we'll do our best not to get in your way," he said.

"I know." She sighed. "I just want everything to go well this summer."

"Don't rush such an expensive renovation, Amy. Since we discussed your business plan, I did some research. Make sure you know that the local market will support another cidery."

Trust Jonathan to research something she'd only mentioned in passing, she thought fondly. "I discussed it with Alex yesterday."

Did Jonathan seem to stiffen a little? Probably not.

"He said he's almost busier than they can handle

in the summer," she continued. "And yes, he has a distillery, too, but he was frank with me about the customer base. Remember, the retirement community around Charlottesville is growing by leaps and bounds. I saw that up close when I was a Realtor. And at some point, I just have to trust my gut."

She knew she'd been very good at ignoring her instincts for several years.

"Your excitement is pretty evident."

She grinned. "I know. I've just begun to see possibilities. If the cider production and tasting room do well, the sky's the limit. Maybe we can begin a café or restaurant, and talk my brother Noah, who's a chef, into coming home to run it. Wouldn't that be awesome?"

Jonathan watched Amy's happy excitement, and he felt a softening inside him that was becoming far too regular with Amy. He liked her—too much. He thought about her when he should be thinking about his book. She haunted his daytime thoughts; she was a sexy specter in the night, when he ached for her instead of sleep. It was all-consuming. He'd begun to slyly tell himself that sleeping with her again would help, but he knew that was a lie. Nothing would help as he became more and more obsessed by Amy.

And it was even more distracting when she left him to go back to work. He watched in awe and arousal as she drove a forklift into the barn to begin unstacking apple bins and moving them outside. Her hands were confident on the controls, her focus intense. For a man who'd never left academia, he was incredibly turned on by watching Amy do manual labor.

"Hey, Jonathan."

Reluctantly, Jonathan turned away to see Mark striding toward him. Jonathan felt the usual dispassion settle over him. It was better than being angry at the man he'd once thought of as a friend.

The man who'd used Amy as a Realtor to buy a house with Geneva.

The thought just made Jonathan tired, but not as upset as he once might have been. At least that was good.

Mark was polite, even subdued, and for a boisterous man, that was still mildly surprising every time it happened. They hadn't had much to do with each other since the whole scandal, except passing each other in the hall or occasionally attending the same meeting. Considering that Geneva worked with them as well, the faculty of their departments hadn't known what to make of the breakup of the engagement, and then her turning to Mark. There had been whispers and conjectures, and to Jonathan's regret, some people had seemed to take sides, causing even more awkwardness. He hadn't wanted that, and worked hard to treat Geneva and Mark with professional courtesy so that the furor would eventually die down. Four months later, they'd eloped, and everything had started up again.

But that was last year. The department had been on eggshells as they all tried to put it behind them, and things were gradually getting better.

"What do you think of Fairfield Orchard?" he asked Mark calmly. Jonathan had once thought he could never work with Mark again, but to his surprise, Mark had been the first one he'd even considered calling. That was a step forward, Jonathan thought with irony.

"It's a beautiful place," Mark said, looking west at the uneven peaks of the Blue Ridge Mountains, with that infamous blue haze. "And to think Thomas Jefferson sold them the land."

Jonathan nodded and restrained his answering excitement. They'd been such history geeks together, immediate friends who'd understood each other. Jonathan had never had a lot of friends as a child. It had been hard to relate to kids his own age, because however hard he tried, it was difficult to hide his intellect. He'd met Mark in a physics class freshman year of college, and by second year they were rooming together, his first "best friend." Jonathan was starting to wonder if he'd begun to miss Mark more than Geneva.

And that was a strange thought.

"You'd warned me that Amy isn't thrilled about this," Mark continued, "but she seemed okay."

"Yes, more so than I'd originally thought. So have you decided where to put the test pits?"

Talking about work focused them away from the awkwardness of being together, and soon they had planned four different test pits between the barn and the old homestead. Mark had a couple students lined up for the summer session, and they'd come out the following Monday to begin. Jonathan promised to let the Fairfields know.

Jonathan watched Mark's SUV drive away, hoping the tension in his shoulders would abate now that Mark was gone, but it didn't happen.

Jonathan spent the weekend writing, before heading to Fairfield Orchard on Monday morning. The day was cloudy, with a chance of rain in the late afternoon, so Mark should be able to get a good start on the test pits.

It was getting more difficult to be at the orchard and not show Amy just how interested he was in being more than a researcher interviewing her grandpa. She was in his thoughts to an alarming degree. Apparently he wasn't capable of being a man for whom sexual satisfaction alone was enough.

And there was a faculty reception honoring a guest lecturer Friday night, one he couldn't easily get out of, as he had so many others. Once Geneva and Mark had gotten married, they'd of course attended together. Jonathan had stayed on the opposite side of the room, trying to make it easier for the rest of the faculty not to tiptoe around the three of them. It was damned awkward. Not to mention the pain he'd felt knowing he couldn't give Geneva what she'd needed. Feeling like a failure had been a rarity, except for in his personal life, with Geneva and his parents.

But now that he'd seen Mark, and knew he'd soon see Geneva again, it had begun to bother him that he never attended these events with a date. And soon he was thinking about asking Amy to go with him. The thought of having her on his arm that night just seemed . . . right. Not that he wanted to use her as a buffer between him and Geneva and Mark, or to show her off as if to say, *See, I can date, too. I've recovered.* He just wanted to be with her, for her to meet some of his colleagues and see where he worked.

But at Fairfield, he didn't see Amy, only Tyler talking to Mark as the archaeologist unloaded equipment from his old Suburban. A couple of UVA students, Waylen and Hannah, stood looking around awkwardly, but both smiled when he approached.

"Hey, Dr. G.," said Waylen. "More Jefferson research, huh?"

"What else?" Jonathan replied with a smile.

The elderly Mr. and Mrs. Fairfield arrived next, the "grands" as Amy called them. Jonathan was surprised to see Mrs. Fairfield wearing jeans and hiking boots beneath her dark fleece jacket. She wore a floppy broad-brimmed canvas hat. Mr. Fairfield looked particularly grumpy, not an expression Jonathan was used to seeing. Jonathan was about to excuse himself to see the couple, but Mrs. Fairfield marched right over and held out her hand to Mark.

"Good morning, Dr. Alberici," Mrs. Fairfield said, smiling.

Mark returned the handshake. "Ma'am."

"I'm Mrs. Fairfield. Do you recognize me?"

"You seem vaguely familiar, but I see a lot of people every day."

"I audited several of your introductory archaeology classes."

Mark's eyes widened. "I see."

"I'd like to participate in this summer's field season."

Mark and Jonathan exchanged a surprised glance, a frowning Mr. Fairfield crossed his arms over his chest, and Tyler grinned.

"I'm not an archaeology major," Mrs. Fairfield continued, "so I've never been able to participate. But since this excavation is on our land, I assume you wouldn't mind if I carry things for you, or maybe sift dirt. I won't get in your way."

"Of course you'll be in their way," Mr. Fairfield said.

Mrs. Fairfield ignored him.

Mark smiled. "Excuse me, sir, but actually, I

would be glad for the help from someone who's had some education in the field. Just promise me, ma'am, that when you need a break, you'll take one."

Mrs. Fairfield waved a hand. "I'm from strong stock, Dr. Alberici."

"Please call me Mark."

"This old fart is my husband, Henry Fairfield."

"There's no reason for name-calling," Mr. Fairfield grumbled.

"I'm just exasperated with you," Mrs. Fairfield said. "I want to do this, Henry, and I won't hurt myself. Didn't I just complete a two-mile hike in the Shenandoah National Park with my club girls the other day?"

Mr. Fairfield made some grumbling noises, but no actual words.

"Then it's settled," Mrs. Fairfield said with satisfaction. She went and stood by the two students, who regarded her with interest. "Just tell me what to do!"

Soon she was carrying shovels and hand screens, all while wearing little flowered gardening gloves. Jonathan stood with Tyler and Mr. Fairfield to explain the pin flags Mark was setting out to mark the sites he'd chosen. The two students worked with the compass and paced off the distance between the pits, writing on a clipboard, while Mrs. Fairfield walked behind them, carrying flags. Soon Mark and his students were removing turf or gravel in a perfect square meter, and then beginning a slow dig down with trowels, while Mrs. Fairfield walked to each of the piles of earth excavated and began to sift. Mark occasionally oversaw her work, and spoke to her patiently.

But Mr. Fairfield was not at all happy, so Jonathan decided to distract him with research, especially the trunks and boxes Jonathan still had to sort through in the house. The lost diary was enough to keep the old man in a more positive frame of mind.

Over the next couple hours, Mrs. Fairfield proved indefatigable, and when Amy brought everyone bottled water and a bowl of apples, Mrs. Fairfield was the last one to help herself, so busy was she examining the connects of her sieved dirt.

Mr. Fairfield was talking with Mark and Tyler, so Jonathan was able to get Amy to himself. He wanted to ask her out, but having been rebuffed the previous week, he thought it made sense to check out her mood. And just standing so close felt pretty good. He was sinking fast.

Amy eyed him, then gave him a slow smile that almost made him forget the conversation he'd mapped out. Damn, she was a beautiful woman. He liked the freckles on her nose that her ball cap couldn't quite keep in shadow, and the way the different strands of brown in her hair gleamed almost golden in the sun where they spilled from her ponytail. He got a hold of himself.

"So how did the second contractor appointment go?" he asked.

She took a swig of water. "Pretty good. I liked the first one better. He seemed more excited, and he'd already done several tasting rooms across the state. But I'll wait for drawings and quotes from each before making a decision."

"You're moving right ahead."

She grinned. "We are. The rest of the family is pretty excited. Logan is chomping at the bit for more details, so I'm fleshing the business plan out, too."

He opened his mouth, but she beat him to the punch.

"I know you'll help if I need it," she said quietly. "I appreciate it."

Their brief silence felt so companionable, so easy. As if he could talk to her about anything.

"Amy, there is a faculty reception honoring a guest speaker Friday night. Would you consider attending with me?"

She didn't say anything for a moment. "So . . . you can bring a date to a work-related event?"

"It's more of an informal get-together. I don't usually bring a date, but . . ." He couldn't think of a way to persuade her without sounding pathetic.

"Didn't you bring your fiancée during your engagement?"

Trust Amy to find the heart of the matter without even knowing the details. "She already works there."

Amy glanced at him, her expression going solemn. "Oh. I bet these things have become pretty awkward for you since the breakup."

"It's getting better." Then he faced her earnestly. "Please don't think this has anything to do with her. I just wanted to be with you, Amy."

She swallowed and their gazes didn't break. "I have to admit I'm pretty curious about seeing you in a work setting."

"Then you'll be disappointed. We're talking drinks and appetizers and small talk that I'm not very good at."

"No? Why not?"

He glanced away briefly. "I think it stems partly from not having any idea what to say to other kids when I was a kid myself."

"The old child prodigy predicament?" she asked in a teasing tone.

His mouth quirked in a smile. "I guess so."

"The other boys wanted to talk about catching frogs and you wanted to dissect them?"

He chuckled. "That's close to the truth. That continued pretty much through school. Liking girls in middle school and not knowing what to do about it put me on an even keel with the rest of the boys, but there and into high school, many of them proved far more proficient than me."

"Aha, was this the first time you'd ever been a failure at anything?"

"Frankly, it was. And it was pretty bewildering. I'd always been able to get straight A's with very little effort on my part. My parents were convinced I was a genius they had to nurture, and of course, they thought they were doing a great job. Seeing me flounder in social settings made them doubt themselves. After a while, I think they decided that being like everyone else shouldn't matter to me, that I was born to be above that sort of stuff."

She winced. "That doesn't sound very helpful."

"It wasn't. But it made them feel better."

"Things must have improved. After all, you did fall in love and become engaged."

"I did. But she's a lot like me, after all, considering we're both in academia."

And Geneva now insisted she'd never really loved him at all.

"Have you dated much since the breakup?" Amy asked.

He shrugged. "A few times, but nothing clicked." Then he met her gaze. "Until you."

Those deep blue eyes widened, and he knew he risked pushing her away, that her own breakup didn't seemed to have healed.

Before she could answer, he said, "I know we

talked about not dating yet, if ever, and I don't mean this to make you think I'm pressuring you. Hell, it's not like I ever thought women would disappoint me, although I swear my parents tried to make me think so."

"No!"

He smiled. "Yes. I think they thought women would distract me."

"And are you distracted?"

She was teasing, but he was serious when he said, "You distract me like I've never been distracted before."

Her eyes went round.

"And now I've gone and scared you off."

"No, you haven't." She hesitated. "All right,| I'll go with you."

It was his turn to be surprised. "Even after I sounded a little obsessed?"

"You didn't sound obsessed, you sounded . . . flattering. I think you deal with women better than you thought, especially after our . . . evening together."

And then it was between them again, as if it had never truly left, the way they'd been unable to stop kissing, stop touching, stop needing, regardless of any sense of control he'd thought he had.

He could have sworn Amy was blushing as she turned to regard the excavation.

Jonathan cleared his throat. "Your grandfather

is not exactly happy with your grandmother. Any idea why?"

Amy looked relieved at the change of topic. "Maybe. Grandma has been so excited taking classes, finding new friends, and I think Grandpa felt left out. Then this research project with you came along and it was sort of his baby, you know? Now here she is." She lowered her voice. "I think Grandpa is feeling a little strange after Dad retired from the orchard and left. And he's still here, you know? I'm trying to let him know he's a part of this place, as welcome as ever, but I'm not certain I've been all that successful. Frankly, you've given him so much happiness and something to look forward to."

"I . . . thank you. That makes me feel like I haven't been too much of a pain, after all."

"If you're looking for a compliment, then okay, you've been less of a pain than I thought you'd be."

"And the compliments just keep rolling in."

She laughed and caught his arm in hers, just a little friendly squeeze, but it felt . . . great.

Maybe too great, talking about her grand-parents, her family, like he was intimately involved with them. He had to remind himself that this was Amy's family, not his, and he'd never had a lot of luck where families were concerned.

— *Chapter 15* —

On Friday, Amy had a hard time making Jonathan agree that she could drive down to Charlottesville for their first official date—she didn't want him to have to take the hour round-trip twice. He was far too polite, and only backed down when she insisted she was coming in a little early to tie up some loose ends for her last real estate client. That was sort of a lie, but she could easily make it true by dropping into the old office and seeing some people.

She could admit to herself that she, being a nondrinker, would rather be in control of her own fate after the faculty party. She didn't want Jonathan to feel he had to stay very sober to drive her home. More than once, it had been difficult to get Rob's keys away from him, when he'd had too much to drink and she'd felt stranded. And she wanted to be able to escape if things felt awkward.

That was the wrong word. The things she felt for Jonathan were no longer "awkward." They were overwhelming and inescapable and distracting. Maybe after an evening of it, she'd have to flee home to her orchard.

But she agreed to leave her car in his driveway,

and soon they were both taking the two-mile drive to the campus.

Jonathan kept glancing at her as he drove.

"Is something wrong?" she finally asked. "Do I have a stain on my dress?"

"No, and I've checked it out so much I can state that unequivocally. You look incredible, Amy."

"Thanks," she said, feeling the usual blush he inspired in her. She'd chosen a blue-patterned sundress with a little summer sweater and sandals. "It feels good to be out of my work boots."

"You look good in those, too."

"You can stop with the compliments. I'm blushing enough as it is."

He gave a quiet laugh. "If you don't mind, we'll park in my lot on the campus, and walk up to the Rotunda."

"Oh, I didn't realize where the party was. I hate to admit this, but I've never been inside the famous building."

Jonathan gave her an exaggerated look of shock.

"Now, *you* grew up in Charlottesville and attended UVA," she reminded him. "I did not. I've always meant to tour the place."

"And now you'll see it at its best after the big renovation."

Soon they were walking across the campus, its historic buildings spotlighted to show off the architectural beauty. Amy's arm brushed

Jonathan's, and she wondered if he'd take her hand—or if she should even let him. He didn't. She should be relieved, but . . . oh, she was so confused in her feelings for him. It seemed overwhelming and too soon after Rob, but it had been seven months already . . . Why couldn't she just take things as they happened and stop overthinking everything?

Because when she did that, she'd ended up having sex with him.

Of course, it had been truly memorable . . .

She shook those thoughts away and just enjoyed the view as they approached the Rotunda, the most important building on campus, designed by Jonathan's career focus, Thomas Jefferson. The round building, with its domed roof, originally the main library, had stairs leading up to the massive columns of the portico. Once inside, they walked up curving staircases until they reached the entrance to the Dome Room. There were dozens of people in attendance, but Amy saw none of them as she took in the beautiful white columns lined two by two circling the entire room beneath the dome. She could see there were still glass-fronted bookcases behind all the columns, and Jonathan told her they housed special exhibits. He pointed high above the gallery that circled the dome roof, to the dark spot at the center of the ceiling, the oculus skylight.

"This is incredible," she breathed.

"I knew you'd like it," he said with satisfaction. "Can I get you something to drink?"

"A Coke is fine. I'll come with you."

There were several bars stationed near the pillars, as well as scattered cocktail tables covered in flowing cloths and decorated with flowers and pillar candles across the polished wooden floor. The lighting was low, the atmosphere intimate and elegant. She saw people glance at them with curiosity, and she remembered that he'd seldom brought a date. She hoped she lived up to every-body's expectations.

Soon, Jonathan was introducing her to colleagues, and she relaxed, listening to them talk about university politics, students, and classes. Jonathan always managed to work into the conversation that she was one of the owners of Fairfield Orchard, and to look for a big reopening this fall. It was sweet of him, and she couldn't help smiling up at him.

And then she saw his own warm smile fade a little bit.

"Jonathan," a man at his elbow said, "just wanted you to know that Geneva and Mark just arrived—in case it matters."

"It doesn't," Jonathan said, smiling ruefully. "But thanks."

Geneva and Mark?

She turned her head around and saw the handsome couple on the far side of the room, near the doors. Yes, it was Mark Alberici and his wife, Geneva, a slim black woman with close-cropped hair that emphasized her striking cheekbones—and apparently, by Jonathan's reaction, Geneva was his ex-fiancée. Amy could have clapped a hand to her forehead as everything made sense. Mark was the best friend who'd betrayed Jonathan. And yet Jonathan had still been open to working with him.

Tonight Jonathan had brought Amy. He'd told her he just wanted to spend the evening with her, show her his university, but a small part of her worried just like that night at the bar—could he be using her, even subconsciously, to prove that he'd recovered from the scandal, from the betrayal?

She wanted him to recover, she truly did, but . . . using her in such a way would mean he hadn't. It had been a year, he said. Why couldn't she just believe what he'd told her?

Taking a deep breath, she looked up to see Jonathan's reaction. But instead of looking at the two people who'd been the source of all his pain, Jonathan was studying her.

"Everything okay?" he asked quietly.

She sighed. "I wish you would have told me the truth about Mark and Geneva. Hopefully I didn't look too shocked."

His eyes widened. "You didn't know?" He grimaced. "I thought you did."

"Really?" she asked.

"Really. You'd helped them buy a house, and for some reason, that made me think you knew everything. Didn't I say Geneva's name to you? I could have sworn I did."

"No, you didn't."

"See, my vaunted intellect is pretty dull at times."

She linked her arm in his. "Or you're just as human as the rest of us. It must have been difficult to come to these events."

"I avoided it at first, retreating too far into myself. Work was the only thing I did."

"I can see you'd go that way."

"But I don't want to do that anymore, which is one of the reasons I'm here. You've made me want to change things about myself," he admitted quietly.

Amy swallowed, a bit overwhelmed at such a personal revelation. She put on a bright smile. "So what do we do next? I do know Geneva. It would be rude to ignore her. But I could say hello when you're in the restroom."

"I don't think I need to be that cowardly," he said dryly.

Her voice was gentle. "I didn't mean it that way. I just know this has been difficult for you."

"It's all right. It's not like I don't see her occasionally."

"And now you see Mark almost every day. That can't be easy."

He shrugged. "At first it wasn't, but we were friends and colleagues for a long time. I know it can't be the same between us, but I also know he didn't intend to betray me, neither of them did. And they never took their relationship farther until she'd ended the engagement."

That said a lot about their integrity, and it made her feel better about them.

"I'll try not to embarrass you by getting angry at the woman who done you wrong."

He chuckled. "Even if you were angry, I wouldn't know. A moment ago, you asked if you looked shocked—and you didn't. I'm amazed at how difficult it is to read your face when you don't want me to."

"It was the real estate. I had to be 'on' regardless of whether I was sick or sad or frustrated."

"It's a good way to hide your true self from people," he said quietly.

She bit her lip, dismayed that he could see something that was hard to admit to herself. No one outside the family had ever been able to read her so keenly. What was it about Jonathan?

"Maybe it's a way to keep them from getting too close?" he added.

She frowned and kept looking into his perceptive eyes when she wanted to look away. "Oh, you're good."

He tilted his head. "Not normally, but with you . . . I feel very connected. Are you sure it was real estate that made you good at hiding your thoughts?"

"Not very subtle, are you?" she asked. "You're asking if Rob made me this way. And I have to say—I don't know. Certainly he didn't help. When I was a kid, I always worked really hard at trying to make everything seem normal and right when my dad was drinking."

He cupped her cheek with one hand. "I wish you hadn't had to try so hard. The person you are is wonderful, and doesn't deserve to be hidden."

"Stop it," she said, blinking hard to fight tears. "Let's go say hi to Geneva and Mark. What do you think?"

"I think you're right."

He didn't let go of her arm, and she liked the experience of feeling needed, even by someone as confident as Jonathan.

Or had he needed her here for darker reasons?

Where had that come from, after the sweet way he'd just complimented her? She had to stop assuming Jonathan was like Rob, a man she'd kept trying to help, to "fix," until it had all back-fired. Even a man could like being supported by an ally on occasion. And that's what she should consider herself. Or did sleeping with him, and now dating him, make her his girlfriend? Was that how she should be introduced?

Stop panicking!

Mark saw Amy first, and he smiled at her in the

surprised way of someone who didn't expect to see a nonfaculty face. He leaned to whisper something to his wife, but Geneva's expression didn't change at all, as if none of this surprised her. And all around them, voices seemed to hush.

Geneva smiled at Jonathan, then said, "Amy, it's so good to see you again. I can't tell you how much we're enjoying the house you helped us find."

"I'm glad to hear that," Amy said.

"So you've left real estate behind? We had friends we wanted to recommend you to."

"That's really sweet, thanks, but I'm not taking on new clients right now. I would be happy to refer you to another Realtor I trust. I'll text you the name and number."

"That would be great, thanks."

Geneva looked from her to Jonathan. "Hi, Jonathan. I'm really glad that you asked Mark to work with you again. You always did collaborate well together."

Jonathan nodded, then glanced at Mark. "It won't be the same, but different isn't always bad either."

Mark smiled his relief. "I like that idea."

The conversation turned lighter, as Geneva asked about the orchard, and then Jonathan's book on Jefferson's land. Amy knew the woman was a professor, too, but of anthropology. So ironic that Mark, Geneva, and Jonathan were all interested in fields so closely tied together. Of course, it was how they'd become friends in the first place. Amy didn't think she had much in common with Jonathan at all, compared to Geneva. But sharing the same career hadn't created real love. There was so much more involved in the chemistry of a relationship. And Amy and Jonathan certainly had chemistry at least.

The two couples only spoke for about ten minutes, and then Jonathan was leading her away to find something to eat. Amy looked back over her shoulder to see Geneva smiling up at her husband as she dabbed quickly at the corners of her eyes. Amy tried to imagine what it must feel like to be the woman to come between two good friends. It must have been pretty awful—and awful to have to break the heart of such a good man as Jonathan.

As they munched on bacon-wrapped stuffed dates and chicken satay, Jonathan said, "So you told Geneva you weren't taking new clients 'right now.' "

"And that's true."

"Do you think you'll go back to it, even if only part-time?"

She hesitated. "I honestly haven't made the decision yet."

"Would you miss it?"

She shrugged. "I'd miss some of the people,

many of whom I can keep in touch with, now that I've learned my lesson," she added ruefully. "I wouldn't miss the uncertainty of when a paycheck would arrive."

"Glad the orchard is better for that. So how are you and Tyler doing with your new responsibilities?" Jonathan asked.

"Well, you know how I'm doing, because I spill every detail," she said wryly. "You must really be talking about Tyler."

"And does that mean there's a lot to tell?"

She shrugged. It was so easy to talk to Jonathan. "You know he's in charge of researching and preparing for the cider brewing."

"And he has Carlos to help."

"I have to admit, I'm worried about Tyler. Carlos is busy with his orchard duties, and I just find myself more and more concerned that Tyler is overwhelmed. It's been almost ten days since we agreed to split the duties. He hasn't given me a complete equipment list, and he won't ask for help. I've already chosen a contractor and we're in the final stages of figuring out what we want and how much it's going to cost. We can't have a tasting room and no cider—no one has to remind him of that. The pressure could be getting to him." She let out a deep breath. "I'm sorry I'm going on and on, but Tyler and I have never had these kinds of problems before. We've always told each other everything. But here we are, back living in the same house, and I think he's beginning to avoid me."

"Tyler's never done this kind of work before, right?"

She shook her head. "He's never been in the business world. He dropped out of college—we're not twins for nothing—and moved to New York City to begin auditioning. He was a server in a restaurant, of course, and he was very good at that, good with people."

"I can see that."

Frowning, Amy nibbled the last piece of chicken from its stick, and after swallowing, said, "He got the job on *Doctors and Nurses* within the year. He was supposed to be a secondary character, the extra doctor in the background of the ER scenes, but Dr. Lake proved incredibly popular. Within a couple years he was one of the stars. I didn't think he had trouble making deadlines or memorizing his lines."

"Would he have told you?"

"Yes! We shared everything."

"Especially an alcoholic father."

She seemed surprised he'd said that, and looked around, but they were still alone by a glass bookcase, the window beside them dark with the night sky.

He said, "I'm sorry, maybe I shouldn't have brought that up."

"No, it's all right," she said quietly. "Of course

our dad affected us. But it wasn't what you think," she hastened to say. "He didn't abuse us or hit us."

"But he drank too much."

She nodded. "Surprisingly, it was his hangovers that were the worst. He often couldn't work the next day—he missed appointments, he let things slide, and sometimes the employees did the same because, what the hell, the boss didn't care, right?"

"Did he forget about his children, too?" he asked.

The compassion in his gaze was almost too much.

She shrugged. "Sometimes. My mom did most of the school stuff. Dad made the occasional game or competition, but . . . it was Mom we relied on, Mom we went to for help."

"But he straightened himself out."

Taking a deep breath, she nodded. "He was driving a tractor pulling a hay wagon with a big group of kids and he almost flipped it over on a hillside." She shuddered. "And that was it. He went to AA after that. He's been sober ten years."

"Tyler's problems—they sound a lot like how your father behaved."

Her eyes widened. "No, he's not drinking. I'd know it. It's something else."

He hoped it was. "Maybe it's about the pressure,

how it can feel like the family's legacy depends on you and him."

Amy bit her lip. "I know, I know, but . . . something else is going on. He knows I'd help, yet he's not asking."

"You're very dependable, and I admire that. He knows he can count on you when he finally asks for help."

Amy shot him a smile. "You admire my dependability? Wow, my heart is racing. You know, it's not exactly sexy when your date thinks you're dependable."

He leaned down and spoke softly into her ear. "I think it's incredibly sexy."

He touched her bare shoulder with warm fingers, and she shivered, her eyes downcast. She was afraid to look up at him, afraid of these feelings that swelled so high inside her they might burst if she looked into his eyes, into his soul.

Whoa, she never thought of herself as having a poetic bent, but there was something about Jonathan . . .

"Okay, okay," she said breathlessly, "enough with the touching. A girl can't think."

He nuzzled his nose behind her ear. "A guy either."

But they both straightened, and Amy fought not to blush when she saw several people smiling and whispering as they openly watched Jonathan and her. Well, they were his colleagues, not hers, and if he was okay with arousing her in public—with just a little touch—then she'd have to deal with it.

"So tell me why the fascination with TJ," she said, after taking a deep swig of her Coke.

As if they'd both silently agreed they were parched, he sipped his wine and cocked his head. "TJ? Really?"

"What, you don't like nicknames? I've called him that before."

He smiled. "And it amused me then, too. When my students say it, I lecture about respect."

"Are you going to give me a lecture, Professor?" she teased.

He let his hand slide slowly down her upper arm. "I don't think so. I can think of better ways to correct you."

She found herself trembling as she imagined how. "Stop that!" she whispered.

He gave a start. "Sorry. Amazing how much you distract me—have I told you that enough?"

"Let's get back to TJ—Thomas Jefferson. You've told me why you were drawn to colonial history, but you've never told me why Jefferson exactly. Yes, you grew up in Charlottesville, but three different presidential plantations are within forty-five minutes of us. You could have chosen to focus on Monroe or Madison."

"But you know it's all about Jefferson around here because he founded UVA. It was Jefferson as the author of the Declaration of Independence that first made me realize he'd done even more important things than design beautiful buildings."

"And how old were you when all this dawned on you?"

"Seven," he admitted reluctantly.

She laughed. "Of course you were. At seven I was just getting into cheerleading for our local peewee football program, and learning that girls could actually *compete* as cheerleaders. It just made my day. But do go on."

"I think you must have been adorable as a cheerleader when you were young, and incredibly sexy as you got older. Do you still have any of those short skirts in the back of your closet?"

When he put his hand on her waist, she surreptitiously pushed it away, though she gave his fingers a squeeze before letting go.

"Not one. Those were uniforms I had to hand back in, you know."

"What a shame." His voice was low and husky, and he didn't hide the admiring gaze that swept down her body.

Damn, was it hot in here or what? She'd taken off her sweater a while back, but the dozens of bodies all talking seemed to have upped the temperature ten degrees. Or maybe it was all because of Jonathan's eyes and hands.

"Back to TJ," she said.

He narrowed his eyes at her.

"I have to get your attention somehow."

"Oh, you have my attention."

She was positively going to implode with heat. "Jonathan," she begged.

"Very well. Back to *Thomas Jefferson*," he said, emphasizing the president's name. "Yes, it certainly helped that I knew all about it from schoolteachers as I grew up. And then I learned that he had slaves, and it was like the wind had been knocked out of my sails. My disappointment lasted months, and I remember tearing up a paper I'd already printed for a class about him, and writing a different topic the night before it was due. But I couldn't stop thinking about the very different sides of such a man, that he was so much more than the basic textbooks painted him as. I finally admitted to myself that I wanted to know more. I wanted to understand him as a man of his times and what shaped him."

"Were you eight then?"

"Nine."

She snorted a laugh and almost inhaled her sip of Coke.

"So I began collecting books and read everything I could. I still have quite the impressive collection."

"I want to see them." She didn't even give the words thought, just let them spill.

Their gazes met and held, along with her breath, and she realized saying this meant far more than continuing their discussion about Jefferson.

He simply nodded.

She whispered, "Are you ready to leave?"

His green eyes were half-closed, smoldering like emeralds being melted down. He laced his fingers into hers. "I'm very ready. But I have a few good-byes to my chair and my dean."

"Of course."

The next fifteen minutes gave her a chance to cool down, to think more, but she didn't change her mind. She was going to Jonathan's house, and this time she was very aware of what she wanted to happen. And it was good to know that he wanted it, too.

Desire trembled inside her, and they said nothing, even as they walked swiftly across Grounds, holding hands. Hell, she'd have jumped him in his car.

What was happening to her?

— Chapter 16 —

Jonathan offered his keys to Amy, and she looked briefly surprised, but took them without comment. He was determined to put her at ease, to show her that a man could have a couple glasses of wine and still do the right thing.

They were silent as she drove the few miles, and though he wanted to, he didn't even take her hand. He felt like he had a fragile bird within his grasp, and he didn't want to do anything to scare it away.

And it wasn't about the sex, but about wanting to show her she could trust him, that they were good together even if they were talking about Thomas Jefferson. And if that's all they did tonight, he'd enjoy that, too. Every moment with Amy made him feel alive and aware and ever more certain they should be together on a more regular basis. He didn't try to predict where that would go, didn't imagine it could result in lasting love. He'd been fooled by thinking that already, and wasn't going to make that mistake again.

In his driveway, when she turned off the engine, he almost—almost—leaned over and kissed her, imagining steaming up the car windows. But no, he held back, led her inside, offered her something to drink.

"No, I'm not thirsty," she said. "But I would like to see your Jefferson collection."

He eyed her doubtfully, but she only gave a mysterious smile. He led her past the shadowy living room that already had so many good memories. He could practically see her naked on his floor but for her short skirt around her waist. He was hard already, but he took a deep breath and kept going down the hall, past the kitchen and into the family room.

"Wow, I thought there were a lot of bookshelves in the living room," Amy breathed.

Three of the four walls had bookshelves from floor to ceiling, leaving room for his leather couch, recliner, TV, and coffee table. A big picture window faced the backyard, but now it showed only darkness.

"Show me the first books you collected," she said.

She kept surprising him, but he did as she asked and went ahead of her to the first set of shelves. To his surprise, he felt her hands at his shoulders, and she tugged off his sport coat. But he managed to pull out a small paperback.

"I got this in the school book club," he said, shaking his head as he stared down at the yellowed pages. "After that, I convinced my parents I needed a monthly book allowance at a real bookstore, and they were fine with that as long as I mixed in some science books, too."

He turned around to see if she was yawning her boredom, only to find her wearing nothing but a lacy bra and matching thong, the single light from the side casting intriguing shadows, dipping into the hollow of her belly button, lovingly caressing the lean muscles in her arms. The book fell out of his hands.

As she gave him a mysterious, knowing smile, she tossed her head. Her hair tumbled around her shoulders and brushed her half-naked breasts. He could see the press of her hard nipples, and he reached to touch them.

"Uh-uh-uh," she said, stepping back. "Show me another book."

"Book?" He couldn't even remember what books were.

"A Thomas Jefferson book," she said, enunciating each word. "That's what we're here for, right?"

Unable to turn away from the gorgeous sight of her, he reached behind him blindly and found another book. He held it up and hoped that would be enough.

"What's it about?" she asked innocently. With a shrug, she let one bra strap fall from her shoulder.

His mouth fell open, and somehow he dropped his gaze to the hardcover book. "It's about Jefferson writing the Declaration of Independence."

When he looked up, the bra was gone. Her pink-tipped breasts were full and round, not large, but perfectly proportional to her. She cupped them as if to offer them to him. He dropped the book and took a step toward her.

"Uh-uh-uh," she said again.

He almost groaned.

"This is an impressive"—she looked down at his pants, where an almost painful erection strained for freedom—"collection of books," she finished. "Find another one."

"Amy." He said her name, his voice almost unrecognizable.

She only shook her head.

He turned around and braced one arm on the bookshelf, taking a deep ragged breath, struggling for control. As he reached for a book, her arms circled him from behind to loosen his tie and pull it off. As she began to unbutton his shirt, he felt her bare breasts through the thin cotton. And with a moan he closed his eyes and just experienced bliss.

"The book, Jonathan."

This was torture, but exciting torture, and he'd never imagined Amy could be so inventive. He certainly wouldn't know how to be. His mind was a foggy morass of want and need and desperation.

But he reached for another hardcover. As he bent his head to see what he held, he watched her hands spread his shirt wide, then slide up over his abs to cup and play with his pecs and nipples. He let out his breath in a gasp of pleasure.

"What's the book about?" she asked, her breath a gentle puff against his back just before she pressed her lips to his skin.

She was enjoying this too much, he knew, as his vaunted brainpower went down like she controlled a dimmer switch.

"Jefferson." He gritted his teeth as her fingers caressed a long line downward, dipping into his navel. "As governor."

Her hands played with his belt now, and he found himself silently chanting, *Yes, yes, yes.*

She unbuckled his belt and opened it. "Show me another book, Jonathan."

He groaned aloud. "Amy—"

"Do it." She unbuttoned his pants and played about with the zipper without opening it.

He fumbled for a book, dropped it, and she took that opportunity to slide his dress shirt off his shoulders. He grabbed another book. As she slowly drew his zipper down, he felt like his erection surged at the release. Her fingers traced the long hard line and he shuddered.

"Jefferson?" she asked wickedly.

"His dealings with . . . the Virginia Assembly."

She stilled her fingers. "Nothing about his presidency yet? I'm so disappointed."

He released the book, braced both hands on the shelf, and hung his head as she spread his pants and let them drop to pool at his ankles. Suddenly she was moving again, keeping their bodies together as she slid along his torso. Her hard nipples left an erotic trail that made his flesh quiver wherever they touched, until she faced him. Then she knelt down, and he lost his breath completely.

She looked up at him, head resting back against his books, her smile wicked and full of promise. Her breasts still quivered from her movement, and he watched them hungrily. But he didn't bend to her—he couldn't move, could only wait light-headed for what she'd do.

She gently slid her fingers within the waistband of his boxer briefs and pulled them downward. His erection fell toward her, heavy and aching. God, did she mean to—

She did. She licked the tip of him, and he clutched the shelves for support, his breathing a harsh rasp. She nibbled his length, then licked him in a long line back to the head before taking him deep into her hot, wet, perfect mouth. He shuddered, holding back to enjoy every moment, even as his body urged him to move, to take what he needed.

But Amy was in control, and he wanted it that way, wanted her to know she had this power over him.

He lost the ability to think as she took him in and out, in and out, pausing to torment him, then leaving him alone for a drawn out second of air across his moist penis.

"Step out of your pants," she said, her voice shaking.

He did, and managed, "Condom . . . in the pocket."

"I wouldn't have forgotten this time either."

She rose to her feet, pushed him backward, and then he was slouched on his couch, watching as she opened the packet. She started to take off her thong.

"Keep it on." It was his turn to command.

Grinning, she did, then began the slow, teasing process of sheathing him in the condom. When it was done, she straddled him, still holding herself above him. At last he could touch her as he pleased, and his hands caressed every part of her, sliding along the lacy edge of the thong, dipping deep into the wetness that soaked the lingerie.

"I want you so much," she urged. "Can't you tell?"

"God, yes."

He leaned forward and took one of her breasts deep into his mouth, suckling, then licking, then giving a gentle bite. Every cry, every moan, had the same result as if she caressed him. With his lips and fingers, he played with both breasts, all while stroking her clitoris through the lace of the thong.

"Please, Jonathan, please," she said brokenly.

He let his hands cup her ass, pulling the thong

to the side, then brought her hips down, and thrust up inside of her. They both cried out, hers high-pitched, his hoarse and rumbling. He wanted her to move, God he wanted her to move, but she didn't. He could feel the flexing of interior muscles, clutching at him. Sliding his thumb beneath the stretched lace, he rubbed against her over and over, circling, then taking long strokes. He licked one breast, fingered the other, and then as if her will broke free, she began to move at last, raising herself up and sliding home again, over and over.

She came almost immediately, and he willed himself to hold off as she moved through the climax the best way for herself. For a moment she held herself still, her frantic breathing making her breasts bob before him. And then she was kissing him, hot mouth slanted over his. He gripped her hips again and this time took control of the movement, and after a few thrusts, when she delicately touched his nipples, he came apart on a groan, his strokes more frantic.

She collapsed against his chest, her silky hair sliding along his shoulder and arm. Neither of them said a thing, their hearts pounding chest to chest, their breathing uneven and rapid, their skin damp with perspiration. He was still deep inside her and didn't plan to go anywhere.

She gave a faint laugh, then tilted her face to smile at him. Her makeup was smudged, her skin damp, her lips puffy, and she'd never looked more beautiful.

"And what's so funny?" he teased.

"The books. Damn, you know how to follow orders."

He tweaked her nipple.

"Ow, sensitive," she said, still laughing.

He soothed it, cupped her breast, and gently stroked.

"Better," she murmured, tucking her forehead beneath his chin.

"This . . . you and I . . . this was incredible," he finally managed, though his voice was still hoarse.

"Yeah, I agree."

"I hope you know I didn't ask you out deliberately planning this to happen."

"I know. It was my idea to come to your house. I'm fascinated by Jefferson, as you can imagine."

He chuckled, then ended on a gasp as she closed those wondrous lips over his nipple.

He moved inside her.

"Still hard," she said, sounding impressed.

"Some. If you wait a little bit, I can be Superman again."

"Superman?"

Her turn to chuckle, and they grew silent. He stroked her hair, and occasionally kissed her forehead, unable to help himself.

"I find everything about you incredible, Amy,"

he said at last, "and I don't just mean the sex—although that was beyond incredible."

"Thanks," she said.

He could feel her lips smiling against his chest.

"There are other things I admire about you. You could have panicked when your parents asked for help. Instead, you rode to the rescue, taking control of your life, and heck, helping control the fate of your whole family and its legacy."

"Jonathan, that's too much."

"No, I admire how you maneuver your way between all the different opinions from your family. Me, I had to break away from my family to control my life."

She snorted. "I have to say, I'm hardly in control of my life, though I'm trying to be. I feel like I'm flailing, like everybody else is trying to manage what I do, sometimes even you."

He frowned and lifted her head so he could look into her eyes. "Even me?"

"You were only trying to help, I know that," she said, smiling. "But it's taken me so long to make my own future, to do what I want, and even your suggestions sounded too much like you were trying to guide me."

"I never meant—"

She covered his mouth with her fingers. "I know. You are a giving person, Jonathan, and you wanted to help."

"Everybody wants to help you."

"But why is what I do so important to you?" she pressed.

He felt a little helpless as he stared into the deep blue pools of her eyes. "I don't know." And that was true—and sobering. "When I'm with you, I sometimes feel like I lose my sense of self. I do things I haven't planned, say things without thinking through the consequences."

"Spontaneity is not a bad thing," she said. She hesitated, then glanced back at his messy bookshelf. "Do you think you were drawn to history as a kid because it was the distant past, because it was safe? Your parents' insistence on conformity surely had to feel controlling to you."

He frowned uncomfortably. "I don't know what to say to that. I've told you why I love what I do. I don't think I'm doing it just to piss off my parents."

"I didn't mean that," she insisted, then sighed. "I don't know what I mean. Once again, I'm overthinking things. I do that a lot," she added.

"I might have noticed."

They didn't say anything for a long time. He heard her breathing lengthen, felt the flutter of her eyelashes on his skin. She might have drifted off to sleep first, but he followed her almost immediately.

And when he woke up before dawn, she was gone, without saying good-bye.

— Chapter 17 —

Only a few hours later, Amy couldn't sleep, so she did the one thing she knew would soothe her confused thoughts and help her find some peace. She drove a pickup through the orchard at dawn, Uma at her side, through row after row, just as her father had done every day, and his father before him. The sky was gorgeous, shades of blue from midnight-dark in the west to robin's-egg-bright in the east, framing the sun where it peeked over the horizon. The beauty of it called to her soul, and she had her first realization that perhaps she might stay here permanently. She'd missed her family and the orchard so much.

But she couldn't just admire the beauty; she had to help nurture it. She stopped to check blossoms, looking for the ones that would bear fruit, examined the leaves for disease. She texted the occasional question to Carlos, telling him which block of apple varieties to double-check for her.

But Jonathan was never far from her thoughts. Their last conversation was a raw place inside her. She'd pried too much, asked too personal a question about his life with his parents, had told him too much about hers. Did she want to know that kind of stuff? They were just dating, just sleeping together; it didn't have to be more than that.

No matter how much she hoped she was changing, there was still that need to understand a guy, to help him. And that thought in the middle of the night was what had made her leave, even though she felt guilty. He'd looked adorable, naked and slumped on the couch, his head back, his breathing a faint snore from the awkward position. Or maybe he snored all the time. She didn't know him that well, did she?

When her phone buzzed, and she saw it was Jonathan calling her, she didn't answer.

Coward.

But a minute later, she pulled over and listened to the message he left.

"Hey, Amy, next time wake me up when you leave. I'll take a rain check on breakfast. Talk to you soon."

Her heart did a little twist in her chest, and she couldn't decide if it was painful or wonderful.

But she reminded herself that he'd slept with her right after seeing his ex-fiancée. Had he needed to block out the memory by using Amy?

What was she thinking—the other voice in her head demanded. Sex had been *her* idea, not his. She kept letting Jonathan get closer to her, unable to keep her distance, and she felt a little panicky about that.

When she got back to the warehouse, Tyler met

her outside, then leaned against the bed of her truck as she got out and Uma shot past her.

Sandy hair rumpled appealingly, wearing an old Fairfield Orchard T-shirt, he petted Uma until she got bored even as he regarded Amy with interest. "So, how was the date? You know, the one you didn't get home from until the crack of dawn."

She crossed her arms beneath her chest. "Keeping an eye on me? And how do you know what time I got home—you're never awake that early."

"Did you ever think I might not have gone to sleep until just about then?"

She rolled her eyes. "Whatever. The date was fine, the Rotunda is gorgeous, and Jonathan is a gentleman."

"I hope not too much of a gentleman. Maybe it was you who couldn't keep her clothes on."

Too close to the truth. "I don't kiss and tell."

"You did last time."

"Only because you guessed!"

He grinned. "Fine. I wanted to discuss visiting the few cideries around here, comparing their tasting rooms to what we're proposing, so we can show how our cidery will be different—'the land Thomas Jefferson once owned,' et cetera. Anyway, I thought Jonathan would like to come with us."

And something inside her snapped. "No. We can handle this."

He regarded her thoughtfully. "You know, you've been all weird about dating Jonathan. I can only think it's because of Rob."

She stiffened.

"I wish you'd talk to me about what really happened," he said softly. "You've never kept a secret from me before."

She looked away. "I can't talk about it or I'd feel even more humiliated. I was such a fool and I've promised myself I won't do that again."

"Won't do what—allow yourself to be with a great guy like Jonathan?"

"I'm with him—I'm dating him."

"He isn't Rob, Amy," Tyler said gently.

Her throat was so tight she couldn't answer.

"Rob tried to keep you away from all of us. We noticed and we used to hurt for you. But you got away from him. And Jonathan's nothing like him."

"I really do know that," she said tiredly. "But maybe I keep trying to help him too much, trying to change him or something. I made that mistake with Rob."

"Change his drinking, you mean."

Amy nodded, biting her lip, before saying slowly, "I rationally knew I couldn't do that. I knew from our experience with Dad that no one can make a person embrace sobriety."

"Look at you, with all the big words."

She pushed his shoulder, relaxing a bit at his

teasing. "It was such a slow descent into drinking for Rob. I wouldn't even have called him an alcoholic until near the end. Or maybe I just couldn't call it alcoholism without admitting I hadn't seen the signs, or that I'd ignored them. I don't know." She sighed. "And my worries aren't so much about Rob anymore. Jonathan sees too deeply, Tyler. Sometimes I'm afraid I still want to hide from him, because it feels like . . . too much. No teasing, okay?"

"Not tease you? What kind of brother would I be?"

But he slung an arm around her shoulders, and they both relaxed back against the truck, looking out at the endless rows of trees that had shed their pink finery for the green leaves of summer. It was a peaceful moment.

"Don't hide from Jonathan," Tyler said quietly. "Don't hide from your feelings. It's okay to be happy again, to trust that you've found a good guy."

She wanted to believe that, to *do* that, but had to deflect the serious moment. "Wow, listen to you, wise and all-knowing."

He puffed out his chest. "Yeah, that's me."

She gave a little push and they broke apart. "I'm going to head to the barn and say hi to Mark, see how it's going. Want to come?"

"No, you go ahead. I've work to do here."

"The contractor we chose is coming Monday

to go over all the final details. He thinks if he can get started within the week, we might have it ready by early September, midmonth at the latest." She hesitated. "Will you and Carlos have a list of equipment and a timeline for me soon? We've got to start placing orders."

"You'll have it."

"Tyler, you think I'm not talking enough to you about Jonathan, but I feel like there's something you need to get off your chest. I'm worried about you."

He just laughed. "Worried—don't be. I'm fine."

She told herself to let it go. Tyler would talk when he was ready.

Amy called to Uma, and they both got into the car. Though Tyler went back into the warehouse, she didn't leave. On a sudden impulse, she called her mother.

"Hi, Amy!" came her mom's breathless voice.

"Am I interrupting?"

"Not at all, I just didn't have the phone right next to me. I'm still fighting the insistence of society that it should be glued to my side."

Amy chuckled. "So where are you guys now?"

"Just got to the campground outside New Orleans last night." Patty hesitated. "Everything okay with you?"

Amy stared at the phone in amazement before saying, "Why would you ask that?"

"Because I'm your mom and your voice sounds

strange. And you're calling me in the middle of the day."

"I work for the family business—I make my own hours. Speaking of the family business . . ."

"Uh-oh. What's wrong? Should I bring your father in for this?"

"No, I wanted your honest opinion without having to worry what he thinks."

"Okaaay," Patty said, dragging the word out.

"It's just . . . Dad was pretty hesitant when e first told him about the hard cider idea. He turned it down when Carlos proposed it years ago. How does he feel now?"

"You know we both understand you kids make the decisions now."

"But I want to know how Dad *feels*."

Uma gave a little whine at the intensity in her voice, and Amy ruffled her furry head.

"Sweetheart, he's fine. I wouldn't concern yourself about him."

"Of course I'm concerned about him, Mom! I want him to be happy when he comes back for the grand opening. I don't want him filled with regrets."

"He won't be. He sees that this is a fresh idea to bring new customers to the orchard. That's all he's ever wanted. But how are *you* with the alcohol aspect?"

"Me?" Amy said, leaning back against the headrest and closing her eyes. "It was my idea."

"I know, but you don't drink, sweetheart."

"Other people do. We've already had several tastings of Carlos's cider. I like watching people enjoy it and listening to them discuss. And then I take a sip of my Coke."

"Okay, you've convinced me, but there's still something else bothering you, I can tell. You're not having problems with Tyler . . ."

"Of course not—you know how great we get along." She did wish she could discuss her worry about her brother, but knew that wasn't fair to Tyler. It would be like tattling. She and Tyler had agreed at a young age it was them against the world, so they never turned on each other. But she had to say something, and words suddenly tumbled out of her mouth. "I've told you about Jonathan, haven't I?"

"The professor who's doing research with your grandpa? Sure, you've told me all kinds of stuff about that, but the things you haven't said have made me curious."

"Well . . . we've gone out on a couple dates."

"Aha!" said Patty. "I told your father that would happen, but he didn't believe me."

"I didn't expect it to happen, not so soon after . . ."

"Rob," Patty finished the sentence, her voice laced with sympathy and understanding.

Amy had always been able to confide in her mom, but not about Rob's drinking problem. It had been too close to what her parents had gone through, without the uplifting ending of her dad's recovery. She hadn't wanted to burden them.

"Take things slowly and give yourself time," Patty said. "I could see that things weren't going well with Rob for a long time. He drank, Amy, and I, more than anyone, could see the signs."

To Amy's horror, her eyes welled right up, and she couldn't speak around the band that seemed to tighten her throat. Uma rested her head on Amy's thigh.

"Amy?" came Patty's gentle voice.

Amy took a deep shaky breath. "How did you do it, Mom? How did you get over what had happened and learn to trust Dad again? Oh, I don't mean I would ever trust Rob again, just . . . men in general."

"The professor in particular."

Amy closed her eyes. "He's a great guy, Mom. He's so good to me and I love being with him. But I can't seem to stop overthinking everything."

"That's only natural, sweetheart. Don't push yourself with some sort of imaginary timetable. There isn't one. You'll know when you're ready."

"I made so many mistakes with Rob," Amy said, wiping away a tear. "I don't want to do that again."

"He was the one with the drinking problem, not you. He is responsible for his own choices and has to live with them."

"And I'm responsible for *my* choices," Amy said, raising her voice. "In trying to keep that relationship going because of humiliation and even some sick sense of pride, I let my friends think I didn't care. I pushed my family away because it placated Rob, who was always so jealous when he was drunk."

"Amy," Patty began.

Her mom sounded afraid, as if she'd guessed it had been worse than Amy had told her. She couldn't let her mom be hurt by the truth, so she rushed on.

"But I've accepted and learned from my mistakes and tried to move on, but can I? Is that even fair to Jonathan?"

"Only the two of you can decide that together," Patty said gently. "But if he means more to you than a date to keep you occupied on the weekend, then you need to give it a chance. Give *yourself* a chance to find the happiness that's eluded you for so long. I want that for you, sweetheart."

I want that, too, Amy thought. "Thanks, Mom, just hearing you has helped settle me down."

"Really? I don't think I've done much of anything." Then her voice became muffled as she called, "I'm inside!"

"Is that Dad? Go be with him, Mom. New Orleans is one of my favorite cities."

"Are you sure? We have time."

"No, you go. We'll talk later. Thanks again. I love you."

"I love you, too. Bye."

The phone clicked off into silence, and Amy got out a tissue and blew her nose. Much as she felt wrung out with emotions, and she wasn't sure about her next move, it had been a good conversation, and much-needed. There was something about a parent's reassurance that no one else could duplicate.

She leaned down and kissed Uma's head. Petting your dog really helped, too.

After driving to the barn, Amy saw that after six days excavating test pits—and her grandma was having the time of her life—Mark had begun to spread outward in a grid, part of which was near the entrance to the barn, and more near the test pits right where she planned to put the patio. There were strings and stakes now, and a device on a tripod that looked like something a surveyor would use. If only she had time to be a part of this, on her hands and knees next to her grandma.

Mark saw her coming and climbed out of a foot-deep area he'd been kneeling in. The students and her grandma waved, but all kept right on working, even though Uma joyously greeted each one of them, especially Grandma. Grandpa wasn't around, Amy thought, frowning. Although maybe he had plans to meet with Jonathan later. She guiltily realized she hadn't asked, so focused had she been on other things, when she was with Jonathan.

"So, a late night and you're out here working in the sun," Amy said to Mark.

He grinned. "I only have so long with the students—and I know you need to get this done fast."

"Yes, thanks." She eyed the site again. "Things are different today."

He rubbed his hands together with excitement. "They are. Come see what I found this morning, and why I decided to go to phase two of the excavation."

"Did you find the cabin?" she asked excitedly.

"No, but we did find some items deep enough that give evidence this site was used around the right time period. We haven't done any true testing, of course, but this was enough for us to expand our search." He displayed a shallow box with a few items inside. He lifted each one and spoke. "This is a piece of flint from a flintlock musket, and another broken piece of metal we think was from the same firearm. Or one like it. We also have several broken pieces of pottery, evidence of plates or cups."

She eyed the broken bits and wondered how they'd even been found. And then she glanced up and saw her grandma Fairfield, waving at her and pointing to a much larger sifting screen that had its own frame. They were bringing out the big guns now, Amy thought wryly.

She turned back to Mark and asked, "How do

you know they're not just from my ancestors?"

"We don't know for certain, not yet, which is why we want to keep excavating."

"Oh." She looked at where his grid was closest to the barn.

Mark followed her gaze. "I know we're in your way, and we'll continue to be as unobtrusive as possible. Will you be working on the barn soon?"

"I'm hoping within the next week. It looks like any equipment can get past you. But there will also be a patio at the end of the barn right on top of where you're excavating. The patio can be done later in the summer—I hope. But we're also taking down that wall of the barn, and the heavy equipment will have to get in there."

Mark nodded, frowning.

"I'm glad you're having success, I really am. Sorry if this is pressure on you."

"No, don't think about that. I'm grateful to have this time to work with my students—and with Jonathan again."

They were quiet for a minute, and Amy stared down at the excavated items. It was so amazing to imagine people had used these items two hundred years ago.

"While I have you alone," Mark began tentatively, "I could use your advice."

She glanced up at him in surprise. "Sure, although I can't help with any of this." She gestured toward the excavation site.

"It's about Jonathan."

"Oh." She and Jonathan were an item now, after all.

Mark took a deep breath. "Geneva's pregnant."

Amy smiled. "Wow, that's wonderful!"

Mark gave a tired grin. "Thanks. We're thrilled. But . . ."

"You don't know how Jonathan will take it."

He spread both his hands. "I need to tell him, of course, and I don't want to hurt him."

Amy touched his arm. "I think it's all safely in the past now, I really do. Though it was awkward last night, Jonathan was pretty relieved to at least be talking with Geneva again—the first hurdle, you know?"

"Yeah, I know. It was a pretty big deal for Geneva, too."

"I could tell," Amy said softly.

Mark let out his breath. "Well, that's a relief. I'll still find a private way to tell him, but it's good to know that it'll be okay."

"I think it will."

"The two of you seem pretty close," Mark teased.

She prayed she wasn't blushing. "He's pretty amazing. But then you know that."

He sobered. "I can't help worrying about him. He's never been the kind of man to have many friends, and that's partly because he's just so focused and intrigued by his work. He used to have me and Geneva, but after that, he just seemed so alone. He likes to be alone, don't get me wrong."

"I can see that." But she could also see how it could be a trap to think you never needed anyone. She could say the same for herself, she mused.

"But now, when I see him look at you," Mark said. "It's pretty clear how interested he is."

The blush was surely spread down her neck at this point and she didn't know what to say.

"Anyway," he continued, "I just want to say you're good for him, and since I know what kind of a guy he is, he could be good for you."

"Thanks," she said. "He *is* good for me."

Mark smiled his relief, and Amy smiled back.

"Amy!"

She turned around to see Brianna and Carmen getting out of Brianna's car. Brianna waved and rushed forward, reaching out her arms wide to embrace Uma. Carmen walked at a more measured pace, putting her long black hair up in a messy bun to combat the early-summer warmth.

"Have you guys met?" Amy asked Mark.

They hadn't, so she introduced the two women to him, and then he excused himself to get back to work.

Carmen studied the excavation site, then asked in disbelief, "Is that your grandmother?"

"It's her," Amy said proudly.

She saw her grandma kneeling on her gardening foam knee pad next to one of the new shallow meter-square sections. She was using a hand brush to clear away what must be a layer of loose dirt. Grandma was wearing her floppy hat and gardening gloves again, as well as a pair of khakis that were now dirty at the knees.

"She took some archaeology classes at the university," Amy continued. "She asked to be a part of the excavation, and Mark was very polite to agree. She's been tireless, working many hours every day until Mark insists she rest. I think she's having a blast."

"Have they found anything?" Brianna asked.

"As a matter of fact . . ." Amy held up the box. "You're looking at the pieces of a flintlock musket and some ceramics. I know it's not much but the archaeology crowd has certainly gone wild for it," she added.

Brianna chuckled, but Carmen merely peered into the box. It was still so strange that when they were all younger, Carmen and Brianna hadn't gotten along that well, and now they both seemed joined at the hip, leaving Amy to feel on the outside.

That was unfair. Amy had put herself on the outside after she'd decided some stupid guy was more important than her family and friends. She was never going to make that mistake again.

"Want to take a tour and hear our plans for the tasting room?" Amy asked.

"We'd love it," Brianna said.

Amy walked them among the excavation grids, where they watched Mark and his students—and Grandma Fairfield—carefully remove small sections of dirt, sifting everything. Then the three women went into the now empty barn, and Amy told them what she and the contractor had come up with, including several bars for customers to stand beside and taste, and a big roaring stone fireplace for some ambiance.

"This is going to be great," Brianna said as they stood in the barn doorway.

Amy nodded, turning to stare out to where the road dipped, and the whole countryside of central Virginia stretched before them. "We'll have a deck here and a patio around the side."

"Really helps how your barn is built into the hillside," Carmen admitted.

Amy smiled at her. "I know."

"You should see what Carmen's done inside her work building," Brianna said.

"Well, I don't need anything fancy for the public," Carmen said.

"But it's incredibly organized," Brianna insisted. "Workstations for the soap and lotions on the one side, and the cheese in its own industrial kitchen in the other half of the building."

"I didn't get to see it when we visited your farm to taste the cider," Amy said wistfully.

"Then let's go see it now," Brianna said, giving Carmen almost a pleading look.

Carmen's hesitation was at least brief before she said, "Okay."

Amy was going to take every opportunity she could to make things better. She smiled. "Let me text Tyler and tell him what I'm doing, and then we can go."

She spent the next hour listening to Carmen describe her business, watching the woman's expression gradually morph into one of excited happiness as she showed them her new lotion line, and discussed the part-time help she'd recently hired because things were going so well. Carmen even laughed at something Amy said, and for just a moment, it seemed like old times.

They were walking past the goat pastures, where the animals roamed and nibbled the new summer grass, and past the open barn, when Amy caught sight of something that glinted from within the shadowy interior.

She came to a halt. "I thought I saw . . ." She trailed off.

"What is it?" Brianna asked, craning her neck.

Carmen sighed. "They're just drums. Papa's taking them out tonight, which is why they're near the door."

"Does he play in a band?" Amy asked.

Brianna answered. "It's that drum circle Carlos hosts for men. My dad used to be involved, too, before Alzheimer's—" She broke off, lifted her chin, and kept going. "They meet a couple times a month and pound drums and let off steam and talk about men's stuff. They build a big bonfire—"

"What?" Amy interrupted. "So this is outdoors?"

Brianna nodded uncertainly, even as Amy realized exactly where it was held.

Carmen heaved a big sigh. "I just found out about it, and I was told that your dad gave permission."

The picnic meadow mystery was finally coming to light and Amy was relieved. "My dad gave permission for people to come onto the property and set fires, but no one tells *me,* one of the new owners, anything about it?"

Brianna's eyes went wide. "I had no idea it was at Fairfield Orchard. You didn't know either?"

"Nope." Amy looked curiously at Carmen. "Your *dad* knew I didn't know and promised to look into it."

Carmen shrugged and spread her hands wide. "Papa wanted to wait until you were more settled about everything before telling you. He isn't harming anyone, and he didn't want you to end something that means so much to everyone."

"I wouldn't do that. Because I didn't know exactly what was going on, I was worried that there could be damage, or even worse, someone could get hurt. Did he think I'd be some sort of . . . killjoy?"

"It was wrong of my dad to stay silent," Carmen

said. "And I should have called you yesterday when I found out." She hesitated, then admitted, "I was letting my anger override my common sense." Her voice came out stiff, but mostly sad. "I thought you felt that a goat farmer wasn't sophisticated enough for someone who lived in Charlottesville."

Amy's eyes welled right up. "No! Carmen, I never thought that. I was such a fool about Rob, and I let my feelings for him control my life. And then as . . . as things got worse, I was so embarrassed by what I'd let my life become. I didn't want you to see me so weak and foolish."

"I never would have thought that," Carmen insisted softly. "I might have tried to talk some sense into you though," she admitted ruefully.

"You'd have been in a long line."

"We're all to blame," Brianna added in a wavering voice, even as a tear snuck down her cheek. "Sometimes we felt like we were watching you self-destruct, and when you wouldn't do anything about it, it became t-too hard to watch."

And then the three of them were sharing a sloppy group hug and trying not to scare the goats by crying out loud.

"We are never letting that happen again," Amy said fiercely after they broke apart and were sharing tissues from Brianna's pocket. "We have to promise honesty, because if we can't be honest with each other, then who will?"

"Amen," Brianna said fiercely.

Carmen nodded, wiping at her smeared eyeliner. "I look a mess."

"You look good enough for a sleepover in a tree house," Amy said.

They both stared at her in confusion.

"It overlooks my picnic meadow," Amy explained, "where the men are meeting! Damn if they're going to meet on my property and me not get to watch!"

Brianna covered her mouth on a giggle, eyes wide.

Carmen's grin was slow and wicked. "Let's do this."

By ten o'clock that night, they had sleeping bags and munchies, wine and soda, and several pairs of binoculars all ensconced behind the half wall of the tree house. As they waited for the men to arrive, they kept their flashlights off and just talked and laughed in a way Amy hadn't shared with women in a long time. It felt . . . wonderful.

Soon they heard the sound of pickups and motorcycles and cars, and on their knees, they peered over the railing and watched as the cars all circled around the picnic meadow, pointing into the center to light up the men who made the bonfire. There had to be three dozen of them, Amy thought in disbelief, some as young as preteens, others as old as her grandfather—and speak of the devil, there he was, helping to take drums from Carlos's pickup truck. She thought they'd be rowdier, but since they seemed full of purpose, it was probably why she hadn't really heard them before now.

"My dad's here," Brianna breathed in shock. "Oh, Carmen, your dad brought him. That is the nicest thing—" She broke off to blow her nose, then grimaced at the used tissue she'd pulled from her pocket.

Amy put an arm around her shoulders, and Brianna gave her a grateful look. As the bonfire grew higher, to Amy's surprise, she could see people drinking soda or water bottles, but not alcohol. When she whispered that to Carmen, the woman nodded.

"It's about getting in touch with yourself as a man," Carmen said, "not about losing control of yourself."

"I like that," Amy said.

Carmen grinned. "I figured you would. They also want to remind themselves that as men, they are not conquering heroes, but strong and equal to their women. They want to give themselves a voice and to help each other."

"By drumming?" Amy asked, curious.

"And talking afterward."

After everyone had arrived, the voices died down as the men gathered in a circle. The three women stopped talking, too, not wanting to be caught. Not that Amy felt guilty—it was her land, after all. But still, she admired Carlos for wanting to help his friends. If only he thought she could handle the stress of knowing the truth! It didn't speak well for what he thought of her.

The silence carried for well over a minute, and above, the black night gleamed with millions of stars. Far in the distance, the lights of the bigger towns lit the horizon, but here at Fairfield Orchard, the darkness was velvety and comforting. The fire below crackled, lighting the faces of men, some who looked serene, others fidgety as if they just wanted to drum. Amy couldn't be surprised her grandpa was trying to find himself here. She hoped it worked for him.

And then the drums began to pound, Carlos setting the pace. Some were big snare drums, others bongos, and a couple of the boys pounded boxes with big sticks. It seemed like you could use whatever you found. For a half hour the drumming went on, and many of the men really got into using their whole bodies. It was loud and joyous and uneven. When Carlos called for a halt, the talking began, and Amy didn't try to overhear, just lay on her back, listening to the murmur of deep male voices, and experienced the feeling of community. Her friendships were whole again, and in some ways, the drum circle had helped. Amy felt good listening to it, peaceful even.

Until she remembered that she'd never called Jonathan back.

— Chapter 18 —

Jonathan stayed away from Fairfield Orchard on Saturday and Sunday, and just kept up with the writing and researching. After a brief conversation Sunday, where Amy apologized for not calling him back and assured him she'd had a great time, they only texted back and forth a couple times. He let it go, reminding himself they weren't in a deep relationship, that they were taking things day by day. But . . . Amy made him *feel* again, made him want things he hadn't wanted in a long time, a commitment, more than just dating. He kept remembering how she'd seduced him, and every time he did, he was just as aroused all over again. He'd been haunted all weekend by memories of their playful, sexy lovemaking. But he wasn't good with emotions, and he didn't want to disappoint Amy, who was also hiding parts of herself. He always had the feeling she was holding back—and who could blame her?

Luckily, he had a distraction, his obsession with the possibility of Jefferson having a hunting camp. He kept looking for mention of it among the man's letters and papers. But after a long weekend chained to his computer, he'd had enough with that, and he just wanted to see Amy. He didn't bother calling, just showed up Monday afternoon.

He felt a little bad for Mark and his crew, since it was lightly sprinkling, but even Mrs. Fairfield was gamely continuing to sift dirt as Mark put up a canopy tent over the section they were working, and the two students pulled tarps across the rest of the site. Jonathan waved, but didn't stop to chat.

He found Amy in the nearly empty barn, and he could hear her talking to someone. After dropping to one knee to give Uma a good hip rubbing, he leaned a shoulder against the wide doors as he peered in, but Amy was alone, except for the phone held in her hand. She appeared to be Skyping, because she was looking at another face.

"Logan, I'm sorry it's so dark in here," she was saying. "It's about to rain. I'll try to walk around and show you what I'm talking about. Over here would be the group of bars where people could stand and taste."

As she began to walk, she glanced over her shoulder and saw Jonathan. She gave him a nod and a smile but just kept talking to her brother.

After a few minutes, Logan's distant voice sounded impatient as he said, "Why don't I have the final list of equipment for the cider house? I have some preliminary stuff, but I can't trust that.

I need that finished business plan along with it."

Amy looked again at Jonathan, and he gave her two thumbs-up and a reassuring smile.

"Who's there?" Logan asked. "Tyler?"

"No, it's Jonathan Gebhart, the professor I told you about," Amy said.

"Tyler told me he's been helping when you need it," Logan said. "Introduce us."

Amy came back toward the door, then stood shoulder to shoulder with Jonathan. He leaned his head next to hers, and the instant scent of her lotion or soap reminded him so much of Friday night that he felt a surge of desire that almost made him forget what he was doing.

Amy eyed him, and her cheeks seemed a little red, but she made sure their heads were in the picture and said, "Jonathan, this is Logan."

Jonathan thought he glimpsed an immense window with a skyscraper view behind Logan, who was around his age, with dark brown hair and one of those square-jawed faces women called "chiseled."

There was a frown line between his eyes, but he looked interested enough as he nodded. "Jonathan."

"Nice to meet you, Logan."

"So you know some of what's going on around the orchard?"

"Some. I've been offering my help with the business plan since your sister permits me my research, but honestly, she hasn't needed much help." Jonathan said to her, "I did find a company you can use to research customer opinions in the area."

Logan shook his head. "We don't need that. We're just waiting for the equipment list, now that the contractor's been chosen." He paused, and looked consideringly at Jonathan. "You say you're helping in exchange for the research. Nothing else?"

Amy looked at Jonathan, and he looked back.

"Got it," Logan said with a smirk.

"Hey!" Amy said. "Stop thinking you know everything."

"I do know everything," Logan teased. "Next time we do a family Skype about the project, you should be involved, Jonathan. Sounds like you have good ideas."

So close to Amy, Jonathan could see her tense. He didn't take it personally. He knew how much Amy wanted to make it on her own, how much she valued this new future she was creating for herself.

But Jonathan wanted to be a part of it, he realized.

"I'll talk to Tyler and get back to you, Logan," Amy said.

"Sounds good. Nice to meet you, Jon."

"It's Jonathan," Amy said.

"Right, sorry." And the screen went blank.

Jonathan gave Amy a crooked smile. "Defending my name now, are you?"

She looked up at him. "I know you can be sensitive about these things."

They were still standing inches apart. Their smiles died, their breathing picked up, and then Jonathan couldn't help himself. He leaned down and kissed her, little kisses that nibbled her sweet lower lip, the corners of her mouth. She clutched his jacket and opened her mouth, deepening the kiss for a long, hungry moment.

When he at last lifted his head, he said hoarsely, "I thought about you—your kisses—all weekend." He heard himself change wording in midstride and wanted to grimace.

But she only smiled and stepped into his embrace, resting her head on his chest and giving a contented sigh. Jonathan rubbed her back and smelled her hair and let the peacefulness of being with Amy wash through him.

"So guess what I did Saturday night," she said.

"I have no idea." And it was true. His brain wasn't capable of any deductions, since he was pressed up against her curves.

"Had a sleepover in the tree house with Bri and Carmen."

He lifted his head and looked down at her curiously. "Really? I thought I got the first sleepover out there."

She laughed. "I was actually there to spy on Carlos's drum circle."

"Drum circle?"

"Yep. That's what's been going on in my picnic meadow this whole time—with my dad's permission."

"Wow. I'm not even sure what a drum circle is."

"You'll get a chance to find out. Tyler says he's inviting you. It's a guy thing."

"I like your brother—both of them."

"You've only met two. You should reserve judgment."

"Okay, then, I have something I can tell you." Jonathan glanced toward the big double doors but no one was there. "Mark told me over the weekend that Geneva is pregnant."

She searched his eyes. "And how do you feel about that?"

He shrugged. "It's strange, no doubt about that, but . . . I want them to be happy. Geneva always wanted kids, when she was ready for them."

Her smile slowly grew again, and Jonathan figured he must have passed some kind of test.

"Okay. Sounds cool," Amy said. "And now that you're here, come read the business plan. It's almost finished. We want Logan to look it over soon. We don't want his partners to have any concerns about where the investment is going now that the contractor is involved."

Jonathan was surprised how pleased he felt that Amy wanted to include him in her future—the future of her orchard, that is. He followed her and Uma to her office, and they spent a couple hours looking everything over. It was difficult to keep his hands off her, but he respected her professionalism and wanted her to know it.

When she closed the document with a contented sigh, he pushed to his feet.

"I have to go," he said reluctantly. "Your grandfather is waiting for me in the homestead. He swears he found a box that might very well contain the lost diary, and wants me to be there when he opens it."

"Sharing history with you," she teased. "You must be in your glory."

He gave a nonchalant shrug, then began to walk backward toward the door. "No, it means little to me, of course. No reason to leave my girl and rush over there."

She blushed as she laughed, and with a nod, he left. This felt good, he couldn't help thinking, seeing Amy share his happiness. It had been so long coming, and it still felt fragile, but he had to accept that life was full of uncertainties.

He jogged across the orchard grounds, past the tarps stretching across the dig, and waved at the crew working beneath the canopy tent. Mark was dedicated, all right. Jonathan was already looking forward to the paper they'd write together. It felt good, as if a shroud had been lifted from his heart.

The old wooden screen door of the homestead slammed shut behind him as Mark entered the house. He took off his raincoat and hung it on the coat tree. Sheets were draped over the sparse furniture in the "parlor," as Mr. Fairfield called the living room. With the faded white lace curtains drawn, the place had an air of neglect that always rubbed Jonathan the wrong way. He wanted beautiful old homes like this to be in use, but he knew it needed too much upkeep for the elder Fairfields, and right now, it was just Amy and Tyler living on the property. Maybe someday . . .

"Mr. Fairfield?" His voice echoed through the quiet house.

No one answered.

Frowning, Jonathan called again, then jogged upstairs to the door to the attic. It was closed, but just in case, he opened it again. The light switch was off.

"Mr. Fairfield?"

No answer. Did Jonathan have the time right? He pulled his phone out of his pocket and checked the text. Sure enough, Mr. Fairfield wrote he'd be in the house all afternoon, and Jonathan had seen his car out in the parking lot. Just to be certain, Jonathan flipped on the light and jogged up a couple steps so he could peer into the attic, but it was empty. He checked all the second floor rooms, then went through the first floor. In the kitchen, the door to the basement was open.

And then he heard a faint groan.

"Mr. Fairfield?" Jonathan cried in alarm.

The light was on, and at the bottom of the stairs, he could see the old man lying awkwardly.

"Mr. Fairfield!"

Jonathan raced down the stairs, then vaulted over him. He knew not to move him, but Mr. Fairfield was doing that all on his own. His eyes were closed, as if he wasn't totally conscious, but he was moving his head back and forth, grimacing. One leg was bent beneath him, and Jonathan thought it didn't look good.

"Mr. Fairfield, I'm here. Try not to move. I'll call the ambulance." He pulled out his phone and almost dropped it by hurrying.

No cell signal.

"Damn," he said, then raised his voice. "I have to leave you for a moment to make the call. Don't try to move. I'll be right back."

Mr. Fairfield grimaced and shook, but Jonathan had no choice except to jump over him and head upstairs. Cell service was difficult enough at the orchard, but on the front porch, he was able to call 911 and explain the situation. Then he ran the short distance to the public grounds of the orchard and waved down Mark, who, thankfully, was with Mrs. Fairfield.

"Ma'am," Jonathan said, "I just found your husband at the bottom of the basement stairs. He's moving around, but he's in pain."

Mark and the crew all gasped their alarm. Mrs. Fairfield blanched, and used a shaky hand to grab hold of Mark, who steadied her.

"I called the ambulance and they're on their way," Jonathan continued. "I don't want to leave him alone, so I'll run back. Mark, can you escort Mrs. Fairfield, and can someone go tell Amy and Tyler?"

Everyone broke apart in a rush, and Jonathan ran back to the old house. After tugging a sheet off the couch and love seat, he found some pillows and a folded blanket, which he brought downstairs with him. Mr. Fairfield hadn't moved, but he kept grimacing and mumbling. Jonathan covered him with the blanket, then had second thoughts about using the pillows. What if he had a neck injury? So he threw the pillows aside, and continued to talk in a calm voice, in case the old man could hear and be comforted.

Mrs. Fairfield came to the top of the stairs and cried out when she looked down.

"No, don't come down, ma'am," Jonathan called. "There's no room. I'm with him."

"Bullshit," she cried, coming down the stairs at the brisk pace of a woman who kept herself in shape.

Jonathan got out of her way, after leaving a couple pillows there for her to kneel on.

"Henry, can you hear me?" she demanded, taking his limp hand.

He didn't answer, but he did keep mumbling and trying to open his eyes. Soon they could hear sirens, and then pounding footsteps overhead. Jonathan peered over the railing and saw Amy, looking pale and distraught, and something inside him twisted at the thought of her fear. Their gazes met briefly; she frowned and seemed as if she would say something, but then she moved out of the way for the EMTs.

And Jonathan suddenly realized that if it weren't for his quest for historical artifacts of the Fairfield family, the old man would have never come down here looking for the diary. Amy didn't need to blame Jonathan—he could manage that all on his own.

Amy thought it was kind of Jonathan to volunteer to drive her to the hospital in Charlottesville, but she insisted she needed her own car—which was true. Tyler came with her, and they were mostly silent during the half-hour drive, where Amy had to keep reminding herself to slow down. Every time she looked in the rearview mirror, there was Jonathan's car right behind them.

It had been terrible to see her grandpa pale and

nearly unconscious, to see her grandma fighting tears as she tried to stay strong for her husband. Jonathan had looked pale himself, and Amy knew it must have been a shock to see her grandpa at the bottom of the stairs and wonder if he was still alive.

The EMTs had been calm and professional, and Grandpa had even awoken after they had the neck brace on him and strapped him to the gurney.

"I don't need all of this," he fumed weakly.

And that had made Amy's eyes sting with relieved tears. The grands were so important in her life; she wasn't ready to be without them.

But now that she was away from Grandpa, imagining the long ride to the hospital in the ambulance—she had never realized how scary it was to not have a medical facility closer—her imagination was doing terrible things to her, wondering if his heart had stopped or—

"I can tell that your mind is in overdrive," Tyler said as they reached the hospital. "Get it under control or you'll drive yourself crazy."

"I know, I know."

They got out of the car, and a couple spots down, Jonathan did the same.

As they walked into the ER, Amy said to Jonathan, "I'm so glad you found Grandpa quickly. I can only imagine if he'd lain there—" She broke off with a shudder.

She wanted him to put his arm around her, to comfort her, but he didn't, only looked solemn and grim as he nodded. Tyler went to the desk to discover what they could, and Amy pulled Jonathan to hold back.

"I don't like what you seem to be thinking," she said, staring up into his face.

"I'm thinking what any rational person would think," he said stiffly.

"If you're thinking this accident is somehow your fault, then you're not rational."

He remained grimly silent, looking past her toward where Tyler still waited.

"He could have fallen down the steps in his own home," Amy said in a gentle voice. She touched his arm and it was like touching iron, so stiff was he.

"But he didn't. He fell trying to get a diary we don't even know exists, just for me."

"Are you crazy? He didn't try to get that just for you, but for his family legacy. He goes into that old house all the time, remember."

She could see him grinding his teeth, then at last some of the tension went out of him. Remorse seemed to deepen the lines in his forehead.

"I never deal with grandparents," he said in a quiet voice. "My mom's parents are dead, and my dad's . . . well, they agree with their son where I'm concerned."

She squeezed his arm a little tighter. "I'm so sorry."

"Being with your family . . ." He paused and cleared his throat. "It seemed overwhelming at first, so many people, each with their own opinions."

"Surely you've learned the art of compromise in the world of academia," she said, trying to sound lighthearted, though she wasn't feeling it.

"Sure. And then I got used to your family, I guess. I liked seeing your grandmother never give in to tiredness, your grandfather so willing to help me however he could." He paused. "It made me . . . remember. I've tried a few times in the past to reconnect with my family," he continued, his gaze unfocused, "but all I usually get is silence, or maybe a message on my machine when they know I won't be home to actually answer the phone."

The pain she felt for him was sharp and unrelenting, as if her heart cracked in two. Even with her father's alcohol problems in her youth, he was still around, still there to talk to—as long as she timed it right, of course.

But Jonathan—his dysfunctional family had actually given her some perspective on her own. His parents had only one child, and because they hadn't gotten their way, they'd cast him off like clothes one would take to a donation center, as if he was of no use to them.

Jonathan let out his breath slowly. "I've been thinking recently that maybe I should try again, actually go see them in person. The relationship you have with your family made me want something more of my own. But I don't know, maybe it's too late," he added wearily.

"Too late only happens when people are dead," Amy said firmly. "Your parents aren't dead, and if you think you want to try again, I'd be happy to go with you."

He gave her a look of faint surprise, and she felt the same about herself. She was thinking how much he needed her, needed a family around him, that he was such a good man—that it was all up to her to help him.

She waited for the immediate feeling of fear because of the past, but it didn't come. Oh, that wasn't good. She needed her fears, she needed her defenses. Without them, she was vulnerable to this soft tenderness Jonathan made her feel.

Tyler suddenly gestured, and she and Jonathan went forward to hear the news.

A dark-haired nurse with an Indian accent spoke patiently. "Your grandfather is still with the doctor, but he's in no danger. His leg is broken, and he might have a concussion, although we still have tests to run."

"Should you run all kinds of tests, in case he's bleeding internally or something?" Tyler asked.

"We are being very thorough because of his

age," she said. "Your grandmother is quite firm about what she wants. I'll have the doctor speak to you when he's finished."

"And then we can see our grandfather?" Amy asked.

"I believe so."

Feeling a little weak with relief—the old cliché really was true—Amy took the arms of both men and let them lead her into the waiting room, half-full with people, some looking hopeful, some scared, some in pain.

"Should we call everyone now?" Amy asked as they found three chairs together.

"Let's wait until we have definitive news," Tyler said. "Who's up for a candy bar for dinner?"

"I should let you guys wait together," Jonathan said.

Amy felt selfish—she wanted him here. "If you have something you need to do . . ."

"I don't, but—"

"Then choose a candy bar," Tyler insisted. "My treat."

It was a couple more hours before they were able to see their grandpa. His skin had more color, and his eyes were alert, and Amy was surprised to feel her own eyes fill with relieved tears. She was crying a lot lately.

She leaned down to kiss him. "Grandpa, I'm so sorry you fell."

He grimaced. "I'm an old fool, sweet pea. I

didn't use the railing, and I still feel like a twenty-year-old who can bound down stairs."

"Maybe thirty now," Grandma teased.

"Hmph," was his answer to that.

They spent a half hour discussing the broken leg and the concussion, and how he could go home in the morning, using a wheelchair for a while and eventually crutches.

When Amy, Tyler, and Jonathan were leaving, they could hear him insisting he didn't need a wheelchair.

Outside the hospital, Jonathan gave her a kiss on the cheek and left, after promising to call Mark with the news. Amy watched him go, thinking he was doing a good job hiding his sadness, but she could see it. Damn.

She and her brother sat in her car and called the rest of the family, glad they'd waited so they could sound reassuring about the whole thing.

When they were done, Tyler looked at her curiously. "It was almost like you were talking everyone out of coming home."

"I didn't want them to drop everything, thinking we can't handle it."

"Was that really it? Or do you like being in charge, Amy Fairfield?"

She gave his arm a push. "That's ridiculous. I know I'm one of six owners, after all."

She started the car and tried not to wonder if there was some truth to his words.

— *Chapter 19* —

Late the next afternoon, Amy was just shutting down her computer so she could go see her grandpa get settled back in at home when she heard raised voices out in the warehouse. The packing line machinery was silent today, and everything echoed, magnified.

Curious, she shut off the lights and left the office, followed by Uma, only to find Carlos and Miss Jablonski facing off against each other. Carlos was leaning against a forklift, with that deceptive casualness that made you feel he didn't care. Amy knew differently. Carlos's dog, Barney, had a rare burst of speed as he rushed to stand behind Amy. Carlos just shook his head at his dog.

Miss Jablonski must have come directly from the high school, because she was wearing a sweater, skirt, tights, and loafers. Her gray hair was in a bun—Amy didn't think she'd ever seen it any other way. The woman, usually a model of polite control, was now frowning as she spoke to Carlos, pointing at his chest.

But Amy didn't get to hear what she was going to say, because Miss Jablonski saw her coming and drew herself up stiffly. She did let some of it go when she leaned down to pet Uma.

Amy smiled. "Hi, Miss Jablonski." She held out a hand.

Miss Jablonski politely shook it. "It's good to see you, Amy. I wasn't certain you'd ever come home from big-city life."

"I think my brother Logan would take exception to hear you call Charlottesville a big city."

The principal shrugged. "I guess it's all perception."

Amy looked at Carlos curiously, but he just gave her another lazy smile. "Miss Jablonski, is there something I can help you with?"

"Mr. Rodriguez—"

"Mr. Rodriguez?" Carlos interrupted, eyes wide with disbelief. "We've known each other since first grade, over fifty years."

"I was trying to be professional," Miss Jablonski said between gritted teeth. "This has to do with Spencer Hollow, not friendships."

"Oh, we have a friendship now?" Carlos countered.

Miss Jablonski didn't answer that, just faced Amy, took a deep breath, and said, "Mr. Rodriguez was at school yesterday, helping to teach his son's class about civil disobedience with some experiences from his past."

"Sit-ins and demonstrations," Carlos said sarcastically. "You remember those."

Amy regarded Carlos with surprise. He'd always been so laid-back, so good-natured. And here, he seemed like he wanted to go toe-to-toe with Miss Jablonski. She'd heard they had run-ins before. Maybe he enjoyed them. It seemed Miss Jablonski did not.

"I do remember what went on in the sixties and early seventies," Miss Jablonski said with the patient tone one might reserve for ignorant freshmen. She turned back to Amy. "And he could not resist stopping by my office to annoy me with his presence."

Carlos rolled his eyes.

Miss Jablonski continued. "He proceeded to tell me about your plans to begin a cidery here at the orchard."

Amy expected Miss Jablonski to be happy for them, but the woman's frown only deepened. "Yes, the contractor hopes to begin within a week."

"And the necessary permits or licenses have been applied for?"

"Of course."

"I wish you would have discussed it with the board of supervisors of Albemarle County."

"You think I should have done that . . . why? I've done the applications."

"Because I am on the board."

Amy blinked at her. "Oh. I didn't know. A county supervisor and a principal."

"She likes to be in charge," Carlos said dryly. "She's not in charge at Fairfield Orchard."

Miss Jablonski ignored him. "Our village is

much concerned by the impact a cidery will have on our way of life."

"Impact?" Amy echoed. "Won't it bring more money into the area?"

"And tourists, and traffic, and more inebriated people. Residents value our peaceful country lives here."

"It will mean more jobs for local residents," Carlos pointed out. "Tourists would eat at Jefferson's Retreat, and at the diner. People would shop at the antique store and the bookshop."

Amy couldn't stop thinking that the woman had raised the issue of their permits. "Would you actually try to block our permits, Miss Jablonski?"

She looked taken aback. "I did not wish to go that far. But the village deserves to know your plans."

"Then I will send you details," Amy said, hoping she sounded pleasant rather than tense.

"Thank you. Have a good day."

As Miss Jablonski left without saying good-bye to Carlos, he watched her go, shaking his head.

Amy let out a heavy sigh. "Is she going to cause problems?"

"To be honest, I don't know," he said, scratching his chin whiskers. "There are some in the village who are upset when a car drives by their property. They want their quiet, their horses, their birds."

"But if no one comes here, don't the local businesses suffer?"

"They do. I told Bill, who owns the diner, about the cidery, and he was excited. He's spent an evening or two hanging in my garage, drinking my cider." He grinned.

"So he'd be on our side."

"I don't think there are sides." But he was frowning, and staring at the door.

Another thing to worry about. Amy's shoulders were starting to feel bowed by the weight.

That afternoon, Jonathan stopped by the elder Fairfields' home in Spencer Hollow. He saw several cars there already, and almost changed his mind, but he really needed to see for himself that Mr. Fairfield was doing better.

He crossed the porch and knocked on the door. It was Amy who answered, and she smiled up at him. Just seeing her pretty face eased his spirit. It was perfectly natural to lean down and kiss her.

"Come on in," she said, tugging on his hand.

"You sure I'm not interrupting?"

"He'll want to see you. Just ignore our crazy commotion for a while. Everyone's talking to Grandpa."

She led him through a door into a living room decorated with a surprisingly modern flare. Amy's grandparents just kept surprising him. Tyler and Mrs. Fairfield were there. Mr. Fairfield was in a recliner, his leg up, a wheelchair next to the wall. He had a laptop on a portable desk across his thighs, and he was talking to it.

"Stop asking! I'm fine."

"It's the family," Amy whispered. "A group chat thing."

Jonathan would have been content just to sit and watch the old man with relief, but Mr. Fairfield saw him.

"Hey, it's Amy's boyfriend, Jonathan! Come say hi."

Jonathan froze and glanced helplessly at Amy. Was she blushing?

"He's the one I've been doing all this research with," Mr. Fairfield continued. "You could say I brought them together."

Several voices talked at once through the screen, but Jonathan couldn't understand them.

Amy pushed him forward from behind, laughing, and he was forced to squat beside Mr. Fairfield and briefly stick his head into the camera shot. On the screen, he could see several boxes, all with different heads of the Fairfields. He waved.

"Amy has a new boyfriend!" Rachel said. "Strange she didn't tell me that."

A man snorted. "She doesn't tell you everything. She reserves that for Tyler."

Jonathan glanced up and saw Tyler frown at Amy, who studiously ignored him.

"What do you do, Jonathan?" a middle-aged man asked.

This must be Bruce Fairfield, Amy's father.

"You already know this," said his wife. "Dad's been telling you all along about the family research."

"Oh, right. I just didn't hear the boyfriend part before."

Jonathan was feeling back in high school again. "Nice to meet you all. I'll let you talk to the patient now."

"Patient," Mr. Fairfield scoffed. "I'm fine."

Jonathan retreated and sat down in a chair.

He found himself listening to the chaos with all the voices in the laptop and in the room. They spent a little too much time discussing him as if he couldn't hear them, but their teasing of Amy wasn't mean-spirited. There was concern and love for their grandfather, excitement for Amy and Tyler and their plans to transform the orchard. He was a little surprised Amy didn't bring up the excavation and how it was in the way, but she let it go.

Next they debated a name for their cidery, and the few times Tyler was asked a question about the equipment, it was obvious he was reluctant to go into detail. Amy frowned at her brother more than once, and then pulled him into the hall as, one by one, their family got back to the topic of their grandfather's health.

Jonathan couldn't miss the twins' discussion, since he was sitting right beside the hall.

"Tyler, I don't mean to pressure," Amy whispered in a low, concerned voice. "I need the rest of the list. I'm worried about our fall grand opening—I'm worried about you!"

"So I'm not dependable enough," Tyler shot back.

Jonathan was surprised by the anger in his voice, when Tyler was normally so affable.

"But let's get to something more important than cider," Tyler continued, "your real life. At least I'm not hiding anything from you."

"I'm not certain I believe that."

Tyler ignored that. "You need to face up to what happened with Rob and just talk about it, before bottling it up inside makes you miserable."

She gave a groan. "This isn't as important as the future of Fairfield Orchard."

"That's what you think. Amy," he added, lowering his voice, "you're scaring me."

Jonathan strained to hear if something more was said, but Amy strode back into the living room, passed him without even seeing him. Her expression was both frustrated and sad. He wanted to help her, but if she wouldn't even let Tyler help . . .

Jonathan turned and blocked Tyler from entering. "Can I talk to you for a minute?"

Tyler sighed. "If this is about Amy—"

"No, it's about you—and it's not about cider."

"All right, all right, what is it?" Tyler asked, backing up into the hall.

Jonathan followed him. "Of course I overheard some of what you and Amy just said, but it only reinforces what I've been thinking for a while. Have you ever been tested for ADHD?"

Tyler frowned. "What? Isn't that a kid thing?"

"No, adults are being tested, too. It's Attention Deficit Hyperactivity Disorder. I see it in my students. Some have trouble getting organized, or they're easily distracted. It's hard to prioritize things, you know?"

Tyler pressed his lips together, but said nothing.

"Just . . . give it some thought, maybe do some research. It might help."

Tyler opened his mouth, but before he could speak, the front door opened and three men pushed their way in.

"The drum circle has arrived!" called one of them.

"It's getting crowded," Jonathan said, backing up to let the men pass him. "Guess it's time for me to head home."

When he said good-bye to Mr. Fairfield, the old man tried to tell him where he thought the diary was.

"No," Jonathan said. "I'll wait until we can look for it together."

Amy was talking intensely to her grandmother, so Jonathan didn't disturb her, just waved good-bye. He got a distracted wave back, and soon he was out on the street. Yes, it was much quieter outside, but . . . he glanced through the big picture window, saw everyone gathered around Mr. Fairfield, and knew the chaos inside was worth it.

He kept telling himself that he and Amy were just dating, that this was casual, but more and more his heart wasn't listening. He was involved with a capital *I*—with a woman who couldn't even trust her own brother, let alone Jonathan, with the secret that gnawed away at the vulnerable depths of her.

Over the next week, things began to happen with the barn, and Amy was excited to watch the dirt floor dug up, the foundation strengthened, water pipes added. Eventually the construction workers poured smooth flat cement, upon which they would build everything else. Mark and his team had sifted the dirt that was removed from the floor of the barn, and mostly found a lot of nails and broken tools, making her feel both disappointed, and relieved.

The archaeological excavation went on regardless, and Amy was amazed at their patience for so little reward. Mark and his students showed her more musket pieces, as excited as if they'd found gold.

By the end of the second week, Tyler presented her with a completed equipment list for the business plan. She stared at the money involved and winced, but Logan took it in stride. Apparently he'd been doing his research, too.

But always in the back of her mind, she thought of Miss Jablonski and the village's concern about the effect of a cidery on the local economy. After she'd told Jonathan what had happened, he'd agreed with her that the benefits outweighed the risks, but the worry never left her.

Jonathan was able to make her stop thinking about it. They had a couple lovely meals together in Charlottesville, and even scoped out some cidery competition. He told her about the diary's continued absence. She didn't think too much about what was going on between them, trying to perfect the ability to just enjoy the moment.

Amy decided she could use the summer festival in Spencer Hollow as a way to gauge how the village would accept the cidery. The village turned out in force at the park. There was an early-season farmer's market, crafts, music, games for kids, and food booths. It drew people from Crozet as well, so Amy used the first of her permits and sold tastings of the cider Carlos had spent the last few months brewing. Surely this would tell how popular it would be.

People loved Carlos, of course. He was active in the community, a volunteer fireman, a member of the Catholic group in the little community church. Amy and Tyler stood beside him, and she was impressed with the brochures Tyler had printed up: "Big News at Fairfield Orchard." People were interested, and most seemed intrigued, even happy for them. Uma serenely lay within the booth, accepting the petting as if it were her due.

Amy went to the rear of their booth and counted how many boxes of cider they had, but she could see Miss Jablonski at the high school bake sale booth, eyeing them with concern. Amy had sent the woman a detailed explanation of what would be happening at Fairfield Orchard, but hadn't heard back.

"Should I ask her if she wants a taste?" said a voice in Amy's ear.

Startled, she turned and saw that Jonathan had arrived. Immediately, it was as if he settled something inside her, gave her a peace of mind she didn't always feel. And of course, as she took in the width of his shoulders, and those charming green eyes, she did a little inward swoon. Smiling, she said lightly, "Not sure that'll help, not if Miss Jablonski is determined that our cidery will destroy the wholesome neighborhood."

"You've always been a popular orchard," Jonathan said.

Amy shrugged. "I know. And she hasn't openly come out against us, but . . . she looks unhappy."

"Must be hard to represent the entire county with so many different interests," he said sympathetically.

Amy rolled her eyes. "Trust you to see it objectively."

He glanced past her toward the front of their booth, where Tyler had a line of women waiting o see him. "I forgot about your brother's popularity. Look at him, signing autographs. And what's that he's signing on?"

"The brochures he had made. Nice, aren't they?"

"He did this without your help?"

Amy nodded, thrilled.

Jonathan eyed Tyler with interest.

"What?" Amy asked.

"Nothing."

"You seem guilty, or like you're hiding something."

"Not at all."

But the way he kept watching Tyler had Amy curious. At last, Tyler took a break from his fans and came over for a glass of cider.

"Miss Jablonski has been giving me the 'principal' stare," Tyler said.

"Ooh, that bad?" Amy said, smiling, pushing aside that niggling feeling of doubt.

"Did you know that she and Carlos have a history?"

Jonathan put an arm around Amy's shoulders and waited. Amy liked it, liked the feeling of being pressed against his warm side.

"How did you find out?" she asked.

"Carlos and I have been hanging out quite a bit over planning the cider house," Tyler said.

"He wasn't shy about discussing the past. Seems back when they were eighteen, they were an item."

"No!" Amy breathed, glancing again at the straitlaced principal/supervisor who was showing the high school girls how to align the baked goods just so.

"You know why he was perfect to talk about civil disobedience with the schoolkids? Because he and Miss Jablonski protested together."

Amy's mouth fell open.

"Sit-ins, marches, you name it. And then Carlos got drafted. Miss Jablonski wanted him to run away to Canada with her."

Even Jonathan seemed shocked. "Well, we know he didn't go to Canada."

Tyler nodded. "He said he couldn't desert his country. But Miss Jablonski never forgave him. They've been estranged ever since."

"Estranged?" Amy echoed.

"I like them big words," Tyler said, the corner of his mouth quirking into a grin.

Amy shook her head. "Well, that's pretty sad. And she never married, right?"

"Nope."

"First love is powerful," she said, then deliberately kept herself from glancing at Jonathan. Neither of them needed to be reminded of what had happened to their first loves.

But he didn't seem to notice as he said to Tyler, "Nice brochures."

"Thanks." Tyler took a seat on a bench and put his arm along the back in utter relaxation. "I was inspired. I needed the Jablonskis of the world to understand what we were up to." He paused, then eyed Jonathan. "I have you to thank for it, of course."

Amy looked at Jonathan. "You helped him?"

Jonathan frowned. "Not at all."

Tyler waved a hand. "Not for the idea exactly, but the ability to come up with it."

"Huh?" Amy said.

A slow smile transformed Jonathan's face. "So you gave my suggestion a try."

"What suggestion?" Amy demanded, looking from one man to the other. "You just said you had nothing to do with—"

Tyler interrupted. "I went to a doctor for a consultation."

Amy's frustration morphed into cautiousness. "Are you okay?"

"Never been better. Jonathan thought I should get tested for ADHD, and he was right. I've been on meds for about ten days now, and I tell you, the world is a different place."

Amy sank down beside him, shock overwhelming her. "ADHD? Tyler, why didn't you tell me you thought something was wrong?"

"I didn't think that at all," Tyler said. "I just thought my behavior was . . . me. It's always been hard to concentrate, hard to focus. It was easy to forget about it when I was acting, because I loved what I was doing. The doc said that's another thing—when you enjoy something, you can focus, but in everyday life, everything seemed as important as the next thing, and I was incapable of prioritizing. I didn't realize how much it was still hurting me until we decided to open the cidery."

"Why didn't you tell me any of this?" Amy asked with bewilderment. "I could have helped."

"I don't know what you could have done," Tyler said. "I couldn't even help myself, didn't know there was anything that *could* be done. I was starting to think I couldn't be a good enough partner for you. And besides"—he eyed her knowingly—"I thought we weren't telling each other our secrets anymore."

Amy felt herself go pale. Tyler had spoken right in front of Jonathan. She didn't want Jonathan to think he wasn't important enough for her secrets.

But neither man knew them all. And she knew they felt bad about that. The destruction of her relationship with Rob had seemed so personal, so intimate—she'd thought it was no one's business but her own. But now her secrets were affecting not just her, but everyone. But how could she bear to expose her stupidity?

"I don't like keeping secrets," she finally said in a soft voice.

"So you feel you have to?" Tyler asked curiously.

She didn't say anything. What could she say?

"Excuse me," Tyler said. "I think Carlos needs me to help tame the masses."

And with a grin, he headed back to the front of the booth, where the sound of feminine voices raised to a squeal.

Amy sat still, looking at the crowds of people gathered in the park, but not really seeing them. She was damaging her relationship with her brother—with Jonathan. But how did you tell someone what a fool you'd been?

"You know," Jonathan said casually, "I gradually realized that I'd been taught one very cruel thing about family love."

She raised her head tiredly and looked at him.

"I learned that love was conditional, that I only earned it by doing exactly what my family expected. And when I eventually didn't, it was taken away."

"Jonathan—" she whispered.

"No, I don't mean this in a pity-me way. What I'm leading to is what I've learned from your family. You all love each other regardless. Tyler knew he could tell you such a personal thing, because your family shares everything, the good and the bad."

"I don't know if it's going as well as you think," she said dryly.

"Then tell Tyler what he wants to know, so he can help. Nothing is too bad to share with your twin."

Amy stared at him. He wasn't even asking for himself, as if he didn't think he deserved to know every deep bit of despair about her.

Though surrounded by people, she took his face between her hands and kissed him softly, gently. There were things she knew she should say to him, but not here, not now. How did you let a man see all of your flaws, if you didn't love him?

But did she love him? She looked into the deep green of his eyes, and waited for the feeling of panic, but it didn't come. She wasn't tempted to back away, to run. This was Jonathan, so steady, so trustworthy. He never hid anything of himself from her; he never tried to change her.

But the people in his life hadn't treated him fairly. His parents had been self-absorbed, and wanted him to orbit them, doing only what they wished. His ex-fiancée hadn't ever truly loved him for the man he was. He'd been such a solitary, lonely man when she'd met him.

And what about her? She was dating him, yes, but she wasn't letting him all the way in. She'd pushed away her friends and her family for so many years, had it become a habit she was continuing with him? Could she change that about herself and risk being open and vulnerable once more?

He asked nothing of her, she saw that now, just her companionship, her tenderness—okay, and great sex. He was a fixture at the orchard, and she wasn't sure how it would feel if he wasn't there regularly. What had started as "just dating" was feeling like a lot more than that.

But that secret she was keeping, that ugly part of herself—was she ready to let him know that?

Walking through the festival with him later, holding his hand as well as Uma's leash, it felt good to be a part of a couple. She didn't have to panic if he had a drink—it wouldn't lead to another and then another. Jonathan wasn't a man who needed taking care of, though in some ways she wanted to. She wanted to comfort him, to show him he wasn't alone, to make him feel like he was the only man for her.

And after he'd helped them take down the booth that evening and pile everything in the pickup truck, she'd invited him home. They'd all unloaded together quite easily, and when Tyler headed back into town for the evening, it only seemed natural to bring Jonathan up to her room and make love with him. They chuckled together over her teenage memories on the wall, and he swore he was going to make her look for that cheerleading outfit. He said it was almost as if he was waiting for the grown-ups to catch them. But *they* were the grown-ups, and it was incredible to fall asleep beside him, to wake up in his arms, pillowed on the shoulder she'd admired from the moment she'd first seen him.

Could the rest of her life be like this?

— Chapter 20 —

When Jonathan got Mark's text Tuesday morning, he didn't dare get too excited.

The text had been short and sweet: *Found something. You need to see this.*

This couldn't be more pieces of musket, or the charred debris of a long-ago fire, not the spot in the ground where a fence post had once rested, all things the excavation team had found. At the orchard, Jonathan jumped out of his car, and he saw immediately where the group was gathered—Mark and his students, Waylen and Hannah, along with Mrs. Fairfield. They were in the part of the excavation right where the tasting room patio would eventually go, where the barn wall would soon be torn down. They didn't have much more time, he knew. He'd been starting to resign himself to just including these small broken bits and pieces of research in his book. But maybe now . . .

Mark looked up and saw him, and his excited expression raised Jonathan's own anticipation.

"What is it?" Jonathan called as he jogged closer.

Mark gestured, the crowd parted, and Jonathan was able to look the two feet down into the meter-square pit, sectioned off from adjoining squares by strings staked in long lines. Hannah was taking photographs, but backed up. Jonathan could see the dirt flattened all around something that protruded upward. All other debris had been swept aside, leaving that . . . something . . . sticking up at an angle.

Mark pointed. "That's it."

"What is it?"

"Notice how sharp it is, how perfectly angular? Doesn't it look man-made?"

Jonathan nodded. "What do you think it is?"

"I think it's a tin box. It might only be another broken piece, but I wanted you to be here just in case."

Jonathan watched Mark climb back down and squat over the item. He used a pointed trowel to slowly dig dirt away from the edges, then brushed away the excess to the side. Jonathan knew they'd sift that dirt the moment it was removed. Occasionally, Mark straightened so that Hannah could take another photo. It was tedious work, and with the June sun beating down on them, Jonathan was thinking he'd been stupid not to wear sunscreen. He was about to ask to borrow some when Hannah gasped.

"Is it intact, Dr. Alberici?"

"I believe it is," Mark said, not quite concealing his awe.

Intact? Jonathan thought with disbelief. A tin from the early nineteenth century?

In another half hour, they had it totally unburied and lying on its side. Jonathan wanted to pick it up, but let them all write on their clipboards, take more pictures and measurements.

Then Mark lifted it and brushed away more dirt, being very, very careful. He revealed the top rim, then glanced at Jonathan. "Should I open it?"

"What are you waiting for?" Jonathan demanded. The shared laughter momentarily broke the tension.

"Do you want to do the honors?" Mark asked.

Jonathan stared at him, and it took a moment to realize it was another attempt at peace between them. Mark didn't need to do that—Jonathan had accepted everything that happened, had long since understood that hurting their friendship had been one of the worst things Mark felt he had done. And it had only been because of love, as corny as that sounded.

"You open it," Jonathan said. "It was your hard work."

Mark nodded, even as he gave a crooked grin. "Thanks."

With gentle hands Mark tried to pry the tin apart but it resisted a long time.

"Is it rusted together?" Jonathan asked.

"It might be. But that also could have preserved the contents, too."

Mrs. Fairfield looked up at Jonathan with excitement. She'd only recently returned to the excavation, now that her husband was on crutches, and better able to take the drive to the orchard.

"Where's Mr. Fairfield?" Jonathan asked.

"Inside the homestead," she answered. "I didn't want him out in the heat until we knew if it was anything important."

"It's important," he said. "I'll go get him."

By the time he returned with Mr. Fairfield, a chair, and an umbrella, the whole group was looking impatient.

"Sit down, Henry," Mrs. Fairfield said. "We loosened the lid."

As they all gathered around, Jonathan was pleased when they made sure Mr. Fairfield could see.

Mark very gently pried the lid off, pieces of dirt and rust falling off. He peered in. "There's something inside," he said with awe.

After sliding his glove-covered fingers inside, Mark removed several sheets of folded paper.

"Will they fall apart?" Waylen asked.

"They're brittle, but they seem okay," Mark said, sounding as if he was so focused he barely heard the question.

On a camp table, he set the paper in the center, then gently unfolded both sides.

"There's legible writing on it," Mark whispered.

They all gasped. Jonathan wished Amy were there to share in the excitement.

"I can't make out all the words, but I see 'assembly,' 'the enemy,' 'flee Richmond.'" Squinting, he peered closer. "I think I see part of a date, seventeen-something."

"Wow," Hannah breathed with reverence. "A letter from the eighteenth century."

"When Jefferson still owned this land," Jonathan said. "Anything more?"

" 'General' . . . something," Mark said.

Jonathan stiffened. "General Cornwallis?"

"I can't tell. That might be the correct first letter of the last name. Why?"

"We have the words 'assembly,' 'flee Richmond,' and reference to a general," Jonathan said slowly, then decided to explain his theory for those who didn't know the details. "During the American Revolution, when Jefferson was governor of Virginia, he was in Richmond, and was sent a warning that General Cornwallis had ordered him to be taken. When he and the Assembly fled capture, the Assembly went west to Staunton. It was believed that Jefferson went to Poplar Forest, a plantation he owned. I hypothesized that he might have come here instead, which is why we've been digging. Could this actually be proof?"

There was not a sound as they all contemplated this possible revision of history. Even Mr. Fairfield, normally grumpy about his wife's preoccupation with digging in the dirt, as he liked to say, stared at the yellowed papers with awe.

"I don't know if we can assume . . ." Mark began.

"Of course not," Jonathan said, "but we can surely decipher more of this note with better equipment, right, Mark?"

Mark nodded. "This will be the most important chapter in your book."

Jonathan ran a hand through his hair and tried not to feel too excited.

And then a forklift rumbled by, carrying boxes into the interior of the barn. He and Mark exchanged a suddenly sober glance. This find was right in the middle of Amy's patio.

"I'll go talk to her," Jonathan said.

He ended up driving to the warehouse office, where Amy was staring hard at her computer screen. She glanced up and smiled, lighting the room with her special glow. Jonathan petted Uma distractedly.

"We found something in the excavation," he said with no preamble.

Amy looked intrigued. "Something besides broken pieces of muskets and cups?"

He nodded. "A tin with papers in it, and what little we can read says it's eighteenth century."

She gasped, then clapped her hands together. "Definitely before we bought the place. Oh, Jonathan, how exciting!"

"It mentions fleeing Richmond and references a general. We should be able to read more of it using a special process, according to Mark."

"That's wonderful. This sounds like the proof you've been looking for." Her smile faded. "And you want to keep digging."

"We'd like you to consider delaying this area of the renovation. It's right within your proposed patio, near the barn wall you plan to remove."

"It's killing me to say this, but I don't know if we can do that, Jonathan."

He slowly sat down in the chair opposite her desk. "Can we discuss this?"

"Of course!" she insisted. "But the equipment for the cider house is ordered. Carlos has long been fermenting batches on the small-scale equipment he has. I've been working on marketing, getting the local magazines interested."

"And you already have a name for your new company?"

Her eyes widened. "Yes, we decided to go with the brand we've been building for over a hundred years, Fairfield Orchard Ciderhouse. The family just settled on it a couple days ago. I didn't tell you?"

He shook his head, hiding his surprise. He told himself that she was dealing with five other siblings, parents, grandparents; it was probably hard to tell who she'd told what to.

But they talked every day.

Wow, he was sounding like an insecure jerk even in his own head.

"I like the name," he told her sincerely.

She smiled with relief. "Thanks! It was a group effort. You were there for one of the brainstorming sessions."

"I remember. But, Amy, you have to give us a bit more time."

"You don't have enough to go on now?"

"It's a good start. But if you let the backhoe and the rest of the equipment dig through there, you'll destroy any chance we have to salvage more."

"I understand," she said, coming around the desk.

He stood up, and she slid her arms around his waist.

"Let me discuss it with the family."

He held her briefly, but that wasn't the answer he wanted to hear. The Fairfields were focused on bringing their orchard to the next level, and that, and profit, mattered more than anything else. History—and his work—couldn't be as important to them. The rest of the family hadn't even met him, and he wasn't sure Amy would fight on his behalf. The future of the orchard was never far from her thoughts, and much as she tried to hide how the weight of responsibility affected her, he knew it did.

He shouldn't be surprised by her focus on her

own goals. After all, work had always been more important than anything else in his life. It was just that he was seeing the conflicts of that now, in Amy, in himself.

"I'll let you get back to work," he said, disengaging himself.

Amy lifted her face for a kiss and he obliged her, then headed for his car. He wanted to trust her, but it seemed so risky. He should back off, protect himself, but it suddenly felt too late. He'd ignored all his own reminders to keep things casual. He sat down in his car, hands on the steering wheel, and just stared at nothing. This horrible yawning feeling of disappointment was because he'd fallen for her; hell, he'd fallen for her whole family, and the thought that they might let him down . . . the pain made it too hard to contemplate.

Before meeting Amy, he'd felt he needed to earn love. Then everything had seemed so different with her, with her family. But was it really?

Back at the excavation, he spoke privately to Mark and explained the uncertainty of the situation.

Mark looked gravely at the excavation, where even now his team was pulling tarps over their work as the rain came down harder. "We'll try to work faster. We'll focus right where we found the tin. Do you know how long we have?"

Jonathan shook his head.

"Got it. Well, we've worked this way before," Mark said.

He sounded like he was trying to brace both himself and Jonathan. It wasn't working.

Amy went to bed that night feeling uneasy. Jonathan had looked so . . . impassive when she'd told him she'd have to discuss the situation with her family, almost as if he didn't believe they could be objective. It hurt her feelings a little, but she had to remind herself of his past, that he'd been let down by so many people. But she thought they'd built more trust between them.

No, her fears were ridiculous. He wasn't the most emotional of men, after all.

But she had a hard time falling asleep. She'd called him right before bed, as they'd been doing lately, but he'd seemed . . . preoccupied. He'd said he was up late, writing, but it had been more than that, she knew it. And she didn't know what to do about it. From the moment he'd first mentioned excavating, she'd let him see her reluctance. She looked back now and winced.

Certainly she had to discuss his request with her family, but it hadn't been what he wanted to hear. He may have perfected the unemotional exterior, but she could read him now. And he thought he was on his own.

That should piss her off. They'd been incredible

together these last few weeks. Why couldn't he trust her?

And the truth hit her like a blow. Like she'd trusted him? she thought with irony and sadness. She still hadn't told either Tyler or Jonathan about her last night with Rob, about the torn photo, about her stupidity. And Jonathan knew it. It was time to prove to him that she did trust him. It was time to come clean about the mistakes of her past. And maybe that meant she really did love Jonathan, after all.

She fell asleep with the wonder of that, especially since the fear seemed gone.

But two hours later, Tyler was pounding on her door.

"Fire!"

— *Chapter 21* —

When Jonathan's phone rang in the middle of the night, he heard it immediately, but had a groggy sensation that he didn't know what it was. And then clarity struck, and he fumbled for the cell on his nightstand.

"Hello?"

"Jonathan?"

Amy's voice was high-pitched and trembling, nothing like herself.

He stiffened. "What's wrong?"

"There's a fire," she said.

"A fire?" he echoed stupidly, as even his brain seemed to seize up with a fear he'd never felt before.

"Not the house, we're okay."

"Oh, thank God." He felt himself shuddering, even as he put his feet on the floor and rubbed his hand through his hair. He was struck with such a desperate need to hold her that it overwhelmed him. "What is it? Not the barn."

"No, it's the old Snack Shack. It's closed off for the season. The fire trucks are here, trying to keep the flames from blowing toward the barn . . ."

Her voice trailed off into bewilderment, as if she could see her hard-fought future might very well fade.

"I'm coming right now."

"You don't need to, honestly," she said.

But it was a feeble effort. She needed him, she wanted him there.

"I'm coming."

"Okay."

The whisper broke his heart.

He threw on some jeans and a T-shirt, grabbed a fleece, and was on his way. He didn't remember much of the ride, except thinking he was glad it was the middle of the night, because he was driving too fast. When he got on the back roads past Crozet, he watched for deer out of habit, but he was really thinking about Amy and what was happening to Fairfield Orchard. When he'd first met her, he'd thought she didn't care about history, that only the future mattered to her, but he'd been wrong. Her family's past, present, and future were all the same thing to her. It was the legacy of the Fairfields that mattered, and bringing what they'd always done, their history, their traditions, into the future. If they couldn't compete now, their history could very well be lost. He'd been so quick to judge just because she hadn't thought exactly like him.

On the drive up the final hill, he could see light against the horizon—too yellow and orange, just wrong against the night sky. The lights of several fire trucks blinked as he pulled through the parking fields that lined the sides of the main road. He left his car in the last lot and jogged past the trucks and their long hoses. The Snack Shack was still ablaze, but fire-fighters were training water on it, and they'd wet down the sides and roof of the barn, just in case.

"Jonathan!"

Amy was running to him, Uma on her leash loping at her side. He caught her hard against him, lifting her clear off the ground.

"Amy, sweetheart," he whispered against her ear.

Then he had her face in his hands, and he was kissing every part he could reach—her cheeks, her forehead, her trembling lips. As they watched the firefighters work, he continued to kiss the top of her head every so often. Tyler and Carlos stood next to a firefighter, talking.

"That's the fire chief," Amy said, as if reading his mind, "Hassan Ali, who also owns the funeral home in the Hollow."

"Multitalented," Jonathan murmured.

She gave a chuckle, though it was weak. After a brief silence, she whispered, "Do you think someone did this deliberately?"

He lifted his head from hers and met her anxious gaze. "Arson?" he asked.

She bit her lip and nodded.

"Why would you think that? Has the fire chief said anything?"

"No, but . . . isn't it a coincidence? Some people

are upset we're expanding. What if . . ." She trailed off, and she looked a little wild with fright.

"They're your neighbors," Jonathan assured her. "If they have a problem, don't you think they'd go to the county board?"

"And apparently some did, but our permits came through, regardless. I'm sure it helps that we've already been regulated by the FDA for years and years because of the cider and food we make. We're a known quantity. But new people move in all the time. What if . . . what if . . ."

"Stop," he said gently, holding her arms to give her a little shake.

"I know, I know, I overthink everything. I always have."

"It's endearing. You care."

She gaped up at him. "Endearing? You're kidding."

"I'm not kidding."

And he almost told her that everything about her was endearing because he loved her, but had to stop the words from coming out at the worst possible time.

"It's just . . ." she began, "it's just . . . this is everything my family has built for two hundred years."

"I know."

"From the beginning you realized how much more important it is than I did."

"That's not true. I—"

"Amy!"

Uma barked, and they both turned, only to see Miss Jablonski fast-walking out of the darkness past the fire trucks.

"Is everyone okay?" the principal demanded anxiously.

"We're unhurt, all of us," Amy reassured her.

Miss Jablonski briefly closed her eyes in relief. Her gray hair hung wild about her head, no demure bun tonight. She wore a pair of yoga pants and a big bulky sweater over them, as if she'd grabbed the first things she could find.

"What happened?" Miss Jablonski asked.

Amy explained again, then added, "I can't imagine what caused this. We inspect all our buildings every year."

"I'm glad it wasn't the barn," Miss Jablonski said.

"You are?" Amy said, not hiding her surprise.

"Well, of course. It's where your tasting room will be."

"But . . . you aren't happy about that."

Miss Jablonski looked surprised. "Why would I be unhappy? I love hard cider."

Amy just blinked at her for a moment. "But . . . you weren't happy on the village's behalf."

"That's just a few people in the town, not the rest of us. Certainly there's concern about increased traffic, but I've been discussing it with the businesses and . . ." She looked past Amy.

"Are you sure you want to discuss this now?"

"What else do I have to do except stand here and worry?" Amy asked, her smile not full of much real amusement.

"Very well, then. Fairfield Orchard is our history, too. I met with various business owners, and Carlos came to speak to all of us."

"He did?" Amy said in surprise. "He never told me!"

Miss Jablonski rolled her eyes. "He assumes too much sometimes."

Jonathan hoped that he'd someday hear more about the strange relationship between Miss Jablonski and Carlos.

"Everyone agreed that the pros of what you're doing outweigh the cons," Miss Jablonski continued. "And if a few residents grumble"—she spread both hands wide—"you can't please everyone."

Jonathan smiled down at Amy, who sagged against him as he put an arm around her.

"I've been so worried," Amy said.

"You probably have far too much to worry about," Miss Jablonski said briskly. "Where is the rest of that family of yours?"

Amy gave a crooked grin. "We can't all be here at once—we'd drive each other crazy!"

"So you'll be going back to Charlottesville when your siblings come home?" Miss Jablonski asked.

Jonathan's gaze shot to Amy.

"No," she said with no hesitation. "I'm here to stay, and the rest of the family will just have to work with me."

Then she looked at Jonathan, and he gave her an approving smile. He was glad that she'd made the decision, that she'd realized her family was more important to her than ever. She was meant to be here, at Fairfield Orchard.

They were interrupted by a loud crash as part of the roof of the Snack Shack fell. A whoosh of flames and sparks shot up, and the hoses were trained on it. Jonathan kept his arm around Amy, who gave an occasional little tremble as she watched part of her childhood, her heritage, die.

Tyler came over to them and stood on Amy's other side. Amy slid her arm around his waist and the three of them stood linked together.

"I knew Mom and Dad really trusted us when they started to let us work in the Snack Shack," Amy said, her voice catching.

Tyler nodded. "We were allowed to handle money, make change. I thought I was awesome at cooking hot dogs."

Amy gave a halfhearted chuckle. "Like it was so difficult."

And then they were quiet again, and it gave Jonathan a strange, tight feeling in his chest to be part of this threesome, like he was a member of the family.

"What will you do about food service for the customers this fall?" Jonathan asked. "Or is it too soon to start thinking about that?"

Amy and Tyler glanced at each other speculatively.

"We've been wondering how we'd pressure our brother Noah to return."

"Ah, and he's a chef," Jonathan said, nodding. "So you might think bigger than just snacks."

"With the tasting room, we'll eventually want people to have a good meal along with the cider," Amy said.

"I'd be quiet about this," Miss Jablonski said. "It'll sound to the insurance company as if you had reason to set the fire yourself."

They all turned to stare at her.

She raised both hands and, without cracking a smile, said, "I was kidding."

Amy and Tyler groaned, while Jonathan just shook his head.

"I need to be doing something," Amy said at last. "Let's make some breakfast for the firefighters."

So Miss Jablonski said good-night as the fire was slowly dying within the charred walls of the shack. Amy called Brianna, who agreed to open the store so Jonathan could grab some more eggs, bacon, bread, and muffins, while the twins started cooking what they already had. Within the hour, they were feeding their exhausted firefighting neighbors, who'd kept the rest of Fairfield Orchard safe. The fire chief assured them that although he'd have the place inspected, he was pretty sure it was just old electrical wire failing, and that they'd need to check the other buildings, too.

After the firefighters left and the three of them cleaned up, Tyler went up to bed. Jonathan leaned his hip against the counter while Amy wiped down the big kitchen table.

"I should probably let you get some sleep," he said, although he didn't really want to leave her.

She set aside the sponge and turned to face him. "Don't leave. I have something I'd like to show you."

"Okay," he said, curious at the serious tone of her voice.

She took his hand, and after quietly ordering Uma to lie down, she led him outside. The sun had come up over the eastern horizon, and the hills of apple trees seemed to shimmer after the rain they'd had yesterday.

To his surprise, she led him to the barn and opened the big door. On one wall, scaffolding had been built in preparation for taking down the external wall and leaving the ax-hewn original support beams. Ladders and boxes and work-tables full of equipment were strewn around haphazardly, but she ignored all that and headed to the loft. She climbed the old wooden ladder and he followed, enjoying the view of Amy from below, of course, but far too curious.

"Nothing has been done up here yet," she said, "so I've been able to put off doing something about . . . this."

She went to the corner, reached behind a wooden beam, and as he squinted, he could see a narrow opening.

"I used to hide things up here when I was a kid," she admitted ruefully.

She straightened, and he saw that she was holding a manila envelope.

"This loft was like my own personal space to get away from my sister and brothers when I needed to. They didn't bother me up here—they enjoyed the tree house more, especially the boys."

"So you've found something you hid long ago?" he asked.

She shook her head. "No, I hid this when I moved back home. Its existence bothered me for the first few weeks, but gradually, it lost its hold over me, which is a good thing, I now realize. Yet . . . I couldn't throw it away."

"You've got me pretty curious."

Amy looked at the envelope, bit her lip, and gave a shrug. "I've never showed it to anyone. But you and Tyler both guessed I was hiding something. This was it. I need you to see it, to under-stand, so you know that I trust you," she added simply.

When she held out the envelope, he took it, surprised to feel nervous, as if whatever this was could blow up in his face. He opened the clasp, looked in, and saw something torn up in the bottom. He dumped it out onto the wooden table built into the wall. It looked like the pieces to a very old photograph. Glancing at Amy, he saw a single tear slide down her cheek. Alarmed, he reached for her, but she held up a hand.

"I'm okay. It's just . . . that's a photograph of Grandpa Fairfield's grandfather and siblings. I know you'll find this hard to believe, but I was once a genealogy buff. I was Grandpa's prized pupil and we had long conversations that bored my sister and brothers to death. But you . . . you brought it back to me. With every discovery, I felt my interest come back to life. But this photograph . . . it's the reason I originally backed away from it, why I didn't think I deserved to be intimately connected with my own family history. I had these plans to have the photo copied professionally, frame some for the whole family, and use it as part of the celebration of our two-hundredth anniversary next year."

"How did it get torn up?"

"My ex, Rob, did it."

Jonathan heard a wealth of sorrow in those

words and, to his surprise, shame. She couldn't even meet his gaze.

He swore softly under his breath, and she rushed on.

"I took too long, don't you see? I—I kept making excuses for him. I kept ignoring what was right in front of my eyes, the escalation of his drinking, the way he was keeping me away from my family, my friends."

She looked tense, as if he touched her, she would shatter. He wanted desperately to gather her against him, to promise no one would ever hurt her again. But he had to let her do this her own way.

At last she raised desperate eyes to his. "I was trying to fix him, don't you see? The worst hallmark of someone who's had an alcoholic in her life. I could never truly depend on my father when he was drinking. It was an uncertain, frightening way for a kid to live. After that experience, I never thought I'd enable another man to drink. But . . . I did."

"Amy, if you loved Rob—"

"But that's not a good enough reason. I didn't even love him by the end. I just wanted to help him, thinking if I did, it would make me less of a fool for sticking with him all those years—those wasted years. But it didn't work out that way. I was . . . trapped."

She hugged herself and briefly closed her eyes,

and he had to make tight fists to keep from touching her.

"I finally couldn't take it anymore," she said at last. "I knew I was making a mistake staying with him, that I couldn't change him, that he had to want to help himself. I shouldn't have confronted him about leaving when he was drinking, but by this point, he always seemed to be drinking."

Jonathan felt the first chill shiver across his shoulders and up his neck.

"He—he slammed around the apartment, and when he saw what I was preparing for my family, he flipped out and tore the photo into pieces before I'd had it copied. All my plans . . . gone. And then . . . he hit me."

She closed her eyes as if she anticipated being hit again, just saying those terrible words.

"Amy, sweetheart," Jonathan whispered, hearing the pain in his rough voice.

She slowly sagged to the floor and covered her face with both hands. Jonathan couldn't stay away, couldn't let her do this alone. He sat down with her, drawing her into his lap as he leaned against the rough wooden wall. Still covering her face with both hands, she pressed into his chest, but made no sound. They sat that way for a long time, his arms holding her tight as he wished desperately to let her know she could let her fear go, that he'd never let that bastard hurt her again.

At last, she sighed, dropped her hands, but kept her head resting tiredly against him.

"He didn't beat me up, if that's what you're thinking," she said.

"He hit you!"

"Once. And then I told him to get his things and be gone when I got back or I was calling the police. And I left. The next day, when I came home, he'd done what I wanted. He even left a note saying he was sorry. Like that helped," she said sarcastically.

"How badly were you hurt?"

"A bruise. Makeup covered it."

"You should have called the police."

"I know. But I felt so stupid, like I'd brought it all on myself by staying with him though his drinking was getting worse. I'd always thought women were idiots for staying with abusive boyfriends—but I never considered myself one of them, oh, no," she said bitterly. "He hadn't hit me then, of course, but his treatment of me was nasty when he was drunk." At last she looked up at him. "It's been so hard for me to even think about this, let alone admit it to anyone. And I never have, until right now."

He gently tucked a strand of hair away from her damp cheek. "I'm glad you told me."

"You deserved to know. I was so short with you about my family history when we first met. It was all because of what had happened with

Rob and the picture. I was so disappointed that I'd let him ruin my plan for the anniversary. Can you forgive me?"

"Forgive you?" he answered in surprise. "There's nothing to forgive. You were hurting."

She searched his eyes, her own damp with unshed tears. "It's taken me a long time to trust anyone with this."

"I know that. And it sounds strange, but I'm honored." He kissed her forehead gently.

"I trust you, Jonathan, and I want you to know that you can trust me. I'd never deliberately hurt your life's work."

He frowned. "What are you talking about? I know that."

"No, you don't. When you told me about the tin and what it meant to you, you thought I didn't understand, that I wouldn't support you."

He grimaced. "I overreacted."

"Maybe. But it was what you feared. I told you I'd go to my family to discuss it, and I did. They're fine with Mark coordinating with our contractor, to help us preserve the site as much as possible. We still have to dig, of course, but I chose the contractor partially because he's worked on these kinds of sites before, and can be sensitive to the chance of more archaeological discoveries."

Jonathan simply stared at her for a moment. "But . . . that'll cost you more time and money."

"It's worth it. We all agree."

He cupped her face in both hands, let his thumbs caress her cheeks for a long moment. "I think I was afraid to trust you," he said at last.

"I know. I was afraid to trust you."

He gave a crooked smile. "A fine pair we make."

He kissed her gently, and she rested her head on his shoulder and kissed him back. It was slow and tender and so good. He was afraid to hope—but he knew at last that he wanted to trust her, and be trusted in return.

"I'm in love with you, Amy," he said.

Her eyes grew all soft. "Jonathan—"

"Let me say this first. I honestly thought I fell in love with Geneva. When she told me she'd never really understood what love was until she experienced it with Mark, I didn't believe her. I thought that was just her way of letting me down easy, maybe even protecting me from my own flaws."

"It doesn't sound very easy to me," she said, resting her hand on his chest, on his heart.

He covered her hand with his own. "But it's like a light has gone on inside me, corny as that sounds. She'd tried to explain it to me, and I didn't believe her. But all along, she knew more about love than I had. Now I know why, because I've found that rare sort of love with you, Amy. I wasn't looking for it, didn't really want it, but it happened so unexpectedly. I'd never experienced the power, the terror, of being so vulnerable, of trusting someone with absolutely everything about me. Being with you has made me realize I don't have to remake myself just to make you happy, that you can appreciate me just as I am. And it's made everything in my life worth living for."

"Oh, Jonathan, this makes me so very happy."

He chuckled and wiped away her tears. "Then why are you crying?"

"Because . . . I can't believe you love me. Because . . . I love *you*. Because you're perfect for me just like you are. Because I can tell you everything about me, and you'll never hurt me, never judge me. There's an honor about you, and I saw it from the beginning."

She threw her arms around his neck and kissed him with eager passion. For a long moment, he exulted in the wonder of being the one Amy loved, of knowing they could go forward and explore this relationship because they trusted each other at last.

He broke the kiss and rested his forehead against hers. "You know, in case you're wondering, there's a special process to fix antique photos. We can make it look almost as good as new."

"Really?" she gasped, and those big blue eyes shined with happiness. "I knew you were the perfect man for me!"

He held her close. "I intend to be. For the rest of our lives."

— *Epilogue* —

Amy stood in the center of Fairfield Orchard Ciderhouse's new tasting room and watched with wonder as the crowd of people milled about. The sun shone through the giant glass wall that was one end of the barn, crisscrossed with only the original beams that held up the walls and roof. A stone fireplace was the center of that wall, faced with deep leather couches, cocktail tables, and chairs. Through the center of the barn, several long tasting bars rested side by side, constructed of weathered barn wood and stone, crystal glasses on racks within easy reach overhead for the staff serving the customers.

At the other end of the barn was their temporary food display, and rather than hot dogs and pizza, there were fresh fruit, exotic Rodriguez cheeses, the best local chocolate, and everything a customer would need to make their own special picnic basket to enjoy on the grounds. Amy had even more plans for how best to feed their customers, but that could wait for another day . . .

All of this had happened because she and Tyler had come together to spearhead it. She was closer than ever to her brother, had confided everything she'd been hiding, then cried in his arms. They'd both agreed they'd never keep secrets again.

Now Jonathan was at her side, a place she hoped he'd never leave. Even now, she was looking for the perfect house for them to buy. She took his hand. "I want you to see something special."

He laughed. "More special than what you've already done here?"

"You bet!"

She led him to a corner she'd kept protected by a screen. Uma nosed behind, but didn't disturb it. Family and friends gathered around them, and Jonathan looked over his shoulder in surprise.

"Amy?"

"Shh!"

She pulled the screen away, and there, on special shelves protected behind glass, beneath a sign reading "Thomas Jefferson and Fairfield Orchard," was the fruit of all of Jonathan's hard work. She'd framed the original deed to the land; with Mark's help she'd displayed and tagged the musket pieces, the pottery, and the two bottles they'd found in the site that could have been used for cider two hundred years ago. In the center was the framed photo of her grandfather's family. She hadn't been able to wait another year to display it. The grands had both teared up when she'd shown them.

Now it was Jonathan's turn to look shocked, and everyone burst into applause.

"When your book is published, we'll put it right here," Amy said, pointing to the center part on the top shelf, "along with the tin and the papers when they're done being examined."

A tag read "Coming soon, the story of President Thomas Jefferson and the beginning of Fairfield Orchard."

Jonathan's mouth worked, but he didn't say anything, only swallowed heavily and gathered Amy against him. There were more applause and chuckles, and Amy reveled in it.

"We'll find that diary," she promised. "Grandpa won't let that go."

"I know he won't," Jonathan said in a husky voice as he kissed the top of her head. Then he straightened. "Hey, there's Mark and Geneva. We need to show them what you've done here."

Amy felt wonderful watching Jonathan shake his best friend's hand, then turn and give a very pregnant Geneva a kiss on the cheek. Mark and Jonathan had become close friends again, as they'd been long ago, and it made Amy so happy because it brought Jonathan peace.

And then a half hour later her last surprise walked in the door, and she watched Jonathan's shock when he saw his parents standing there uncertainly.

Jonathan clutched her hand. "How did you . . ." But his words died away.

"I told them about your new book, and all the work you've done here," she said, giving his hand a squeeze. "I admit, I didn't know if they'd come. I don't want you to think they gushed all over me, but . . . they came. Maybe it's a start?"

He gave her a quick kiss. "Today has been . . . incredible. This should have been about you and your family."

"You are my family," she told him.

They stared into each other's eyes for a long moment, then kissed again.

Amy grinned. "Now let's go talk to your parents."

An hour later, Amy and Jonathan escaped the crowds and the noise and left his standoffish parents in the capable hands of her own parents.

Outside, the sun was shining; happy parents and children walked the grounds, picked apples in the orchard, browsed in the store, and took rides on the hay wagon, but Jonathan tugged Amy away, toward the first row of apple trees, already long cleared of apples. As usual, Uma raced off to chase bunnies.

He took both her hands. "This is where I saw you for the first time. Or I should say, I saw your muddy boots."

She giggled and grinned up at him. "It can be our special place."

"Let's make it even more so." He pulled something out of his coat and got down on one knee in the dirt.

Amy gasped, and her hand began to tremble in his. "Jonathan?"

"Amy, will you marry me?"

He opened the box, and a lovely diamond—the setting looking like an antique itself—twinkled at her.

"That ring—" she began.

"You can't wear it until you say yes," he teased, but his voice was soft and full of love. "And I have a Jefferson quote that's perfect for the occasion."

She groaned.

"He wrote this to John Adams: 'I like the dreams of the future better than the history of the past.' That's how I feel about you, Amy. You're my future. Say you'll marry me."

"Yes, oh, yes, I'll marry you."

He put the ring on her finger, and she was crying, and to her surprise, people were applauding. She looked up to see that all their family and friends had "somehow" known to follow them.

Jonathan stood up, then bent over her so she could fling her arms around his neck.

"Forever," she whispered into the warmth of his neck.

"Forever."

About the Author

Emma Cane grew up reading and soon discovered that she liked to write passionate stories of teen-agers in space. Her love of "passionate stories" has never gone away, although today she concentrates on the heart-warming characters of Valentine Valley and Fairfield Orchard.

Now that her three children are grown, Emma loves spending time crocheting and singing (although not necessarily at the same time), and hiking and snowshoeing alongside her husband, Jim, and their rambunctious dog, Uma.

Emma also writes *USA Today* bestselling historical romances under the name Gayle Callen.

Center Point Large Print
600 Brooks Road / PO Box 1
Thorndike, ME 04986-0001 USA

(207) 568-3717

US & Canada:
1 800 929-9108
www.centerpointlargeprint.com